# The Return of
# Captain Vampire

# The Return of Captain Vampire

by
**Brian Gallagher**

based on the character created by
**Marie Nizet**

A Black Coat Press Book

# TABLE OF CONTENTS

## *Foreword*

This foreword should be read after reading this book as it contains many plot details.

I came to Captain Vampire whilst looking for a story idea to pitch to *Tales of the Shadowmen* Editor Jean Marc Lofficier. I needed a central character, and spotted the short novel by the Belgian writer Marie Nizet, published by Black Coat Press.[1] It's a great story, very much overlooked in any examination of vampire literature. The titular "Captain Vampire" is the Russian Army officer Boris Liatoukine, and relates his sinister activities in Romania. The novel is a critique of Russian imperialism in that country, as well as being an enjoyable horror story. If you haven't read it, pick up Black Coat Press's translation by Brian Stableford, who also writes a superb introduction on the background to the story. Having read it, I quickly realised that Boris Liatoukine had great potential for further exploits. However, the stories need to work in their own right as supernatural tales, all the historical themes had to come second, hopefully adding more for the reader.

The concept of *Tales of the Shadowmen*, where all these stories first appeared, is to use characters from fantastic fiction, but including Francophone characters and concepts. The Vampire City Sepulchre—or Selene to humans—is another overlooked vampire concept. It was created by the French writer Paul Feval, in his 1875

---

[1] ISBN-13: 978-1-934543-01-6.

work *Vampire City*.[2] The story is an enjoyable romp—and it's also available from Black Coat Press. Aside from the City itself, it provides a number of other things to the Vampire mythos such as green tints in windows to denote vampiric presence are around and their being able to absorb people and churn them out again—but changed. The latter provided an ingenious way of explaining how Count Orlok and Dracula could exist in the same universe, by Dracula using that power. There are also meta parallels with the Bram Stoker's wife suing the makers of Nosferatu for making a copy of the original.

Something that I wanted from the beginning was that both the fictional universe and history in the real one should be adhered to. Dracula was dead and would stay that way. Further, the vampires would not be seen to be controlling human affairs: world events would be due to humans not supernatural beings. I borrowed a little from Tolstoy's idea of history being a force in itself, in this case to the detriment of the supernatural.

A thread through many of the stories has been the Austro-Hungarian Habsburg Empire. It's often overlooked, but it had a significant role in history that has its influence today. Vienna still has influence—especially economic and generally positive—in its former empire in places such as Croatia, which we see briefly in the final story.

Something established in the first story was Liatoukine's interest in politics. He is very interested in power for himself but also for Russia. He is concerned that vampires may go too far, triggering the very real power of the Empires that existed at the time. The se-

[2] ISBN-13: 978-0-9740711-6-9.

cond story, *The Trial of Van Helsing*, I decided to show Liatoukine as fallible in his political thinking. The background to the trial of the famous killer of Dracula by a city of Vampires—an irresistible idea—is the looming spectre of World War One. In Vampire politics, Boris came out on top. However, it is clear by the end of the story that he—and Van Helsing—have absolutely no idea what is coming next and arrogantly believes he will end up in a position power.

The next story, *The Stake and the Sickle* sees Liatoukine humbled. The catastrophe of the Great War sees him fighting on the losing side in the Russian Civil War. Orginally, I had thought of setting this in World War II, with Romanian fascist vampires, but Jean-Marc pointed out that World War II vampires are far from an unused idea. He was right of course and setting it during the Civil War gave the story a great direction, really putting Boris under pressure. It was also interesting to see that there is very little in the way of fiction about that particular war compared to others—Doctor Zhivago pretty much dominating. A story about vampires in this conflict was thus a necessity. Boris here is very much in trouble. His dreams of being the power behind the throne of a more powerful Russia are gone, and we see him turn into more of a survivor than anything else.

The story sees the introduction of Von Bork. This was a Sherlock Holmes villain from the short story *His Last Bow*, It's a wartime propaganda piece and a not very good one. Von Bork, the German spy villain of the piece, seemingly planned the First World War to the precise month. That hardly stands up today, and so I made clear from Von Bork that it was indeed propaganda. Also, I thought it likely that he would be disgraced on his return to Germany, so much so that he would be recruited by Bolsheviks keen to use his talent. Being very embittered he accepts their offer, ending up in the Cheka, the forerunner of the KGB. He gets the better of Liatoukine, hunting him down in Paris after the war and recruiting him to his department—turning Von Bork into a formidable character.

Liatoukine has no choice, but he even sees an opportunity, as things may change as inevitably, they do.

In *The Berlin Vampire*, Liatoukine is doing reasonably well as a Soviet agent—but still under the firm control of Von Bork. The setting was inspired by trip to the German capital, and seeing monuments dedicated to the 1953 uprising in East Germany against communist rule—a revolt which was put down by the authorities and the Soviet Union. This event is surprisingly little known outside Germany. It's a forerunner to the invasions of Hungary and Czechoslovakia. This made it an excellent background for this story, with Liatoukine quite happily joining in the repression of the Germans— his only concern being to leave them in a state to be able to produce things for the Soviet Union and himself to later loot. Liatoukine is very much still the character Nizet created. The destruction of the Vampire City was due to it being inevitable that the modern world would soon see it one way or the other, regardless of then being in Communist Yugoslavia. It had to go, and obliterating it in an atomic strike is suitably dramatic. Here we see how history is simply rolling over the supernatural. Incidentally, the Church of Reconciliation featured in the story was destroyed by the communists in 1985—church members retrieved the cross when it fell off the tower and hid it from the authorities. A new Chapel of Reconciliation has since been built on the site.

By 1979, many of the old guard were dying off in the Soviet Union, and this was reflected in Von Bork. He was aged, and wanted to cling on—hence his wanting to become a vampire. Tied into this was the approaching war in Afghanistan, which Von Bork was keen on, but not Liatoukine. This was simply because Boris is no fool; he had seen history and did not think Afghanistan could be won. He is all in favour of conquest—but only when it is successful. In this story I introduced the character of Countess Irina Petroski. She is a descendent of her namesake from the 1972 British/Spanish film *Horror Express*, set in 1906. She is an adventurer, a touch like the Nyree Dawn Porter's Contessa Caroline di Contini in the Gerry Anderson series *The Protectors*. In keeping with the time, and her Polish nationality, I give the Countess a strong anti-communist viewpoint.

In *Horror Express*, an order comes from Moscow to send the train—which has a marauding alien on board—into a ravine. How did Moscow know of that situation to be able to order such a drastic action? The universe of the Shadowmen provides the answer - it is here revealed that it was Boris Liatoukine who gave the order. This makes perfects sense. If anyone would know the murders on that train were more than they seemed, it would be him. In this way, Captain Vampire may have saved the world!

*The Skull of Boris Liatoukine* takes place in London, during 1998. Here, Boris has left the KGB and became an oligarch. He is certainly not the first to do so. London becoming a playground for wealthy Russians—some rather dubious—was actually encouraged by government policy at the time, as the story makes clear. The rise to power of Vladimir Putin, which our Skull protagonist senses, was accelerating at this time. Despite being set over 20 years ago, the whole thing feels relevant due to Putin's continued position of power, and various UK-Russian political clashes and assassination incidents.

*The Vampire President* proved a challenge on a number of grounds. Unlike many locations in previous stories, I have yet to visit either Moscow or St. Petersburg. I thus had to rely on two swiftly purchased guidebooks, and I hope that I have served those great cities well in my description of them. All previous stories took place in the past, whilst this would take place in the near future. However, I wanted the story to be plausible, and so the dates used are the ones that—at time of writing—are when the next presidential elections are due to take place. The incidents such as Drubetsky flinging water live on TV on Liatoukine's face was taken from actual event that happened. The idea of Liatoukine being a candidate solely to drain votes from more popular rivals to Putin's successor (not a real person I hasten to add), was something that some commentators believed had happened at a previous election. Whilst the story does not do any favours to Russian politics, I was keen to show up Western hypocrisy in having some seeing Liatoukine as pro-human rights for no other reason that he, ostensibly, opposed the Putin candidate. This sort of thing goes on, and certainly has been seen in other ex-Communist countries.

I put in a joke about Jeremy Corbyn being UK Prime Minister. I am certainly not sympathetic to his politics, but when this was being written, the outcome of the inevitable general election was not seen as certain. The joke would have worked as well, or as badly, with Boris Johnson, but I have resisted the temptation to change it.

However, President Vladimir Putin is on course to thwart the final story. As I write, a referendum is due which, amongst other things, will change the constitution which will let him run again for President. There is little doubt the referendum will go his way. That was a development I had not foreseen, but I suspect it is one that Captain Vampire's creator, Marie Nizet, would have.

Brian Gallagher
June 2020
London

# City of the Nosferatu

*Transylvania, 1830*

The journey from Vienna to Transylvania had been straightforward, pleasant even, Boris Liatoukine thought. This diversion to see the Count was a minor delay, but a necessary one. Count Dracula was not a figure to be ignored in a matter as delicate as that which was to be discussed.

They were high up in Dracula's castle, overlooking the Borgo pass, sitting opposite each other over a table. It was night, Dracula's preferred time. Liatoukine knew that the Count could exist in the day—just as he himself could. However, Dracula's powers were far greater at night. Far more than his own, in fact—which was perhaps the point of making him wait until darkness fell to see him.

The Count decided to sum up their conversation thus far.

"The Habsburg Emperor Francis in Vienna believes that vampires are infiltrating his Austrian Empire? And your Tsar Nicholas as well?"

"Quite so," replied Liatoukine. "It's based on a number of incidents, usually involving a vampire being caught. More often than not, they seem to be influential members of society."

Dracula did not seem impressed by this.

"This is hardly new," he said. "I myself wield some authority here. And you too carry some small influence at the Imperial Court in St.Petersburg—despite being a mere Captain in the Russian Army." The unkind comment regarding Liatoukine's rank was delivered with a little smile.

Liatoukine knew it was best to ignore the remark; Dracula was not one to annoy or be trifled with. "It is the scale of incidents that concerns them; they are all too frequent," he replied. "Of course, some of us are captured and destroyed on occasion but…"

"*Us*?" inquired Dracula.

Liatoukine decided to choose his next words very carefully. It would not be wise to imply that the Count was just another vampire who might be destroyed by mere humans. His history was substantial for anyone, human or vampire. Had he not studied at the Scholomance, where he'd learned the secrets of the Evil One himself?

"Forgive me, Count. I meant the vampires of the Sepulchre. They have long had their people in positions within human society. Their being caught from time to time does have the benefit of ensuring a certain degree of fear amongst the populace. There have never been enough incidents to provoke the authorities into action. Some even harbor doubts as to the existence of those like us."

"What, then, has changed? Why are the great powers starting to take the existence of vampires seriously?" asked the Count.

"Because the frequency of such incidents has recently multiplied. We know that the Sepulchre always have had their people hidden amongst the humans. So far, so good. But now, the Emperors seem to think that they are under threat. Their police have captured some minor vampires who were, frankly, just too careless. The large recruitment the Sepulchre appears to be indulging in is not providing the best quality of converts. From interrogation, scraps of information have emerged. The Sepulchre is being mentioned regularly. This only matches the rumors that the humans already knew—although they call the Vampire City, Selene. The Emperors are communicating with each other via their Royal families—this helps avoid any political issues. Action is underway in several countries: the Austrian Empire, Russia, the Ottoman Empire, France... even England."

"England?" said the Count. "I have an interest in that country."

"The Sepulchre has placed one or two of their people there in the past. A few years back, an expedition led by an Englishwoman to Selene led to chaos and the death of Otto Goetzi," said Liatoukine.

"I am aware of that incident. The Radcliffe woman was a remarkable individual. I am intrigued by a nation which can produce such a woman. Goetzi was a fool—how could he permit her and her associates to cross Europe to destroy him in his very lair? What she did in invading the Sepulchre was another factor that brought her country to my attention. The British are now of great interest to me, especially their science and their ambitions. They do not limit themselves to Europe. They fascinate me, because they are the future. Here," he gestured at the window to the country outside, "we are still backward and mired in superstition."

Liatoukine thought that perhaps the local superstition was not so backward, given who was residing in this very castle, but he kept the thought to himself.

The Count pondered, stroking his large moustache.

"I have little time for the Sepulchre's foolish games. I have my own dreams of the future in England. I do not wish to see them disrupting that country, or Central Europe, for that matter. Do they wish a full-blown war with the humans? Fools! What will they do when the Imperial armies stand outside Selene with their cannons? Yes, I know that the Sepulchre only exists in our reality for an hour every day, but do they think that no damage can be caused in that hour? Every day?"

Liatoukine nodded his agreement. The Count considered him, gazing at him with his red eyes.

"Pray, tell me... (they both smiled at the use of "pray") What precisely is your involvement in all this?"

It was time for Liatoukine to expose his own interests.

"The Tsar has been in touch with the other Monarchs in this matter. There have been certain incidents in St. Petersburg. Indeed, I myself had to swiftly execute a nobleman. There are many who fear me there. Some are even aware that I am not what I seem. This works to my advantage. A more mistrustful, ever fearful, atmosphere, however, could achieve the opposite and destroy all my efforts."

"For myself, I most certainly find fear to be useful," Dracula said.

Liatoukine ignored his remark and continued:

"Fortunately, the Tsar feels he can still rely on me in certain matters. I have been of use to him in the past, especially in the recent successful war we waged against your ancient enemies, the Turks. So he suggested that I should look into the matter, and see what should be done. I was dispatched to Vienna to discuss the 'vampire problem' with the Habsburg Emperor himself. The Austrians have a prisoner in their Croatian city of Zagreb, whom they are not even certain how to kill. I would speak with him, and then destroy him myself. Our position is especially perilous in the Austrian Empire, as such prisoners only increase the humans' knowledge of us."

"Even here, in Transylvania, I have become aware of the growth of these inferior vampires within the Austrian Empire," interrupted Dracula. "Lawyers, petty officials, and so on. Wisely, they have avoided all contacts with me, presumably believing that I am still unaware of their presence. However, they have not been widely detected by the humans. I assume this recent increase is due to the infiltration strategy by the Sepulchre that you mentioned earlier?"

"Yes, I suspect so," said Liatoukine. "The infiltration has been most intense in areas where our kind has traditionally been the strongest, such as the Magyar lands. My concern is that, if the humans are pushed, they will retaliate. We are powerful, but there are millions of them, and we are but thousands, if that. Hidden as we are, lurking in the shadows, our very existence denied by men of science—some in our employ—we thrive. The lower orders of life fear us as spectres of the night. But if we were to take over, resistance would quickly replace fear; we would be right in front of them—an open target. Using selected humans as our servants would no longer work; some of them are already being exposed. And as you said, human weapons could smash even our strongest holdouts."

Dracula rose and strode to the window, gazing out. He placed his hand on the stone wall, as if to reassure himself of his castle's strength. Tall, thin and pale, like many of his kind, he also had pointed ears and red eyes. Perhaps it was just as well that he was rarely seen outside his castle nowadays, thought Liatoukine.

"Yes, yes… this is so," said the Count at last. "Vienna thinks it rules here. They would no doubt muster their troops against me if they felt my existence was a threat to them. I would prevail. Nonetheless, it would be extremely inconvenient. However, I sense that you are not simply here for discussing the problem, Boris Liatoukine. You have other intentions in mind, don't you?"

"Indeed I have, my Lord Count," replied the Russian. "A name has occasionally been mentioned when the Austrians have interrogated the vampires they captured, prior to their destruction: Orlok. I believe I have heard the name before, always in relation to this region…"

"So you think I may be connected to all this?" asked Dracula.

"No, my Lord, not in the least. Your independence—as well as mine—from the Sepulchre is well known."

"Quite." Here Dracula started to almost look amused, "However, the name Orlok is indeed familiar to me, and it explains much. You may, in fact, be able to resolve matters far more easily than you might have thought…"

On horseback, Liatoukine approached Zagreb. What Dracula had told him was most useful indeed. He came to a military building in the center of town, where he knew he was expected. He was immediately taken to a commander named Sponsz. The soldier couldn't help but wonder about his visitor. How was it that this mysterious, tall, gaunt Russian with his strange burning eyes had been granted such liberties? He had been ordered to extend every courtesy to him, and tell him whatever he wanted to know. In his career, Sponsz had come across many strange things, but always kept quiet. His masters knew that he could be trusted.

"Tell me how your prisoner came to be in that cell?" inquired Liatoukine.

"Yes, sir," Sponsz began. He was unsure on how to address a Russian army nobleman and officer, but "Sir" seemed to evoke no rebuke, so he continued: "Baron Grando was captured at the home of one of the mayor's most trusted advisers, alone in his office. Horrifying cries and screams were heard. Some of the servants burst in to see the Baron drinking the adviser's blood from his wrist whilst holding him down by his neck.

"Given that the Baron is seventy, this was a considerable feat. In fact, it took ten men to overwhelm him. Six others were killed in the process. A lamp was knocked over, causing a fire. We made use of this to tell the public that there had been an accident and that the deceased were burned to death. The survivors, who had helped subdue the Baron, were only too glad to keep quiet."

Liatoukine nodded. He rather suspected that the fire was started later on, rather than being the result of a genuine accident, but kept silent.

"I understand that the Baron was injured?" he asked instead.

"Indeed, sir. A number of men tried to kill him. It is best that you see for yourself"

They headed downstairs, to a long corridor, along which there were doors leading to what clearly were cells. A number of these seemed to be made out of the same stone than the building. Clearly, no ordinary prisoners were kept here. They stopped at one such cell, which had its own guard standing outside. The guard opened a spyhole and checked on the prisoner. He confirmed that all was well. Sponsz, however, took a second look to make sure. With a little difficulty, the young guard opened the heavy stone door.

"You may wait outside," Liatoukine told Sponsz.

"I regret, I cannot, sir. The regulations say that if a dangerous prisoner is to be visited, there must be a soldier present."

Liatoukine did not know if this was true, but Vienna clearly wanted their man to report back on what would be said. *Very well*, he thought, *they have sealed their servant's fate.*

Liatoukine strode in, followed by Sponsz. The guard closed the door behind them. The cell was bare, without any natural light. There was what appeared to be a block of stone with a figure sitting on it. It was tied down to the stone by chains. On a table nearby, a lamp flickered. Sponsz went over to it and turned it up. The increased light provided more details of the figure. Thin and pale, the creature smiled at his visitors. To anyone else other than Liatoukine and Sponsz, this might have come as a surprise—if they had recovered from the shock of seeing a stake sticking from the man's chest, where his heart should be.

Liatoukine pointed to the stake.

"The men who overwhelmed the Baron attempted to destroy him by traditional means," explained Sponsz. "As you can see, it failed, but I thought it best to leave things the way they were."

Liatoukine also noticed several holes in the Baron's shirt that looked like bullet holes. Clearly, other methods of destruction had been tried, which had also proved unsuccessful. Not all vampires could be killed in the same way, although the stake was the most common method.

The Russian was surprised they had not tried decapitation. Perhaps orders had already come through that the prisoner needed to be interrogated first.

"Come to see what cannot be killed?" sneered the Baron. "Another servant of that useless Emperor in Vienna?"

Liatoukine looked at him more closely. Grando seemed to shrink back. From that look, he had not only understood that the Russian Captain was a vampire, but also a powerful one. The Baron did not know how he knew. He just did.

"Are you here to free me, my lord?" he asked.

The sneering tone had gone. Sponsz picked up on this and shifted uneasily. Clearly, this Russian was of some significance.

Liatoukine ignored the question. He looked at the floor. There was a layer of ash on it. He crouched down, touched it, and sensed the remnants of departed vampire spirits.

"My Lord," said the Baron, "what you feel is what's left our kind—the ones killed over many years by the Austrians. They leave their ashes here to intimidate those of us they capture."

Clearly, the Austrians and their Croat subjects knew more about vampires than they'd let on, thought Liatoukine. Something to be remembered.

"*Our kind*? Does he mean, noblemen?" asked Sponsz, although his real suspicion was painted on his face.

Liatoukine turned to him. He grabbed him by the throat so he could not scream. He didn't bother answering the question. He stared deep into Sponsz's eyes. The Commander felt waves of terror flood through him. He could no longer move. He realized what was strange about the Russian's eyes: the pupils had turned into vertical slits, like a cat's!

Then, he could no longer think of anything. His heart had given out.

Liatoukine dropped him to the floor.

"That is how I dispose of people," he said.

Grando looked awestruck. "What of his blood?" he asked.

"His life-force is what I take. I do dislike having blood on my uniform." He went over to Grando and removed the stake. The hole started regenerating. "We must move fast to leave here…" He went to the chains and pulled at them. "This will take a few moments…" He grappled with the chains behind the Baron.

Grando was clearly pleased with these developments.

"Of course, you are obliged to help me. Vampire is loyal to vampire, vampire does not kill vampire! Not like the humans, who slaughter each other for no reason. They would have killed me if they could, but they couldn't find the right method…"

Liatoukine ignored his talk.

"Tell me," he said whilst seeming to grapple with the chains, "it is clear to me that you have only recently become one of us. I sense a familiarity about you, although we have not met before. Perhaps I am aware of the one who created you. Who is he?"

"It was Orlok, my lord, *Graf* Orlok."

Was the emphasis on the title of "Graf" supposed to impress him? Liatoukine thought? "Orlok!" he exclaimed. "A dear friend of mine. I have not seen him in many decades. I hear he has some new plans?"

"Yes, yes, my lord! He has plans to extend our influence into the Empire. He is selecting many of the more influential of us for his purpose. We will soon control the Empire and will not have to hide anymore. He has promised me that I will be a young man again."

And Orlok is doing all of this himself? From the Sepulchre?"

"Yes. From time to time, he visits certain cities, changes select people such as I, and then we carry on with his work in our areas. He intends Selene to become the capital of the new Empire. He has great ambitions for Russia, too, which is perhaps why you've heard of his plans?"

Liatoukine had heard enough; this confirmed what he already knew. Best to get onto the other reason why he was here. He noted that the hole in the Baron's chest had already healed. Good.

Liatoukine pulled a knife from inside his tunic and plunged it into the Baron's chest. There was a gasp from the uncomprehending nobleman. Then, the Russian Captain proceeded to cut out the Baron's heart.

"What are you doing?" cried the Baron.

Liatoukine ignored him. He never felt the need to explain himself to fools. Besides, time was a factor. The last thing he needed was for the guard outside to wonder what was going on, although he could hear nothing through the heavy door.

Once finished, he placed the heart in the small box he had brought in with him. Inside was a bottle of oil, which he poured over the heart. Lighting a small splinter, he set it alight. It burned with extreme intensely— the oil had special properties that made it so. Nothing was happening to Grando; sometimes the burning of the heart would destroy his kind of vampire. *No matter*, thought Liatoukine.

He placed the stake back into the Baron's body, where it had been previously, even though the hole was now rather larger. The utterly confused Baron piped up again.

"My lord, I am uncertain as to the meaning of all this. Why are you burning my heart?"

Was Grando really so ignorant? The oil had almost done its work. Since he had some time, he might as well enlighten this idiot, he thought.

"You are the kind of vampire whose heart, when burnt, provides a fine ash with certain properties— properties that are not present if you are ordinarily destroyed and reduced to ash"

"Properties, my Lord? I do not understand?"

Liatoukine looked inside the metal box. The oil had done its work. Carefully, he closed the airtight box. Then, with one swift blow, he decapitated Grando with his sword. The head spun in the air. Liatoukine caught it with one hand. The head pulled away from his hand and rested back on the body, re-attaching itself. No doubt, the Croats had attempted this method before then.

The Russian Captain had no particular idea on how this vampire could be killed, and no time to find out. His own powers would have to do. He took a gold coin from his pocket and smashed it into the Baron's skull. Half of it stuck out.

"My Lord, I must protest... this is no way to treat a fellow vampire! Graf Orlok will not be pleased! Vampire is loyal to vampire!"

Liatoukine just stared into the Baron's eyes, using the same power he had used on Sponsz earlier. The Baron was going to say something, but suddenly, his head started to decay. It turned into a skull. Liatoukine let it fall to the floor, with the gold coin still lodged into it.

The body had similarly rotted away. He went over the chains that still restrained the body and now broke them effortlessly. Liatoukine kicked the Baron's skeleton, which further disintegrated into ashes, with the stake still in the middle of what was left of the ribcage.

Taking his sword off his belt, Liatoukine went to the heavy metal slot on the door and banged on it with the handle of his sword. The slot opened. Liatoukine shouted through it:

"Quickly, man! Open!"

With some effort, the door was duly opened and the guard from outside rushed in and looked in horror at the scene.

Liatoukine pointed at what was left of Grando with his sword. "You fools! The chains were not strong enough! The creature got free and attacked me. I could have been killed." He gestured towards Sponsz's body. "This one died in terror—his heart must have given out."

"How were you able to kill it?" the stunned guard asked.

Liatoukine pointed to the gold coin sticking out of the skull. "Gold, man, gold. To be pressed into the skull only. Are you people here not aware that some vampires can only be killed in this way?"

The guard shook his head. The humans needed an explanation for Baron Grando's death, and that gold nonsense was as good as any other. Orlok would no doubt sense the death of his minion, and may even suspect who was responsible, but he would not know for certain—let alone be able to prove it.

The Russian Captain left the cell, affecting to be in need of wine. He was, of course, full of energy, as always when he drained another vampire. What drivel had

Orlok fed Grando? "Vampire is loyal to vampire, vampire does not kill vampire?" Indeed!

If the local Croat authorities doubted Liatoukine's story, they did not show it. In fact, the Russian Captain made great play of how he had been put at risk, and so on. He used his powers of influence just to make sure to be believed. He was further assisted in his task by the attitude of some officials who were only too glad that the Baron had been destroyed, and displayed their thanks in a most embarrassing manner. Liatoukine pretended to be mollified and instructed that the Emperor in Vienna should be told that this unfortunate outbreak of the "vampire plague" would be swiftly dealt with by Liatoukine himself.

The Austrians provided him with a military escort of four cavalrymen, led by a lieutenant, to the border between their empire and Serbia. They rode out of Zagreb and through the fertile lands of Slavonia. They stopped at a small town for a few hours of rest. Liatoukine made himself popular with his escort by treating them to free ale at a local inn. Whilst his escort was busy drinking, he saw to some business with a local smith, a task that he had not wished to have done in Zagreb, in order to avoid spying eyes. He needed some work done in order to help him make a certain point with the rulers of the Sepulchre, when he got there.

After a night's sleep, they arrived at Zemun, known as Semlin in German. It was the last stop before crossing the border, and then onward to the Sepulchre. Liatoukine had given some thought to simply going around the town in order to maintain the element of surprise when he would arrive at Selene's gates. However, if Orlok got wind of his coming, due to his spies—incompetent as they seemed to be—it would be best for Liatoukine to suggest that he was in no way afraid of the other vampire.

Zemun contained a number of discreet spies who had been working for the Sepulchre for many years due to its proximity to the Vampire City. These spies would soon report his arrival. Liatoukine considered that this news might, in fact, unsettle Orlok and, more importantly, other powers in the Sepulchre.

To make sure that his presence was known, the Russian Captain met with the mayor—calling it a courtesy call, as the Austrian cavalrymen were escorting a Russian officer on a diplomatic mission. A surprise early morning call for the mayor, pleasantries exchanged in his office, nothing more.

Liatoukine could not help but notice the occasional green tint on the window in the mayor's office. The Russian Captain knew well that this was a sign of vampiric infiltration—not surprising for a place with such strong connections with the Sepulchre. It confirmed that, beyond using human informers, there were also vampires here. Perhaps the mayor himself was one? This was reckless indeed. Human settlements around the Sepulchre had traditionally been left largely alone in order to prevent any unwanted attention. The humans certainly feared Selene, but such fears did not turn into any aggressive intent. If this had changed, Orlok's influence was indeed proving to be baleful.

Liatoukine also noticed that the cavalry lieutenant had glanced occasionally at the window. Further, he had noticed the use of languages amongst the men who comprised escort. German, of course, but they also spoke in Croatian, and the officer had betrayed his knowledge of Latin. Educated men... No doubt some among them might even know French, and perhaps Russian too? Clearly, these men were more than mere cavalry men in the service of the Emperor... Perhaps, they suspected his true nature? No matter. Today, they were allies, after a fashion. Nevertheless, it would be wise to remember this in the future.

They concluded their business and headed to the Serbian border. Soon, they reached it and came to a halt.

"This is where we must leave you, sir," said the lieutenant.

"Of course. I should be able to get to Belgrade to continue my mission without any difficulties," replied Liatoukine.

More to the point, he thought it was important that the secret of the Sepulchre be kept from these humans. He had, in fact, no intention of going to Belgrade, although he had arranged for Vienna to be told that he was.

After his escort had gone, Liatoukine moved across the border and rode towards Selene, eventually reaching its outskirts. The Vampire City, of course, was neither visible, nor tangible. Where it stood, all that could be seen was barren land, with dead trees and no life of any kind. It gave off a feeling of death and corruption. This was how humans were deterred from approaching it. The city somehow co-existed in the same space as that barren marsh, but on another plane of reality. As a vampire himself, he could enter either space, but he waited an hour or so until 11 a.m. for, at that time, Selene became visible for an hour to all.

It duly appeared on schedule, materializing slowly. A city of dark shapes, buildings at strange angles, and any such movements that could be seen inside were fleeing and disturbing to human eyes.

Liatoukine looked at the Vampire City. Some thought this was God's way of signaling its existence to the humans. For centuries, the locals had barely spoken of it, simply keeping well away from its dark walls. However, there were many legends. With the humans' rapid scientific and military development, Liatoukine wondered not only if the secrecy would last, but if confrontation would not become someday inevitable—a confrontation that vampires couldn't hope to win. Perhaps that was God's plan as well? Perhaps that was also why Orlok was behaving as he was—trying to control the humans before they became a threat?

Whenever that confrontation were to take place—and the later, the better—Liatoukine had every intention of being far away. And preferably, on the winning side.

Liatoukine now entered the Vampire City. He tethered his horse to a tall, dark pole made of some unknown substance, with no apparent purpose. The beast was clearly afraid, but the Russian Captain simply placed his hand on its neck and it became utterly docile. He did not leave all his weapons with the horse. Instead, he took his sword and two pistols. He then proceeded on foot.

He walked through the dark streets, encountering strange figures as he walked. They let him pass, looking at him strangely. Vampires tended not to enter the city when it was visible to humans. Liatoukine had done so deliberately, in order to unnerve. Further, he could have proceeded to where the middle of the city was and let it materialize around him, but he wished to take in the current atmosphere of the Sepulchre. He had not been here for a while. It was as unappealing as ever.

He knew some of the figures he passed by reputation. A number used the city as their base. Others had fled here from lands where they had been exposed. Some had "retired." He was unimpressed by the city and its inhabitants. He did not share his kind's love of the extreme macabre. Humans were weak. However, they provided much in the way of entertainment, pleasure, and a refined society in which to partake and, occasionally, dominate. He considered that much more preferable than skulking around in some invisible mausoleum.

Soon, he came to the central plaza of the Sepulchre. Here was a temple, an imposing chapel of sorts. Its columns were interspersed with statues of tigers ripping the hearts out of young women, frozen in fear. He went up the steps, past the statues. These were actually real women, who, in death, had been transformed into statues by their vampire killers for the express purpose of being displayed here. Liatoukine was responsible for much death, but could not see the point of this spectacle. Vampire art was never his thing.

He was greeted—if that's the word—by what appeared to be little more than a skeleton dressed in a Russian military uniform. The skull had vampire fangs. Presumably this was Orlok's own effort to unsettle him. The skeleton wordlessly gestured to follow him, and led Liatoukine into the hall. At the end was a raised platform, on top of which were five stone stands, with figures behind them. This was the Vampire Council, those who currently governed the Sepulchre. They were bathed in a dull green light.

Liatoukine recognized them. There was Count Szandor, Baron Iskariot and Baroness Phryne. He noted one, wearing garments that were fashionable in Europe a few years back. This was the second Otto Goetzi; the first being infamous for letting humans intrude into the city and almost getting himself destroyed in the process. There was, however, no mistaking the one in the center:

tall, bald, large ears, with rat like teeth, wearing a long coat... They had not previously met, but this was Graf Orlok, no doubt about that.

Littered around the hall were a number of vampires of all kinds. This was unusual; the Council tended to meet and hold its audiences in secrecy. Presumably Orlok was expecting trouble and had gathered his lackeys?

Orlok stared at Liatoukine.

"Welcome, Boris Liatoukine. I am Graf Orlok. We have heard of your journey here. What brings you home?"

This was certainly was not home for Liatoukine; but Orlok was clearly playing to the notion held by the other Council members that the Sepulchre was the home of all vampires—and thus, that it had power over all of their kind.

Liatoukine got the pleasantries out of the way. "Greetings, Orlok, fellow council members…" Then, he decided to get straight to it as it seemed they knew full well why he was here. "Vampires have always infiltrated human society in the past. We need to, if only in order to protect ourselves—and of course to gain enrichment and nourishment. However, it seems that we are increasing such operations far more aggressively than in the past. It appears as if we are trying to take them over completely." Liatoukine used the 'we' simply to imply brotherhood. He didn't mean it, of course.

"Quite so," said Orlok. "It is long past time we took control. Our city appears every day for an hour. Currently, only fear and our influence keep its existence at the level of rumors. But this will not last. As the humans develop their sciences and communications, too many will come to know of the Sepulchre. News of its existence will spread. The human empires are large and powerful. One or more may decide to move against us. This may prove perilous for us. I trust, then, that you do not disagree with our new strategy?"

"As it happens, I do disagree. It is *your* strategy, Graf, is it not?" Something that passed for a smile appeared on Orlok's withered face, and he slowly nodded his head. The other Council members said nothing. Liatoukine noted this. Perhaps they were not too enthusiastic about the new strategy, and happy for Orlok to take the blame if anything went wrong?

Liatoukine pressed on. "You are pushing too hard. The humans are becoming far more aware of us, at every level of their society. I can assure you of this. In my own Russia, officials have destroyed many of your agents. The Emperors themselves have been secretly conferring about us, notwithstanding their political rivalries in other, more mundane areas."

"I know of this," responded Orlok, "but it does not matter. Control will pass to us, overtly or with the humans acting as our marionettes."

"No, it will not," Liatoukine stated. "Even if you manage to enslave all the royal families of Europe, and all their ministers, it is foolish to think that you could control millions of humans. Do you think the God-fearing masses will put up with vampire control? Operating in the shadows, having us dismissed as mere superstition is one thing, but this aggressive push towards mastery of Europe will bring us into open conflict. We cannot fight millions of them. What will you do when they surround the Sepulchre and bombard you with their cannons every day for an hour?"

Some of the council looked unsettled. Liatoukine pushed his advantage.

"They are already destroying your agents. I come from Zagreb; there, they held one of your infiltrators prisoner; they interrogated him, then destroyed him. It is clear to me that the Austrian Empire has far greater knowledge of us than we thought. They have prison cells made especially for us. I suspect they may even be aware that the Sepulchre is real, and not just some local peasant's tale. There can be no doubt that a confrontation is coming. Rather than put it off for decades—time during which we can perhaps find a solution—it will be upon us within a few years, maybe even a few months."

"And you, of course, are completely loyal to us?" responded Orlok. "Perhaps you can explain your greater loyalty to the Russian Empire? Your fighting for them? Even now, you are on a mission for them. You think I did not know? Is it really the case that you are here for our benefit? Or for those of your masters in St. Petersburg?"

Liatoukine's loyalty was to himself above all. However, he certainly preferred St. Petersburg to the Sepulchre. And he had much sympathy for the Russian Empire. The assimilation of other lands into the Empire, the crushing of the lesser kinds, especially the peasants, yes, that was real power! Perhaps, one day, they would take control of the Sepulchre itself—under his guidance of course. However, there was the more immediate problem of Orlok's activities. It was time to go further on the offensive.

"My loyalty to my kind is not in doubt," said the Russian Captain. "Your spies seem to know that I am on mission to look into the so-called 'vampire plague' on behalf of my Tsar, working in tandem with the Habsburgs. But it is only the ideal cover to protect our own interests, which is why I am here. At least, I have not been uncovered, unlike so many of your servants." He paused. "Aside from your competence, perhaps it is your own motivation that we should question?"

This was an open challenge. Orlok hissed back in anger, but Liatoukine did not let up.

"How did you become a vampire, Graf Orlok? Does the rest of the Council know?"

They clearly did not. Orlok was known to have mysterious origins and that it was best not to inquire about them. They gave no answer, and Orlok was certainly not going to enlighten them. His hands were now outstretched, his long fingers with their razor sharp fingers moving as if digging into Liatoukine's neck. The Russian Captain pressed ahead. There was no going back now.

"Most of us became what we are by having been converted by another vampire's bite. Some of us have the power to absorb humans into themselves and to then release them, changed into whatever their masters want them to be. Their physical form can be changed, to be made grotesque, to even destroy the memories of who they once were…"

Otto Goetzi intervened. "We know this, Liatoukine. I myself was converted by a Great One in such a manner. I have taken his name to match his appearance, the very form in which he shaped me. Get to your point."

Liatoukine knew this; in fact this second Goetzi assisted the accursed Radcliffe's human incursion many years before. Somehow, he had been forgiven by the Council after the first Goetzi's death. Liatoukine did not know—or care—about how that had been accomplished. The first Goetzi was, in fact, not that well regarded, despite what his successor said. He was known for his sadism; this version of Goetzi had been a young village woman once known as Polly Bird and Goetzi turned her into a copy of himself.

"Of course," responded Liatoukine. "But first, I wish to be clear about who Orlok is—or was. There was once, some time ago, a young Transylvanian nobleman…" The atmosphere in the room changed a little. An element of fear and foreboding could now be felt from the Council. More hissing from Orlok. "I do not need to bore you with the details, but Graf Orlok, then a handsome young man, thought that he could displace the power and influence of Count Dracula himself."

There were stunned gasps from the Council. All knew Dracula. All knew that he was the most powerful vampire of all.

"Orlok of course, had no idea that Dracula was a vampire. He had scoffed at the local peasantry's fear of him, dismissing it as mere superstition. Hearing of his attitude, Dracula invited him to his castle. Orlok was not much seen after that. His family all seemed to die mysteriously, disappeared, or became seen only at odd hours. Orlok himself was also rarely seen. And soon, the locals started to fear Orlok, with good reason.

"For Count Dracula had not merely killed him, of course. He had absorbed him. He then allowed him to reemerge but only as a copy, a doppelganger of Dracula himself. Orlok would carry out business on his behalf, the things the Count considered to be lesser tasks. And when these tasks were carried out well, Dracula would let Orlok out of himself not just in the form of a copy, but in the misshapen shape we see today, in which he would terrorise the locals."

"Are you saying that Orlok is a servant of Dracula?" interjected Goetzi. "That he is here serving him now?"

"Far from it," replied Liatoukine. "A few years ago, Dracula dismissed Orlok from his service. No reasons were given. Perhaps we can infer a degree of incompetence on Orlok's part? After all, Dracula left him in his current, charming form... Orlok became resentful at having been cast out. He left his land and came here. Where he seems to have done quite well."

"What do you know of these matters?" Orlok finally said. "You're but a barbaric vampire from the East?"

*Barbaric?* Orlok would pay for that, swore the Russian Captain, who resumed addressing the rest of the Council.

"Forgive me, my lords. Orlok has already questioned my loyalties, and now he mocks my very knowledge of him. Please be assured that my information comes straight from Count Dracula himself. Indeed, he has authorized me, if it came to that, to present you with this letter..."

He handed the letter not to Orlok, but to Goetzi. The latter noted the seal, and opened it. The note, no more than a few words, was handed round the Council. Was that a trembling of their hands Liatoukine thought he saw?

"As you can see," he resumed, "Dracula himself has authorized me to speak on his behalf in this matter. He and I share the same concerns over the current strategy. I trust that settles any doubt over my knowledge, or indeed my loyalty to our kind. Unless, you doubt the word of Dracula?"

The Council said nothing.

The note had been passed to Orlok. He shook it at Liatoukine with his outstretched hand.

"Dracula does not rule here!" he screeched. "He rarely leaves his castle! His days of power are long gone!"

But Liatoukine was not intimidated.

"Do you intend to test him on that? He remains part of you, Orlok. Dracula is both fascinated and intrigued with the British Empire. He thinks in terms of the decades ahead, and some here know that he wishes to have... interests in the heart of the British Empire. You, yourself, know this, Orlok. You think you can do better than him. Be faster than him. Thus, your policy of recent years."

Orlok crushed Dracula's note and shredded it with one hand before casting it aside.

"I offer power and security to our kind. Dracula offers nothing. Nothing!" he said.

Liatoukine ignored this and continued:

"You appear to have focused mostly on the Habsburg Empire. Perhaps you have an ulterior motive for this? You hate and fear Dracula. You resent him, but cannot destroy him. He is, after all, your creator. His lands, at least nominally, come under Austrian governance. Perhaps you seek control of the Habsburgs not for our kind's benefit, but to control their armies which you plan to use to attack Dracula's castle? They would do something you are too fearful and weak to do yourself?"

This accusation moved Orlok to sheer rage.

"You dare question me? How dare you!"

He gestured to one of his larger minions standing in the hall, who then moved towards Liatoukine. The vampire in question looked like a peasant, probably converted by Orlok himself. *Perfect*, Liatoukine thought. Time to make the point for which he had prepared with the smith he had visited earlier.

He drew his pistol. The peasant vampire sneered. After all, everyone knew that bullets were harmless to a vampire. Liatoukine fired. The peasant exploded in a fireball. All present were shocked.

Liatoukine was most satisfied. Had this not worked, his powers would still have been sufficient to deal with the attack, but he was inordinately pleased with his success. He swiftly made his point:

"Clearly, I was merely defending myself. Please notice, however, that I destroyed that upstart using bullets containing the ashes of a vampire's heart. Such ashes are a known weakness for many of us. Imagine the humans with their pistols—their bombs even—containing such ashes. They would be many casualties on our side. These weapons the humans are capable of devising are beyond our imagination. Let us not provoke them into using them against us now by stirring a foolish campaign they are already aware of."

The argument was clearly running away from Orlok. All could sense the mood, in the way that only vampires can, amongst themselves.

Liatoukine pushed harder.

"What is Orlok? He is nothing but a copy of Count Dracula. Trying to outdo him. He is a counterfeit, not the real thing at all. His very ideas are derived from his creator!"

The taunt hit home. Orlok screeched again. His one chance to retrieve the situation was to demonstrate his power and impose his will by killing Liatoukine. He started moving towards his intended victim.

Liatoukine was prepared. He swiftly used his other pistol and fired. The bullet smashed into Orlok, sending him flying backwards, but did not destroy him as it had his minion was. Liatoukine could see why: his foe's coat had been reinforced in some way. *Very well*, he thought. He would simply use his own powers. Or decapitate him. Or both.

He issued one final taunt: "I see. You protected yourself with your coat, but did not provide such protection to your minion, for all your talk of our kind."

Orlok levitated forward, ready for the final confrontation, but Goetzi intervened. "Enough! There must be no more disunity here! Orlok—it is over. We can no longer afford the risks of your strategy. It could bring destruction upon us all. It must end." He seemed to speak for the Council, for they certainly did not disagree.

Orlok hung in mid-air. He floated down. His coat was damaged where the bullet had hit him. He waved his hand across it and what was left of the bullet fell to the floor harmlessly. The coat itself seemed to regenerate. He turned to the Council, slowly looking at each of them in turn as he spoke.

"I will not stay to witness your destruction. All of you will die at the hands of the humans some day, but not I. I shall leave the Sepulchre tonight. I will not return." With that, he walked out of the hall.

Liatoukine wondered about Goetzi. Why had he taken his side? His taunting of Orlok as a mere copy could have been applied to Goetzi too. It must have struck a nerve. Then, again, perhaps Goetzi intervened out of kinship, to save Orlok's existence?

"Where will he go?" wondered Goetzi.

"I care not," answered Liatoukine. "His time is, I suspect, limited. He can never be free of his old master's subconscious. He will forever be influenced by it, and try to outdo him in some way. And he will no doubt fail. Dracula plans decades ahead. Orlok attempts to rush things, as we have seen. I will leave the winding down of his strategy in your hands and will take my leave. Unlike Orlok, daylight does not affect me"

Liatoukine rode away from the Sepulchre. He had a long journey back to St. Petersburg. On the way, he would send word to Dracula of his success.

He had served many interests well that day: the Empires, Dracula, his fellow vampires, but, above all, his own. His stature and influence with the Sepulchre and Dracula, on the one side, and the Royal Courts—in particular, St. Petersburg—on the other, would both benefit. And he had enjoyed himself, too. The defeat of Orlok had not been guaranteed. He was a powerful foe. Liatoukine had enjoyed the danger, the thrill of it.

However, Orlok was not entirely wrong. At some point, the humans would cease to ignore the Sepulchre out of fear and disbelief. Something would have to be done. Exactly what, Liatoukine did not know. Even in Russia, some suspected him. They would soon call him "Captain Vampire," if he was not careful. But for now, however, he was secure and able to use his influence to ensure that his not aging never became an issue. Lone vampires such as himself and Dracula could remain safe, but would an entire city?

*Van Helsing's phonograph, Wisborg, Germany, 10 August 1901.*

My studies of the Undead, and of my late adversary, Count Dracula, have revealed the existence of a Graf Orlok who lived some years previously in Transylvania. He, too, had a fearsome reputation, although not as great as Dracula's. It would appear that, after a period of absence, he returned to his home in 1830, but a few years later, left to come here to Wisborg.

Following his trail here, I have been taken aback by subsequent events that occurred in 1838. From the documents I have found, it appears that Orlok had similar intentions to that of Dracula, although here in Germany and not in England. Even his adversaries were people similar to those of us who fought Dracula. And his strategy was the same. This Orlok even had the same desires as Dracula—taking an unholy interest in Ellen Hutter, the wife of Thomas Hutter. However, things did not end well for her as they did for our own Mina Harker. Ellen gave her life to trick Orlok into consuming her blood until dawn. The rays of the Sun then destroyed him without trace. Not a weakness that Dracula had, and a very different conclusion to our adventure. She did not survive.

However, the coincidences are too much to be ignored. Furthermore, in the records I have found here, Orlok mentions something called the Sepulchre—a city of his kind. I have heard other rumors of such a city, whispered amongst communities in Central and Eastern Europe plagued by vampires. It is sometimes referred to as "Selene."

There have been too many references for me to ignore, and this Orlok affair of years past has unsettled me. There must be some connection to Dracula. I have not, in the past, been inclined to try to convince the world of the existence of such creatures as vampires. But I may have to reassess matters. The existence of Selene, or the Sepulchre—whatever it may be called—is a matter too great to be ignored. I must research it further.

There can be no graver a threat to humanity than a City of the Nosferatu.

## The Trial of Van Helsing

*St. Petersburg, 1913*

Rasputin considered his visitor, tall, upright and thin. There was something about the eyes—like those of a cat. In some circles, he was known as "Captain Vampire." However, he was now a General of the Russian Imperial Army. Yes, thought Rasputin, up close he could tell that the General was not quite human. But many did not listen to the rumors. Liatoukine was a man of influence. And it seemed he wanted the help of none other than himself; also influential in certain circles, although perhaps a lot less liked.

For his part, Boris Liatoukine was also considering Rasputin, but he thought him to be nothing but a degenerate. They were both at a particular lady of the court's home. Rasputin was sitting on a divan. He was leant back, his shirt undone, with a semi-clad noblewoman on either side of him. Liatoukine was not above such behavior himself, but he disapproved of it in others. Especially peasants—and he considered the monk Rasputin to be little more than that. But his influence was unquestionable. Liatoukine had, in fact, expected to find a supernatural being, but he had found someone who was only human and nothing more. Given the peasant's power, he found that unsettling. One day, something would have to be done.

They had already exchanged pleasantries when

Liatoukine finally got to business.

"I understand you can help me find a certain individual, a renowned professor named Van Helsing—a Dutchman. You are aware, of course, that the Tsar relies on me to look into areas of... er, *special interest*, shall we say? I firmly believe the Professor could assist in these matters. We have approached the Dutch government, but they say he is studying and does not wish to give private consultations. I am sure I could persuade him to help, if only I could speak to him myself."

"My dear General Liatoukine," cackled Rasputin. "No need to be so coy. You advise the Tsar on supernatural matters. I, too, advise him—and the Tsarina—on many matters. We both do God's work." Rasputin looked heavenwards, rolling his eyes upwards. Liatoukine, too, felt like rolling his eyes, but restrained himself.

"Of course, I can help you," the monk continued. "In recent years, Van Helsing has become known in many religious circles for his esoteric knowledge. I have already obtained the information for you. Of course, I had to incur certain expenses..."

Liatoukine tossed a small pouch at Rasputin. The monk took a quick glance inside. He was not greedy, but money helped him be the center of attention. Satisfied, he placed the pouch on a table in front of him, then took a small envelope which he gave to Liatoukine.

"I think you will find the information necessary to assist you in finding Van Helsing," he said. "Now, if our business is concluded, I have many spiritual matters to discuss with my guests."

Liatoukine was displeased with the monk's attitude. Had it not been for his closeness to the Tsar, he would have drained him of his energy, giving the peasant an excellent opportunity to have a real spiritual discussion with his maker. Instead, he simply bade him a good day and left.

Liatoukine entered his carriage and looked at the document he had just been handed. Van Helsing's location was a surprise to him. It was a place he had visited in the past, whose master was now dead, but somehow, it seemed appropriate. Of course, Liatoukine had no real intention to merely have a conversation with van Helsing. He was to capture the Dutchman and take him to the Vampire City—The Sepulchre, sometimes known as Selene amongst the humans. There, Van Helsing would stand trial for his role in killing the greatest vampire of all—Count Dracula.

### Castle Dracula, Transylvania, the Austro-Hungarian Empire.

On a mountain high above a village, a most foreboding castle stood. Within its corridors, soldiers of the Austro-Hungarian Empire patrolled, and certain officials worked. The soldiers would patrol and look into anything odd; a mysterious sound perhaps, or an odd drop in temperature... Nothing was ever found. Such things were unsettling, but only temporarily. These men knew their business and were confident. The one who had once been the master of this castle had been destroyed some twenty years before. They were the masters now, and used the castle for their own purposes.

In one of the many rooms, now converted into a study, two men were having a conversation. Baron Vordenberg, whose office it was, was talking to a distinguished guest. Vordenberg, a man in his late thirties, was experienced in supernatural matters and had gained a high official position within the group tasked by the Emperor to deal with such things.

"Well, we know the vampires of Selene have been looking for you for a while," he said. "They seem to have become a little braver of late, we believe, of which trying to get to you is a large part, but you already know this."

His guest, a noted expert on many supernatural matters, including vampirism, was Professor Van Helsing. It had been a few years since his encounter with Count Dracula, but he remained active.

"I am most grateful not only for informing me of the threat," he replied, nodding his head, "but also for the access you have afforded me to study the many documents and artifacts left behind by Dracula"

"My friend, it is we who should be grateful," said the Baron, laughing. "Your efforts disposed not only of a grave vampire threat, but also provided the Empire with a most useful base of operations. Cost free, too!" he added, slapping his hand on his desk in amusement.

"What about the locals? Do they have any inkling of what you're doing here?" asked Van Helsing.

"Possibly—but only as rumor. Our public face is merely that of minor functionaries with a small troop of soldiers, operating in a part of the Empire that is so remote that no one would think anything of it. The legends of the previous, er, owner, persist of course. However, we do feel some of the natives are slowly becoming impressed by the fact we have taken the castle for ourselves. Such stories serve our purpose. The peasantry is consequently less fearful of the supernatural—and the supernatural is more fearful of us!"

"Hence perhaps the vampires' recent interest in me," mused Van Helsing. "No doubt an attempt to tilt the balance back. Especially now that we know where their city is located."

"And that is something else we are very grateful to you," nodded the Baron. "For your work on establishing where it is was of great importance. The city would be better off destroyed. It is unfortunate indeed that it is situated, as was rumored, in Serbia."

"I understand the political situation remains tense," said Van Helsing.

"Yes. Serbia is promoting an assassination campaign in Bosnia-Herzegovina, which is part of the Empire. They seem to be insisting on a war—one which we would swiftly win, of course, even if their Russian friends support them, which frankly I doubt. In such circumstances, we could then attend to Selene. However, we are beholden to a policy over which we have no influence. Vienna will not institute a war over a supernatural city that can only be seen for an hour a day. Serbian agitators, yes,they are real enough for the world to see, but vampires, no—despite rumors and even some official reports. We can only act covertly, and in such a way to not provoke Serbia or Russia. We still don't quite know what the understanding between Belgrade and Selene is..."

Van Helsing pondered the issue.

"Perhaps some form of non-aggression pact? I wonder what they make of the new ruler of Selene— Mircalla Karnstein. From what I learned, and your own organization have gathered, she is being most assertive. Certainly, it seems she is making a real effort to deal with me. I can only assume my research has eager readers in her domain."

"Indeed," chuckled the Baron. "Especially as they are clearly aware of your dispatching the former owner of this castle! However, we are ready for them. As you know, we have given your location to the Russian General Boris Liatoukine."

Liatoukine was a familiar name to Van Helsing; he had long been rumored to be of supernatural origin and had been known as "Captain Vampire" for decades, although the present holder of the title claimed he was just the latest in family line. It was not an unfamiliar tactic among some vampires... Liatoukine had a brutal reputation. His influence at the Court in St. Petersburg was well known, even feared. Although there was no solid evidence, Van Helsing assumed that Liatoukine was some kind of vampire, but one who drained life-force instead of blood.

"What you perhaps do not know," Vordenberg went on, "is that the General has assumed some kind of role as supernatural adviser to the Tsar. In matters pertaining to vampires he has effectively total control. You could say he is my opposite number. Of late, due to the political situation, our cooperation with Russia on these matters has declined. With Liatoukine assuming this role, it has fallen even further. We even believe there has been some disinformation. We have only just found out about his position..."

Van Helsing wondered if they had just found out, or if the Baron had only just decided to tell him. Perhaps he was just getting older, and more suspicious due to his experiences. The Baron and his people had been very helpful in his research, despite his not being a citizen of their empire.

"Perhaps it is he who will come to kill or capture me?" said Van Helsing.

"I do hope so," said the Baron. "If we can capture him, we may be able to interrogate him, and if kill him, that's one less enemy to deal with. To all, he will have simply disappeared. He is unlikely to have told the Tsar where he is going. But whoever comes, our trap will send the right signal to Karnstein." He paused. "It is brave of you to act as bait."

"Not so. I have no intention of looking over my shoulder for the rest of my life, however long that may be. The vampires have been afraid of me since they realized my involvement in destroying Dracula. Now, it seems Karnstein has emboldened them. Destroying their agent would throw them back into a state of fear."

There was a knock on the door. A guard came in with a note for the Baron. He read it and said:

"It seems we will soon find out. We have word that strangers are approaching the village. We should prepare. Our trap may be sprung tonight!"

"One moment," said Van Helsing. "I am troubled by Mircalla Karnstein. We know she was destroyed many years ago How is it that she has come back to life? Her resurrection is the key to her rise to power—no vampire has ever come back from such destruction before. Indeed, there was an official report on the matter and her last victim even wrote something on it..." Van Helsing paused. "If she can come back, then perhaps others can too..." He paused again. "...Others such as Dracula..."

"Yes, that had crossed my mind too," said the Baron. "Of course, my own family has its own connection to Mircalla Karnstein. Dealing with such creatures is a family tradition. My grandfather was present at her destruction. He related it to me himself. There is no doubt in my mind that he told me the truth. The official reports from Styria confirmed the matter. Even the famous report by Doctor Hesselius leaves no room for doubt. And the account by Karnstein's last victim, Laura—her own descendent!—also confirmed it, although she was not present at the destruction..."

"All of that is only some of the evidence that the public knows about, and it is often attributed to hallucinations, visions, or what have you, in relation to what some believe was the work of a poisoner rather than a vampire."

Baron Vordenberg looked thoughtful for a moment.

"We know Karnstein was not a poisoner. I have been pondering this and I do have a theory—nothing more than that—that would explain it…"

Later, Van Helsing made his way down to the village, accompanied by a couple of soldiers. Other troops were ensconced there. The Dutchman was staying at a rented farmhouse rather than at the castle. That had been the location provided via intermediaries to Liatoukine. In these remote parts of the world, matters could be dealt with quietly and away from the eyes of the public. Van Helsing had approved of this as there were fewer chances of innocents being harmed. The villagers had been told that tonight they may be better off staying indoors.

Van Helsing entered his house and sat at a desk. He hoped the strangers were indeed vampires. It would be best to deal with them as soon as possible.

The horse-drawn carriage with the two strangers stopped before approaching the village. Liatoukine was the main rider. He was dressed as a trader. He considered this ruse somewhat unbecoming for a man of his stature, but such deceptions were unfortunately often needed—especially as not only his vampire senses, but his soldier's experience, told him something was not quite right in the village ahead.

He turned to his fellow rider, also disguised as a trader. Like Liatoukine, she, too, was a vampire. Originally known as Polly Bird, she had been converted into vampirism by one Otto Goetzi—long since deceased. However, he had used his power to change her into a copy of himself. She stayed in that form for many years, even becoming a member of the Vampire Council of the Sepulchre.

However, Liatoukine was well aware of her original form. She had been lower born than him, certainly, but it was said she was rather beautiful previous to her encounter with Goetzi, and he certainly admired the female form. He made an offer: using certain knowledge he had acquired, he would revert her to her previous female form—still belonging to the Undead of course—and, in return, she would support him on the Vampire Council of the Sepulchre.

Things had not gone entirely to plan, however. Mircalla had objected to Polly's continued presence on the Council due to the change, arguing she was no longer quite the same person. Liatoukine found this odd. It was thought that Mircalla had certain tastes and that, like himself, was not averse to the female form. No doubt her attitude was to do with eliminating someone loyal to her from the Council. This was when their rivalry had begun in earnest.

Still, Polly Bird had remained his ally within the Sepulchre, despite no longer being on the Council. Liatoukine could count on her, but knew that she also had a degree of ambition of her own. She desired to reclaim her position on the Council, but not for his exclusive benefit. Observing her long, raven-colored tresses and shapely body, Liatoukine felt pleased with his work.

"I sense something amiss," he said, breaking out of

his reverie. "I will visit the local inn, see what the atmosphere is like and gain information if I can."

Van Helsing was still at his desk. He was not alone. There was a soldier masquerading as his assistant in the room. Upstairs, there were more soldiers waiting. And there were more still, hiding behind a false wall of his study.

The Dutchman suddenly some green light on his window—the sign that a vampire was coming. He rapped on the wall twice. Signals would be passed. All would be warned.

Liatoukine entered the Inn and proceeded to the bar. The establishment only had only a few young men there. At first glance, there was nothing unusual—but the Vampire General noticed the absence of older men and barmaids. He ordered a tankard of ale.

"What brings you here, stranger?" the landlord asked.

The landlord was in actual fact a local, albeit a Sergeant in the Emperor's army. All the men were soldiers dressed as villagers.

"I am just a trader, selling my wares," replied Liatoukine. "What I sell is not cheap: jewels, rare books and so on. I aim for those with enough money to appreciate the better things in life. I understand that to be Castle Dracula outside?"

Nobody reacted at that—the other patrons simply carried on talking. The landlord replied, handing over the drink:

"Yes. The Count died a while back and it's all in the hands of the state now."

Liatoukine had been here before, years ago. The locals were terrified of the very name of Dracula. They may have recovered some of their courage, but surely not to this casual extent?

"However," the landlord continued, "we do have a man of learning in the village, studying books from the Count's collection. He may well be interested in what you are selling."

"My prices are high, but I would like to meet with him. Perhaps I have something of interest to him," replied the Russian Vampire.

The landlord gave him the address of Van Helsing's farmhouse.

The lack of fear, the quick providing of information of Van Helsing's address, the make-up of the pub clientele... All a bit obvious, Liatoukine thought. Still, best not to underestimate these men. He went over to a table and drank his ale—not too quickly—and then left.

He walked back to his carriage and took a case out from the back. Polly was seated there, hidden from view. He quietly and briefly apprised her of the situation.

He then walked over to the farmhouse and knocked on the door. The Dutchman's "assistant" opened it. Liatoukine briefly introduced himself as a trader of books and jewels from St. Petersburg and was let in.

Van Helsing got up from his desk to greet his visitor—crucifix casually in hand. Liatoukine saw no reason to delay matters. It was indeed his quarry. They had met before, just a handshake, at a diplomatic function.

The Vampire General spun around and killed the young "assistant" with a blow to the neck. Another blow to Van Helsing's arm and the crucifix was on the floor. Without a word, he grabbed the Dutchman by the throat and pulled him out of the house. Why delay things with dramatic utterances? That can come later at a more congenial time.

The soldiers behind the fake wall—nothing more than paper—burst through and gave chase. There were two of them; their pistols had bullets which contained the ashes of vampire's hearts—a rare commodity that could destroy vampires.

"Halt!" they cried.

Liatoukine held Van Helsing aloft with one arm. With the other, he shot the soldiers with his own pistol. A bullet to their hearts. Had these humans not yet accounted for the speed and superior reflexes of a vampire? Clearly not.

He landlord and his men came running from the Inn. From the first floor of the farmhouse and other directions came more soldiers—in military dress. They were armed in a number of ways: pistols, swords, stakes, holy water and other weapons known to defeat various forms of vampires.

Liatoukine assessed the threat in but a moment. As indeed had Polly Bird, who burst out of the carriage.

She carried a machine gun in her hand that might have been too heavy for a normal human to carry as lightly as she did. She leapt onto the carriage roof and started mowing the soldiers down. Then she jumped off and ran around, firing at everyone—whilst not hitting Liatoukine or Van Helsing.

For his part, the Vampire General was also moving swiftly, using a knife, cutting and slashing any soldier who got near him. The bloody scene looked like a grotesque speeded up ballet with Liatoukine and Polly leaping and jumping and spinning and killing.

Within a minute, they had won. All the soldiers lay dead or dying.

In the distance, the two vampires could see more soldiers coming down from the castle at high speed, but for a few precious moments, they would savor their victory. This they did by feeding on the dying. Polly went for their throats, taking their blood whilst they were still breathing. She did this to three of them, taking enough to convert them. She did this knowing that their comrades would destroy them as soon as they reached them. It was an act of deliberate psychological cruelty—these Austrian upstarts must be taught as disturbing a lesson as possible.

For Liatoukine's part, he swiftly drained the life force of two soldiers, including the landlord. The man was saying the Lord's Prayer as he died, causing Liatoukine some pain. For that, he left nothing but a skeleton behind, even if it did take a few moments more.

A horrified Van Helsing had already started running towards the coming soldiers, led by Baron Vordenberg. But Polly caught up with him, grabbed him by the neck, and pulled him back to the carriage. There, she threw him into the back and attached him to a chain hanging off the compartment wall.

Swiftly, she jumped next to Liatoukine in the rider's seat. With a crack of the whip, the carriage was away at enormous speed. Both Liatoukine and Polly, intoxicated on their success and their feeding, laughed almost uncontrollably.

At the village, the soldiers lay dead, their blood seeping into the ground. They had come from all over the Empire: Austria, Dalmatia, Slovakia, Ruthenia and Slovenia. They were Austrians, Croats, Czechs and more. They had served their Emperor and indeed their God under one banner. Their loyalty and service had been rewarded with death. Such were the thoughts of Baron Vordenberg as he surveyed the scene. Despite his experience, he found himself shaking in shock at what had happened. They had not been prepared for such tactics. How dare these creatures use such barbaric technology as a machine gun in the heart of civilized Europe?

Meanwhile, after a frenzied ride of no more than an hour, Liatoukine's carriage had come to a halt in a deserted field. There, guarded by a couple of peasants—they had their uses after all—was an aircraft. It was a Russky Vityaz, of which only one was built. However, Liatoukine had had a secret version especially made for him. Furthermore, using certain knowledge gleaned from the Sepulchre's library, he was able to make certain modifications to the machine.

Liatoukine considered himself a modern vampire. He had visited an air show in Brescia, Italy, in 1909, and was fascinated with what he'd seen. Technology was here to be used and, indeed, enjoyed in the furtherance of power. He cared not if it came from the humans. Many other vampires preferred more traditional methods of doing things. Fortunately, Polly was advanced in her thinking and was most enthusiastic about using the machine gun—his idea, of course. Such tactics had given them the edge.

Now, with this other piece of human technology, he would foil the Austrians again. They bundled a protesting Van Helsing into a compartment, not bothering to respond to whatever he was saying, and took their places in the flying machine.

They took off into the dark Transylvanian sky. Liatoukine was still intoxicated by his draining of the soldier's life force. He wanted to demonstrate his superiority over the Empire he had just defeated and test his aircraft modifications.

One of his fellow countrymen had just performed

the first loop the loop. This was a matter of great pride for Liatoukine. He was a proud Russian. Many of his kin suspected his loyalty to Russia outweighed that to the Sepulchre. They were right.

Liatoukine pulled back the control stick and the aircraft started the loop. Liatoukine roared with delight. Polly screamed her joy. On the ground, the plane was barely seen, but their unearthly cries could be heard by many, causing deep fear. Liatoukine was exhilarated. What a joy it was to be Undead in this new era! In his tiny compartment, Van Helsing's reaction was somewhat less enthusiastic.

The aircraft landed in Serbia, where the Sepulchre was based. There, they transferred to a horse and carriage supplied personally by Mircalla. It had no driver—a supernatural trick intended to cause fear amongst the locals. Liatoukine was all in favor of causing fear, but wondered if this might bring too much attention to the Vampire City. The Serbian authorities and the Sepulchre had some kind of informal agreement. He would have to find out what that was; Mircalla's behavior may endanger it.

Liatoukine discussed the current situation with Polly.

"I daresay Mircalla will be most pleased with our results," he said, with more than a hint of sarcasm.

"You mean, your plan was to kill Van Helsing in revenge for his destruction of Dracula?" she replied.

"Yes, his impertinence could not be allowed to stand. Humans have destroyed prominent vampires before—including Mircalla herself before her resurrection—but he was the Lord of the Vampires. A direct insult against all of us."

"And of course, your personal standing and influence amongst our kind would have been most enhanced."

"Naturally such a thought never crossed my mind," he replied with a sly smile. "That would be a pleasant outcome, but my motives are entirely altruistic."

Dracula may well have been "Lord of the Vampires" or whatever, but Liatoukine's respect for him had, in fact, diminished. His actions in Britain appeared almost naive. He seemed not to care if he drew attention to himself, and inevitably was destroyed. So much for that education at the Scholomance, the school of the evil one himself.

"Of course, Mircalla heard of my plans," he continued. "I fear I may have been indiscreet. She commanded that I take him prisoner instead, giving me an arrest warrant for him would you believe. She wants to reap glory as the one who puts him on trial. She even intends to notify the great powers of the inevitable execution. A simple killing without boasting to the Empires would have been better. Her Austrian arrogance will simply increase the danger to us all. Dracula and Orlok were vampires of power; they pushed things too far, and where are they today?"

"Mircalla was once destroyed," said Polly, thoughtful. "Yet she came back. No other vampire has ever achieved that. It is that resurrection that enabled her to awe others into eventually letting her take over Selene. We should not underestimate her."

"Indeed, we should not. Given her position, I am not able to stand against her openly. As for her resurrection, I am not convinced of it. Why has not Dracula returned? Or Orlok? We often know when one of our kind dies and, in this case, the Austrians were obliging enough to produce a public record of the affair. They have been more circumspect since, of course."

"Are you saying she is an imposter?" asked Polly. "Or that she did not die? I must say, there is much speculation about her taste in lovers, and yet she has taken little interest in me." She gave a deliberate fake look of hurt.

Liatoukine laughed. "That could be because she knows you are my ally as much as anything else. It was sensed in the city when Mircalla died years ago. And as for being an imposter... she certainly has great vampire skills, just as the original Mircalla did. She operated alone, aside from her immediate servants, and few knew her. None are Un-dead today."

"In itself, that is most curious," said Polly. "They have all been destroyed, apparently by humans discovering them. A possible coincidence, of course, but most convenient for her, if she is not whom she claims to be. Although these few who knew her were not necessarily her friends—another reason to dispose of them?"

"Whatever the case," responded Liatoukine, "we should assume that Mircalla intends for us to be also 'accidentally' discovered by humans. I have never been impressed by her, and she knows it. Had we failed in capturing Van Helsing, or been destroyed in the process, that would have served her too. No doubt someone would then have been sent to destroy Van Helsing as per my original plan."

The carriage came to halt outside Selene. The gates of the Vampire City materialized. It was both invisible and intangible during the day, except for one hour when it could be seen by all. For Liatoukine, this was a dangerous tactical disadvantage in a world where humans were becoming ever more scientifically advanced. One day, soon, the whole world would know of the city's existence. Unless the Sepulchre could be made intangible for the whole day, some kind of arrangement will have to be made with the empires. The one with Belgrade would no longer suffice.

The carriage entered, pulling the cage containing Van Helsing. Two vampire guards took him from his cage and walked him through the city. The expert in Van Helsing came to the fore, helping to balance his terror. The city seemed constructed from some form of black marble. There were many bizarre-looking shapes and statues. And although it seemed empty, he could feel that he was being observed by many, those who wished to see the man who had killed Dracula. Some psychic effect, probably? This was all most informative.

They came to a rectangular building with many different sized triangles on the roof. Van Helsing was placed in a cell and given some food. He felt he had to learn more about this place. He was also determined to escape, but how?

The next day, the Dutchman was taken to the courtroom. He was placed by his guards in the dock. There, he took in his surroundings. To his right was a high bench for the judge. Past that, also next to him, were empty tables, presumably for prosecution and the defense. Would he have a defense? By a vampire? No! He would defend himself. He was avoiding the sight in front of him, the public gallery. There seemed to be at least a hundred vampires, hissing at him. A particularly hideous crone in the front row was clawing in the air. He could see his captors there too. Liatoukine was, as he had suspected, a vampire, too.

For his part, the Russian was irritated at having to sit next to the peasant crone. He suspected this may have been a local only just converted in order to provide some theatrics.

From a doorway behind the high bench, Mircalla entered. The hissing ceased. All rose, including, somewhat grudgingly, the Russian general.

Van Helsing did not rise. His vampire guard simply grabbed him by the back of the neck, held him aloft, and dropped him back in his seat when she sat down.

She wore elaborate robes, based on those of the judges in Vienna, albeit configured to her comely form. Her Styrian background had not been affected by her time in the Sepulchre. What else might she look to Vienna for? Liatoukine doubted that she intended to create a non- aggression pact with the human empires. If such things were to be achieved, it would be under the influence of St. Petersburg, not Vienna.

He turned his attention back to Mircalla. She had been followed by her lieutenant, Countess Marcian Gregoryi, also known as the legendary vampire Countess Addhema. Rather than immediately sit down, Mircalla hovered above the courtroom.

"We have before us the Dutchman Van Helsing, who is accused of the murder of Count Dracula!" she finally proclaimed.

"Murderer!" shouted the crone, attracting everyone's attention.

Given that she sat next to him, Liatoukine felt rather awkward. He hoped that people would not think she was with him. At least, Polly was on the other side. Lowly born as she was—a failing, of course—her beauty and her fighting prowess made her much respected.

"In two days' time," Mircalla continued, "we shall hear opening statements on the charge of the murder of Count Dracula. In a matter as grave as this, only I am fit to be charged with the duties of a judge."

The crowd roared its approval.

Predictable, thought the Russian general. Mircalla wishes to dominate the masses in such a manner, appearing to control everything. Even the Vampire Council seemed to have disappeared altogether.

"The prosecutor shall be Countess Marcian Gregoryi!"

Another roar. No surprise there: her Austro-Hungarian compatriot, albeit from the Magyar side.

"And the defense shall be..."

"If I may interject," said Van Helsing, causing much hissing, "I will represent myself in this ludicrous farce. I will tell you all about what happened, so that you will have an inkling about what will happen to you all and this foul city soon enough."

Again, this was predictable. Mircalla would no doubt make the most of the opportunity. He had to admire the Dutchman's nerve though.

There was again much hissing. Mircalla smiled, revealing her splendid fangs. How unfortunate she was an enemy, thought Liatoukine.

"Oh no," she said. "You are unfamiliar with our laws, and that would put you at a disadvantage. We are a fair people. You will be assigned counsel—one of our greatest denizens in fact." She pointed at the Russian General. "General Boris Liatoukine shall be your defense counsel!"

That development had not been so predictable.

In the office provided for him, Liatoukine was incandescent with rage. Mircalla had placed him in a position he could hardly have refused. Not if he wanted to get out of the city. He was hardly likely to win the case.

More importantly, he knew this would damage his reputation. Defending the killer of Count Dracula, even
though he had had no choice in the matter, would not be
forgotten. He suspected that Mircalla had plans for some
unfortunate incident to happen to him soon after the trial.

His best stratagem would be to go along with this
trial lunacy and then get back to St. Petersburg as quickly as he could. Let her try and eliminate him there! He
would plot against her from his beloved homeland. Let
the Serbs provoke their war with the Habsburgs. Russia
would come to Belgrade's aid and crush Vienna within
weeks. Then, Russian influence would reach new
heights. And, under his control, St. Petersburg would
make a new arrangement for the safety of the city of the
vampires, taking over from the Serbs. The cost would
not be too high: merely his appointment as military gov-
ernor and the staking of Mircalla in the heart of the Sepulchre! He would even get Countess Gregoryi to do it,
perhaps.

Liatoukine turned his mind to the current situation.
He had had a brief meeting with Van Helsing. He hoped
to persuade him to plead guilty. He was going to die anyway, probably by Mircalla draining every drop of his
blood. Why prolong the wait? He might even be granted
some form of last request. Getting him to plead guilty
could have served Liatoukine well. However, Van
Helsing refused to see reason.

Now, the trial was about to begin. He had a strategy—it was a strong one, but it might fail. If it did, he
would not go down attempting to curry favor. There was
also a slim chance of getting the mob to respect his effort.

Liatoukine left his office and proceeded to the
courtroom. He was clothed in full dress uniform, com-

plete with ceremonial sword. He considered the silver-edged sword a useful precaution. The metal had a powerful effect against most vampires.

Mircalla opened the trial by addressing Van Helsing.

"Professor Abraham Van Helsing, you are charged with the murder of Count Dracula. How do you plead?"

Van Helsing decided to go for theatrics. He got up and, directly addressing the court, responded:

"Certainly, I am not guilty of murder. I plead guilty only to the destruction of a foul creature, nothing more than a bit of vermin extermination."

The crowd went wild with hissing. Liatoukine grabbed the Dutchman and pulled him back into his seat.

Mircalla put up her hand and all went silent.

"Let the record show a plea of not guilty. The manner of his plea, however, will be taken into my consideration. Let the prosecution open its case."

She knew she could have forced a plea of guilty, but she wanted a full trial to glory in—and to force Liatoukine to defend the murderer of the Lord of Vampires.

Countess Marcian Gregoryi, resplendent in her rich Hungarian garb, began:

"Over the next few days, I intend to show how the accused and his compatriots, whom sadly we cannot yet locate..."

Or because Mircalla is not reckless enough to draw the attention of the British Empire just yet, thought Liatoukine.

"...plotted and carried out the destruction of the man known justly as the Lord of the Vampires. Even more foul, they murdered the newly-created vampire Lucy Westenra and those three known as his 'Brides.' I request that he be also charged with those murders."

"I object!" exclaimed the Russian vampire. "My client has only been charged with one murder. We have not prepared for others. Van Helsing must be treated fairly, so that we can all have confidence in our justice."

Mircalla considered this. She intended at some point to widen the system to deal with vampires who opposed her in any way. For the time being, it would serve her just as well to give the illusion of fairness.

"Your point is well taken, General Liatoukine. The original charges will not be expanded..."

The Countess looked startled for a moment. Clearly, this was not part of the plan, thought Liatoukine. Mircalla quickly continued:

"...However, the killings will be considered as part of the evidence for the overall main charge. Please continue, Countess Gregoryi."

The Countess had fully recovered her composure.

"Thank you, my lady. I intend to show how Count Dracula had meant to start a new existence in London. Quite reasonably, he had already taken an interest in English women as his servants. Or brides, if you will. It is the undisputed right of vampires to use humans as they see fit, after all. I will show how the Count traveled to London, passing through the town of Whitby, all the while harassed by Van Helsing and his criminal associates. The Count was eventually forced to retreat from England, but even this was not enough for Van Helsing. He pursued him across Europe..."

The Countess was interrupted by a wail from the peasant woman, accompanied by much hissing from the vampire mob in the public gallery. She continued, coming to the end of her presentation, her voice getting more strident:

"And then, in the final act of this symphony of horror, Van Helsing presided over the driving of a wooden stake through his very heart!"

The Countess dramatically clutched at her chest. The peasant vampire screamed and collapsed to the ground. The mob hissed again, this time seeming to move forward. Mircalla stood up and raised her hand. The hissing subsided at once.

"Actually," Van Helsing said, standing up, "we destroyed him with a knife slashing his throat and another straight into his heart."

He sat back down. Liatoukine almost burst out laughing, but contained himself. Still, he had to grab the Dutchman and exit the courtroom before the enraged mob could get to them.

The court reconvened the next day. This time there were more guards and fewer vampires in the public gallery. Liatoukine was pleased to see that the peasant woman was no longer there.

Mircalla began by addressing the court:

"There must be no repetition of yesterday's disturbances, whatever the provocation. The consequences of any further disruption will be severe." She did not care if the mob destroyed Van Helsing and Liatoukine. It was the challenge to her authority that concerned her. "General Liatoukine, please deliver the opening statement for the defense."

The Russian General rose to speak.

"It is clear that the human Van Helsing did indeed—either by his own hand or by leading others—murder Count Dracula. It is also correct that we vampires can do as we see fit with humans. Yet, there is a natural balance. Sometimes the humans have a right to defend themselves—but only until the balance is restored. The Count had effectively begun an unspoken war against the most powerful force in this world, the British Empire.

"Such behavior is unheard of amongst vampires. We always strive to remain in the background. We have had sometimes had to restrain our own kind. Some here may remember having to deal with Graf Von Orlok, who was himself connected with Dracula, a few years ago. Orlok was going too far with his plans involving our city. They may also recall my own part in the successful conclusion of that affair..."

Here, he gave a meaningful look at Mircalla. This was clearly an unspoken challenge, one that those in the public gallery would understand. It would do no harm to put some doubt about Mircalla into the minds of the other vampires, and remind them about his own considerable abilities.

"What an interesting defense you present," responded Mircalla. "Van Helsing isn't even British. Nonetheless, you will have your chance to present your evidence soon enough. The prosecution will present her evidence tomorrow; the day after the defense will do the same. Two days after that, I will deliver my verdict. Let no one say our justice is not swift and effective."

Van Helsing had been watching this with some interest, as he might, given that his life was at stake. But what really interested him was the rivalry between Mircalla and Liatoukine. He did not quite understand what was going on, but he saw an opportunity. He quickly wrote a note and passed it to Liatoukine: *Get a recess of a few days*, it read.

The Russian vampire wondered what the human was up to. He knew that Van Helsing was no fool. This was not likely to be a simple way of postponing his demise. Further, this was the first time he had communicated with him in any meaningful way.

He decided to see where this led.

"My lady," he said to Mircalla, "I would be like a three-day recess. We need to consider the evidence of the prosecution further, in particular how they have come by some of their information."

Mircalla looked at him. He must be desperate, she thought. He might also be up to something. She decided to give him only one day, in order to be seen to be fair.

"General Liatoukine," she said, "you have already had time to examine the evidence. Nevertheless, I will grant you an extra day."

With that, she left the courtroom.


Liatoukine went to see Van Helsing in his cell.

"You have something in mind?" he asked.

"Quite so," replied the Dutchman. "I think there may be a way out of this for both of us. I have certain information that may—if it is accurate, and I cannot vouch for that yet—let us both come out ahead. It is only a slight opportunity, but at the moment we appear to have none. It is clear to me that you have some problem with Mircalla. I sense she wishes you out of the way as much as me, is that not so?"

Liatoukine ignored the question.

"What is this opportunity?" he asked.

Van Helsing responded with a list of demands:

"I will need assurances regarding my safe passage out of Selene and my return to areas safely under human control. Further, I will require a solemn guarantee as to my own, permanent safety and that of my colleagues involved in the demise of Count Dracula in the future. In return, the information I shall give you will see an end to Mircalla's reign. I assume this trade may be of great benefit to you?"

The General wondered what it could be that Van Helsing had that could result in such an outcome. He could, of course, torture him. However, the Dutchman was hardly young anymore and may not survive the ordeal. It was perhaps surprising that he had already survived his trial without any apparent ill effects.

"If this information of yours gets Mircalla out of my way," he replied, "how do you know that I won't just kill you?"

"I don't," the Dutchman replied. "That is why I need some kind of witness to our agreement. No doubt you will choose your associate, this bizarrely named 'Polly Bird' However, she may not always be your ally, and should you betray me, she will be in a position to reveal your deal with me, and how you broke it. But by keeping to our agreement, you will send a signal to the powers of Europe that you can be trusted. From what you said in the courtroom, I gather that you do not seek a war with Mankind, not least due to your own life of privilege. I suspect those of us who deal with your kind already suspect your true nature. Assassinating you would prove too difficult and diplomatically risky, given your position of power in Russia. So it makes sense to strike a bargain now. That said, my information requires verification—I am not even sure we have enough time..."

Van Helsing was indeed no fool, Liatoukine thought. He was clearly outlining some very good reasons to let him go. The removal of Mircalla would be a prize well worth the Dutchman's freedom. And he was also correct in his assessment of Liatoukine's situation—it was important that the powers of Europe realize that, when it came to vampire matters, he could be a man with whom they could do business. He had certain plans.

"I can agree to a witness," he responded, "and I can certainly get you over the border to Slavonia, in the Austrian empire. I cannot give the assurances you seek regarding permanent safety—you are hardly popular amongst my kind. But you are in no position to guarantee my own safety form various human agencies. However, I think that both of us coming out of this situation victorious should be enough, don't you agree?"

Van Helsing did. Polly was called in to witness everything that was to be discussed and agreed. The Professor began by relating what Baron Vordenberg had told him a few days earlier at Castle Dracula.

"We must indeed move fast," Liatoukine said. "Polly will have to get the evidence we require. Using my aircraft, and her own natural speed, it can be achieved in the next couple of days. She will leave at once. Tomorrow is our oneday of recess and the next day will be taken with the prosecution case. No doubt Mircalla will have her spies follow her, but I am sure she is more than capable of dealing with them."

Polly smiled, and was gone. The vampire and the human then started to prepare for the first day of the prosecution.

The first day of the prosecution proceeded with a vigorous case presented by Countess Gregoryi—matched by an equally vigorous cross-examination by the Vampire General. He knew the ridiculously brief trial could not be won and Mircalla continually intervened, usually in favor of the Countess. However, he remained confident throughout. As well he might, given that word had reached him from Polly. She would shortly arrive back at the Sepulchre, already in possession of the evidence required to deal with Mircalla.

The next day, the trial reconvened for the beginning of the defense.

"General Liatoukine, you may begin your defense," Mircalla said.

He stood and said, "I wish a mistrial to be declared."

"On what grounds?" a clearly amused Mircalla asked. She could not wait to hear whatever desperate reason this Russian barbarian had found.

This was Liatoukine's moment. He addressed the whole court, rather than just Mircalla.

"On the grounds that the judge is not who she claims to be. You are not the real Mircalla Karnstein. You are an imposter!"

Countess Gregoryi and Mircalla threw a swift glance at each other.

"Prove what you say. Immediately," demanded Mircalla.

She knew the shared glance had been a mistake. All had noticed it, and undoubtedly did not interpret it as a glance of incomprehension.

"Mircalla Karnstein is famous in the human world, as most of us are not," Liatoukine began. "Indeed, for those humans who believe in us, this manuscript is of great importance." He waved a book in the air. "This is a study on the case written by one Doctor Hesselius. It contains the official report on the matter. It also contains the manuscript of Laura, Mircalla's last victim, relating her experiences. It makes it clear that Mircalla was destroyed by human hands. That form of destruction is one that our kind never survive.

"Then, some years ago, this person claiming to be

Mircalla Karnstein appeared, claiming that she had returned from the dead. I don't quite know how she convinced so many, but surely her close associate the Countess here," he pointed at Marcian Gregoryi, "had much to do with it. The Countess has a formidable reputation and her vouching for the woman claiming to be Mircalla would indeed help convince many of us..."

"You talk nonsense, Russian," the Countess said. "You can prove nothing—you seem to forget it is your client who is on trial here."

"Oh, but I can prove what I say," Liatoukine simply continued. "The imposter we see here today was helped by a very real link to Mircalla. Her last victim, Laura, also happened to be her descendent. And that is who we have before us—Laura."

Mircalla looked impassive.

"What is your evidence?" she asked. "And may I remind you that Laura was not one of us."

Liatoukine again addressed the court.

"It is true that Laura was not a vampire—not at first. She was only a descendent. She had been bitten by Mircalla. Then after Mircalla's destruction, I believe Laura gradually became one of us. The bite and familial link must have been the cause. Perhaps when she died, she became one of us, or perhaps she did so beforehand and only faked her human death? Certainly, it must happened some years after she wrote her manuscript that appeared in Doctor Hesselius' work. At some point, Laura's vampiric legacy took over. She wanted power and thus took the persona of Mircalla. The details need not concern us, whatever they may be, but the evidence I have should. First, we have a copy a Laura's manuscript and Mircalla's signature—in reality, Laura's—on her arrest warrant for Van Helsing..." He held both items aloft. "Look! The handwriting is the same!"

Many vampires had superior eyesight; those in the public gallery could see that what he said was the truth.

"However, my ultimate evidence was obtained recently by Polly, whom many of you know," Liatoukine continued.

"Your associate!" hissed the Countess.

"Yes, my associate," countered he Russian, "but one who is well known by many of you. And the evidence she procured is incontrovertible..."

Polly entered the courtroom—in a pre-planned manner—with two large portraits, held easily aloft in each hand. She explained their meaning.

"In my right hand is a portrait of Mircalla Karnstein, taken by myself from Karnstein Castle. In my left, taken from her former Styrian home, is one of Laura."

The women in the portraits were similar. However, it was clear who the woman seated in the judge's chair was—Laura.

Many vampires were old. They had a sense of age. Their eyesight could see the details of the art. Those in the public gallery could see within seconds that the portraits were from two different time periods. Laura's would have been painted long after Mircalla's—that was clear to them, as Van Helsing and Liatoukine knew it would be.

He briefly wondered how it was that Laura had not destroyed such evidence years back. Styrian arrogance, no doubt.

There was great unrest in the public gallery. The vampires moved forward, as a mob. The guards did not try to stop them—they joined with them. This imposter had made fools of them. They did not take that lightly.

"I am Mircalla," Laura bellowed.

She looked for support from the Countess—but she had somehow disappeared. It was over. She glared at Liatoukine. She still had one chance—destroy him and perhaps she could restore her authority.

She levitated. The mob stopped, some residual fear remaining.

She swooped down towards Liatoukine, arms outstretched. She would remove his head from his shoulders and crush it. If that did not work, she at least would have had her revenge. But the Russian vampire was ready for her. Aside from his powers, he was a true soldier. Laura could not match his combat experience. The Vampire General drew his sword and, as she came down, sliced her outstretched arms off.

Laura screamed in agony, blood splattering everywhere. Her arms slowly moved back in the air to re-attach themselves, but even before they reached her, Liatoukine had grabbed her by her throat, dropping his sword. He glared into her eyes and started to absorb her life force.

Laura thought of her childhood, her innocence. When Mircalla had come to her, when she was so young, so pure in spirit. It was only years after Mircalla's death that she felt the changes, a corruption taking root within her. She tried to resist it at first, but eventually gave in. How she wished now that she had resisted it more. How she wished now to have remained in that state of innocence, to somehow return to it. Then she thought no more.

Liatoukine had taken her life essence. She became old and wizened, her floating arms became bones and fell to the ground, disintegrating. Even the blood that had gushed from her severed limbs dried away. Held aloft in Liatoukine's arm, Laura rotted into a skeleton; even her clothing disintegrated. Then she was just dust floating down between the Russian vampire's fingers.

Van Helsing watched, transfixed and terrified. He had been silent throughout the trial, as agreed, in order not to antagonize the vampires any further. Somehow he remembered what he had to do—and that was to get out whilst all eyes were on this grim spectacle.

He moved towards the door and was out of the courtroom. He missed the sight of the Russian Vampire casually brushing off bits of dust from his uniform.

Van Helsing left the city and was taken to the border of the Austrian Empire in the same carriage that had brought him to the Sepulchre—albeit this time he was not in a cage. He crossed the border on foot and soon made contact with Croatian officials. He was taken to Baron Vordenberg without delay. Van Helsing considered that a victory had occurred. He was still alive for a start. More importantly for the wider world, the information he had gathered would soon be in the hands of the Austrians, and those they cooperated with on such matters. Their understanding of Selene and its politics—something not really considered before—would now be vastly enhanced. A dangerous vampire, Mircalla, had been removed. It was possible that Liatoukine may be even more formidable, but the information gathered about the Vampire City would outweigh that.

On the journey to Vienna, where he was expected to brief some of the Habsburg Empire's top officials, Van Helsing considered the political situation. He did not believe there would be war. Humanity was moving beyond that, at least in Europe. The incidents in Bosnia-

Herzegovina were just that—not sparks but perhaps cinders of all previous wars. The great powers instead would cooperate to prevent war. Were not all the royal houses related to one another? Was there not new, forward-thinking policies in the empires? Indeed, he expected them to cooperate on matters related to vampirism. There would perhaps be a war—but one of a united Europe against Selene. Despite an experience that may have driven many to madness, he felt content.

For his part Liatoukine was satisfied. He was still intoxicated with the life force of Laura. Now it was time to return to St. Petersburg. As her reward, Polly had been reinstated on the reconstituted Vampire Council, ensuring his influence. He had his position in St. Petersburg to return to and thus could not be on the Council himself. However, his reputation had soared. Perhaps now he was considered almost as great as Dracula?

Laura's lackey, Countess Gregoryi, had fled. Perhaps she may turn up somewhere else. He might even offer her forgiveness, if she agreed to be in his service. Apart from anything else, he admired her countenance.

He took a horse to get to his aircraft. He knew it would be one of the last times he would do so, as he intended cars to replace horses. Modernization was one of many of his plans for the Sepulchre.

He was pleased that Van Helsing had gotten away safely. This would help open lines of communication when needed. His reading of the political situation was that there would be a short war against Vienna. Russia would soon crush the Austro-Hungarians. He would take control of whatever deal Belgrade had made with the Sepulchre. From Russia's position of strength, he could secure their safety in a world ever moving faster with scientific progress. A non-aggression pact was the best option. Vampires would be grateful for the security and look to him for protection. He would use his position to find out all the supernatural secrets the Sepulchre had. These would be put at the service of Imperial Russia, which would become the most powerful force in the world—beyond that even of the British.

In such a position, the political rabble in his country would also be dealt with. The weak who preached democracy and worse would be swept away in days. He foresaw a glorious Russian Imperial future, under his quiet but firm guidance. Whatever could stop it?

## The Stake and the Sickle

*Southern Russia, March 1920*

The Russian vampire Boris Liatoukine, it must be said, did not have a good war. He himself had been thinking this just prior to being shot at by some Bolshevik. Not only had the war concluded with his homeland going nowhere, but also the very country had been taken over by Bolsheviks—whom he was now fighting at that moment.

The Reds were fighting intensely, as well they might, given that the reward for retreat could well be death by order of the political commissar. However, Captain Liatoukine himself inspired terror in his own men, but also a certain respect. He knew his business and demonstrated it by raising his pistol and shooting a number of the Red soldiers dead with a few well-aimed shots. Such accurate shooting was attributed to his rumored supernatural powers. "Captain Vampire," his men called him—they believed he had inherited them from his father. His men were in fact wrong on just one count—he and his father were the same man. Certain difficulties due to the political changes meant that he had to rapidly become his "son"—losing his senior rank in the process.

A grenade landed near Liatoukine, killing one of his men and severely wounding another. Despite Liatoukine being the nearest to the explosion, his wounds were minor and he was thrown off balance only temporarily.

Another couple of well-aimed shot dispatched two more red guards. His men were also doing well. They advanced forward, coming in close contact with their enemy. Bayonets were used. Liatoukine used his powers, speed and prowess—but not to the extent where it was obvious he was not human. He had made that mistake before.

Faced with such firm opposition from this unit of White Russian troops, the Red guards decided upon retreat. Liatoukine did not have enough resources to give chase.

A couple of survivors were left behind. One, an injured NCO, was taken captive. The other was an officer. Liatoukine ordered his men away whilst he dealt with him.

The Red officer was a young lieutenant. He was badly injured, but his situation was such that he could be saved. Liatoukine stood over him, and then kneeled next to him, pulling him up by his tunic, ignoring his pain.

"Brother officer... please... help me..." the man pleaded, looking straight at the vampire's cat-like eyes and pale, bearded face

Brother officer? Liatoukine swiftly understood that this meant the man was likely to have been a former Imperial officer, now working for the Reds. A traitor.

"I was in the Imperial Army," the man said. "I had no choice but to work for them. They had my family..."

"There is no excuse to work with these Bolshevik scum," Liatoukine hissed at him. "None."

The vampire glared at the prisoner, then started to drain him of his life. Liatoukine was a vampire that fed on the energy of human beings. He could take blood, but it was not enough to sustain him. Often, his victims would be found to have died of sheer terror or seemingly natural causes. The officer felt his life drain away.

Liatoukine would often take officers prisoner and interrogate them first, before eliminating them. Here, his anger got the better of him. His men had moved away and would see nothing. Liatoukine's fury meant that he turned the officer into a husk.

*Let the Bolsheviks see the corpse and be fearful*, he thought.

His men had captured an NCO—he would do for interrogation purposes. He took a last look at what remained of the officer.

"You should be grateful to me, 'brother officer.' As you are dead, it's likely your family will be left alone."

He went over to his men. Had they seen anything? They would only have seen a little. And a bit of fear in one's subordinates was no bad thing.

They started back to Novorossiysk, the town on the Black Sea where the anti-Bolshevik Armed Forces of South Russia under General Denikin had their headquarters. Theirs had been a reconnaissance mission, simply to see what was going on behind enemy lines. Their fight with the Bolshevik troops had not been part of the plan.

Suddenly, there was a sound—an aircraft. They all looked up. It was a Royal Air Force plane, heading towards the Reds. Part of the extensive British forces sent by Winston Churchill to help the White Russians' effort.

Back at Novorossiysk, Liatoukine returned to his quarters. At this moment, he was effectively an intelligence officer, spending time trying to find out what the Reds were up to. He also had duties as a liaison officer with the British forces.

He liked to go out and see firsthand what was going on. Hence the recent operation. Really, it was not a good thing to have been spotted and to have to fight his way out. However, he enjoyed combat. It stirred the blood—or whatever it was that ran in his veins. He wasn't sure himself. Regardless, at least the battle had resulted in the capture of an enemy NCO. The man spoke fast on the way back. He begged to join the White Army—but there was no way back for him, now. He feared the wrath of the political commissar, a certain Kostaki.

This Kostaki was ruthless in dealing with those who acted with insufficient zeal. Nothing unusual about that. Reds feared the commissars with good reason. No, what was odd—and the captured NCO confirmed it—was that it was known that this individual liked to rip apart the throats of those who didn't want to fight for the Revolution. Their bodies were found, drained of their blood. Again, nothing too outré by Cheka—the dreaded Bolshevik state security organization—standards. After all, their practices included throwing water over naked prisoners in sub-zero temperatures, turning them into frozen statues for all to see.

What interested Liatoukine was that the draining of blood was usually the mark of a vampire. Combined with the occasional sights of unaccountable green lights and reflections—some vampires caused this effect—that he himself had seen behind the lines, he was in little doubt that that Kostaki was a vampire. Furthermore, Kostaki was a name associated with a Moldovan vampire aristocrat—this was also rather suspicious.

Liatoukine was appalled that a vampire could lower himself to work for the Reds. He was all in favor of murdering and trampling on his lessers, but the Reds were too much. They were ill-bred certainly, but talking of power to the workers and so on, whilst lording over them, was too much hypocrisy, even for him. They also had little concept of the good things in life—although what little there was, they took for themselves.

Still, he did admire their use of terror. It amused him too—Lenin's man, Trotsky, the architect of Red Terror, might even have been considered too extreme by most vampires.

He was distracted from his thoughts by a commotion in the street. Some of the locals were crowding around, talking to each other excitedly and clearly somewhat fearfully. Liatoukine went outside.

He called out to an old woman whom he recognized; she always knew what the street gossip was. She came over quickly to him.

"What goes on, peasant?" he asked.

"It's the White Lady," she said. "She has struck again, attacking two young men. She crushed the throat of a tailor who was walking by the sea with his son yesterday evening—the son barely got away. The body was drained of blood when they found it."

Liatoukine waved her away. Ah yes. His other, more pressing vampire problem. A vampire aristocrat killing locals in and around Novorossiysk and even across the sea in Crimea. The "White Lady," they called her. Nothing wrong with killing a few of the locals for sustenance, but the rate of killing was much too high and providing the Reds with extremely damaging propaganda against the Whites. He would need to see this problem resolved—and swiftly.

At that very moment, behind Red lines, the people responsible for Liatoukine's problems were engaged in a conversation. Their location was a carriage in a stationary battle train of the Red Army. This carriage was a special one, off limits to the rest of the train's operatives, let alone anyone else.

The carriage was rather more comfortable than the rest of the train. A woman—tall, raven-haired and beautiful—was seated in a chair opposite a man with an aquiline face sitting behind at large desk. She wore an elaborate white wedding dress.

"I am so pleased your people have got me this lovely dress," said the woman. "The previous one was covered in blood. Where did you get it from, my dear Von Bork?" she then asked in a fake innocent manner.

"A bourgeois reactionary woman," Von Bork—the man opposite her—replied. "She had no further use for it."

The woman, who was called Polly Bird, knew what that meant. She was intrigued, however, to know more of his use of language and asked him about it.

"Your words…'bourgeois,' 'reactionary...' They do seem strange coming from you—the aristocratic master of espionage who once worked for the German Kaiser. How is it that you are now a Bolshevik?"

Von Bork seemed to bristle slightly.

"And how is it that you, a vampire, find yourself working for me, a mere human"

"I don't work for you. I work on behalf of the Sepulchre, in alliance with you," she replied with a smile.

Von Bork gave as good as he got, she thought. Still, it was good to remind him now and then that she worked for the City of Vampires, the Sepulchre, referred to as Selene by humans.

"Of course, you do," he said. "A little joke on my part. As to your question, I did much work in England, until I was caught by Sherlock Holmes. However, even then, I outwitted him as he rather obligingly informed me of the disinformation he had passed to me. I was handed over to Germany just prior to the British declaring war. But my own government saw me as a failure—the same government who sold Germany out at Versailles. As for the so-called patriots, they, too, saw me as a failure..."

His tone had become increasingly bitter.

"I was approached by German communists. They could see my skills. They were unconcerned that I had been apprehended by Holmes—indeed they were curious regarding my views of him. They were most impressed with my many espionage achievements..."

Von Bork did not say it, but they were also impressed by his critique of the Great Detective—had he been Holmes, he would not have exposed Von Bork but continued the deception, perhaps for many years. The Bolsheviks seemed to appreciate this form of thinking.

"You helped start the war," Polly Bird interrupted, "even working out the date of its start?"

Von Bork waved that away.

"Ludicrous British propaganda. You will find that it was a capitalist war against the working classes."

"And so the Bolsheviks offered you work?" asked Polly Bird.

"They did indeed," he responded. He then added "Naturally, I had begun to see the way in which the war had crushed the working class. They have had much use for my talents here."

His tone had turned from bitterness, to something rather less than convincing. For Polly Bird matters were perfectly clear; Von Bork—she noted he kept the noble "von" in his name—probably cared less for bolshevism than for power. The Bolsheviks gave him great power in return for his skills. Given the international network of the Reds, the Germans probably would come to rue the way they treated him so badly—if they had not already done so.

As if he had read her mind, Von Bork said:

"Germany will fall to revolution of course, and then my old capitalist friends will be dealt with. However, there is much to occupy us here. It appears that my plans are going well. Liatoukine is well aware of my operative Kostaki, including the fact that he, too, is a vampire. When he approaches him, he will be eliminated. The Whites cannot be permitted to have a vampire in their employ, even if they are not aware of it. I know there are rumors about him. It did occur to me to simply provide that information to the Whites and let them deal with Liatoukine—there is enough fear of God amongst them for that—but the possibility of them taking a pragmatic view of his services is too much of a risk. And I have no reason to believe that he would work for the revolution. His enmity to us is too well known, let alone his decadence."

Polly Bird smiled. There was quite a bit of "decadence" where they were, given some of the lavish items in Von Bork's carriage.

"Yes, I can assure you that Liatoukine would never countenance for one moment the notion of working for the, er, 'proletariat,' as you call it,"

Von Bork nodded with a frown.

These Reds took themselves so seriously, Polly Bird thought. She continued:

"I know him well. He was once on the Vampire Council of the Sepulchre. He was ambitious for the future. He did actually think that the Great War was going to be won very quickly by Russia, and that we would be controlling the Tsar thereafter. Well, that went wrong almost immediately, and his influence in our city has now vanished."

"Whilst yours has grown, I gather," said Von Bork, deciding to make a point. "You now are on the Vampire Council?"

"Indeed, I am," she replied. "Poor Boris is behind the times. He has picked the losing side. And we vampires are not losers."

Von Bork nodded. He had some knowledge of the politics of the Vampire City. During his time with the German Secret Service, he had had contacts with the Austrian Empire's organization that dealt with such matters—a Baron Vordenberg was in charge. And it was Vordenberg who had briefed him. The Baron would no doubt have been mortified as to such information being used to help the Reds. He wondered for a moment what had become of that organization. Had it survived the chaos of the war?

Whatever the case, Von Bork was quite happy to use these vampires to create terror and eliminate the formidable Liatoukine. He had a concern that the Whites may reward the Vampire Captain's skills with greater power. Whatever else Liatoukine was, he was good at being a military commander.

"I think it is likely that he will make a move against Kostaki soon," said Von Bork. "But he will find a team of Chekists waiting for him. They have been in place for a few days now."

"Are you sure that these operatives of yours can deal with Liatoukine? They are but human," Polly Bird said.

"They are elite Chekists. With Kostaki's help, they should be able to liquidate Liatoukine, whether he comes alone or with others," Von Bork replied. He then moved onto a related matter. "You are doing excellent work yourself for us as part of our alliance. Much terror has been caused amongst the ordinary people in White-controlled territory—with the aristocracy taking the blame."

Polly Bird smiled. She got up, resplendent in her appropriated dress.

"Thank you. Which reminds me—it is time for the 'White Lady' to go prowling again."

Also going out that night was Boris Liatoukine. It had only been less than a day since his contact with the Red forces. In that time, he and his men had extracted information from their captured NCO. The man had been most forthcoming—so much so in fact that they had spared his life, providing he now fought for the Whites.

His quarry, described to him vaguely as 'tall and bald,' was based in a small village held by the Reds. Kostaki was surrounded by troops, of course. However, he had his own quarters—this was crucial, as there would be no witnesses. Liatoukine knew that, like himself, Kostaki could survive during the daytime. He was still even more powerful at night, but at least the night afforded Liatoukine more cover in which to operate. Operating by himself, he was freer to use his abilities to move surreptitiously into enemy territory. He would deal swiftly with Kostaki; if possible, he would try to question him, but the priority was to neutralize him.

Whilst moving covertly through the village, Liatoukine was conscious of the Red soldiers in the gloom. None had spotted him—or so he thought. In actual fact, they had. They were just waiting for him to go into Kostaki's house, where they would corner him.

Liatoukine went into the house that was his target's headquarters. He went upstairs to the top floor and walked into what he knew to be Kostaki's office. He was completely confident of his ability to deal with his opponent.

Kostaki lounged behind a desk, his legs crossed on it. He, too, was confident, although this was not part of the plan. He was supposed to feign surprise, just to give the Cheka soldiers a second or two of extra time. He even had a line prepared and started it, something about expecting Liatoukine, but the Vampire Captain had begun whirling around.

Up the stairs came Cheka officers, in their distinctive black leather garb One came down through a trap door in the roof.

How could he have missed all this? Overconfidence, thought Liatoukine.

All the Chekists had stakes in their hand. Some had guns—loaded with silver bullets perhaps?

Liatoukine had the advantage of superhuman strength and speed and used it. Those split seconds that Kostaki's arrogance had given him were put to good use. Using his own silver sword, he swiftly decapitated the Chekist who had come through the roof. The Vampire Captain could touch silver and thus used such a sword, but it was any breaking of the skin that could cause difficulty.

Other Chekists were coming in through the door. Liatoukine ran one through, then whirled around and killed another one coming through the window.

Meanwhile, Kostaki was not idle; he was attempting his own attack on Liatoukine. He fired his gun at the Vampire Captain, hitting his shoulder with a silver bullet. Energy fizzled out of the wound, but Liatoukine's body managed to expel the bullet before it could do further damage.

The Vampire Captain realized that matters were becoming a trifle desperate. He would have to call in a reinforcement.

Outside, the house a figure slowly materialized. It was another Liatoukine. It stood only a few foot from the nearest Cheka soldier. This second Liatoukine immediate raised a pistol and shot the soldier. The first Liatoukine had used a sword, as that was already in his hand. This second used his pistol, not only due to efficiency; but also to create a noise in order to distract his opponents.

All the Cheka troops heard the shot.

"Another one! He has an accomplice!" shouted one of them.

The second Liatoukine ran for the cover of the trees, with the troops in pursuit. He knew he would not be able to elude them all, not that that was his intention. As soon he got into the shadows, he faded away in much the same manner that he had appeared. The pursuing soldiers chased him anyway, simply believing that he was just ahead of them in the dark. This took away enough soldiers to improve the odds for the first Liatoukine.

However, it was still not enough.

In Kostaki's office, the gunshot had momentarily distracted the Chekists, giving the first Liatoukine enough time to dispatch two of them with his sword. He still did not use his pistol, not wanting to take any attention away from his doppelganger.

Kostaki now had a stake in his hand, and had maneuvered himself behind Liatoukine. He rammed the stake in the centre of the Vampire Captain's back, straight through the heart.

Liatoukine looked down at the stake protruding from his chest. He looked bewildered. Then, he fell over sideways, crashing to the floor.

He lay there quite still, his eyes staring.

A Cheka soldier swiftly aimed his pistol at Liatoukine's head and fired a silver bullet. Parts of the Vampire Captain's brain splattered around.

"Dead," said the soldier.

"Stay here and keep an eye on him," Kostaki told the soldiers in the room.

He went downstairs and asked the Cheka troops what had happened outside.

"There was another one—somehow we had not spotted him. Some of the men are in pursuit," he was told.

This was not good news. Von Bork would not be pleased. Kostaki did not fear the German, but enjoyed his work as a Bolshevik commissar. It gave him a good cover to feed on humans and thus did not wish to jeopardize it.

"Get everyone onto finding him—at once," he ordered.

All the troops complied. Kostaki left a few men in the house, one directly guarding Liatoukine's body.

He then went into a nearby communications room to relay the news to Von Bork by a special field telephone.

The spymaster was not pleased with the apparent escape of what appeared to be an accomplice. However, he did seem satisfied with the elimination of Boris Liatoukine.

"Yes," the Chekist vampire said. "It went just as you said—the stake through the heart was the way to kill him. A silver bullet in the brain was also delivered."

"Very good," said Von Bork at the other end. "Keep watch on the corpse yourself. I shall arrive in due course to take it away."

Kostaki returned to his office. The first thing he saw was a body on the ground, with blood pouring out of a stake through its heart. But the body was not Liatoukine's! It was that of the soldier who was supposed to be guarding him!

Liatoukine stepped from behind him—very fast—grabbed him by the neck and held him mid-air.

"Not a word," Liatoukine said. "I am sure you know my abilities."

Kostaki kept quiet. He saw that Liatoukine's injuries appeared to be repairing themselves.

"Tell me what I need to know quickly, and I will let you live," Liatoukine continued. "You have my word as a nobleman of Selene. I will also permit you to come to the White side to work with me, should you wish it. I doubt your masters will be forgiving, but I offer you that way out, if you wish it."

The terrified vampire made a sound that Liatoukine took as assent. He put him down and loosened—but did not release—his grip on his throat.

Kostaki told him of how he had preyed on humans in Moscow. He told him of how Von Bork had captured him, and how he had offered him employment with the revolution—an offer he could not refuse, given that the alternative was a stake in the heart—the sure way of killing him. And, of course, such employment meant he was safe, providing he was discreet and followed the German spy's orders. Finishing his story, Kostaki said:

"We must go now. Any further details must come later."

Liatoukine simply re-tightened his grip and drained the vampire of energy. The body turned to dust, its fangs strangely surviving on the floor. The Vampire Captain crushed them contemptuously with his boots. Promises to vampires who worked for Bolsheviks had no validity whatsoever—besides, he needed Kostaki's energy.

Liatoukine proceeded downstairs and left by a back exit. The few Cheka who had remained behind did not spot him; they had no reason to believe anything was wrong. Liatoukine also moved very fast and ensured he headed in a different direction from the search parties looking for his "accomplice."

He moved though the dark countryside, helped by being able to see clearly in the dark. *That had been too damn close*, he thought. He had become too arrogant over the years. The wooden stake had been painful, but no more than that. The silver bullet had passed only through part of his brain, allowing for swift regeneration, his consciousness intact.

He very rarely used his doppelganger power, and only in the most serious of circumstances He barely understood it, for a start, seemingly being conscious in two places at once, something he found very strange. More importantly, he wished as few of his enemies to know of it as possible.

As soon as he realized it had been a trap, he knew there was more to Kostaki than just being a vampire who had opportunistically infiltrated the Bolsheviks. It seemed that Von Bork was after him after all.

No doubt when he worked for the Kaiser, he had gathered much valuable intelligence on vampires, either from within Germany or from the Austrians. The Bolsheviks were such hypocrites! They pointed out with relish the foreign help the Whites were receiving from the British, French, Americans and others, and yet, many in the Cheka were themselves foreign. His assailants had cursed in Chinese, and Von Bork was German. Of course, it was the Germans who had given Lenin safe passage into Russia in the first place...

Still, despite the close call, Liatoukine had succeeded in his mission of neutralizing Kostaki. Further, he now knew of the threat of Von Bork.

As a precaution, some years ago, Liatoukine had placed false information within a certain text in the Sepulchre. It stated that the only sure way to kill an energy vampire such as himself was by a wooden stake through the heart, much like other vampires. It had been a precaution against current and future enemies who would wish to destroy him. Von Bork clearly had great sources from within the Vampire City itself. The spymaster, it seems, was keen to use vampires in furtherance of the Red Terror.

These thoughts were most troubling for the Vampire Captain. Most troubling indeed...

Later, in Von Bork's rail carriage, Polly Bird, too, was troubled. She and Von Bork were engaged in conversation regarding the previous night's events.

"I knew the trap was too weak," she told him. "Liatoukine is not only a powerful vampire, but he has considerable military experience and skills. He is still alive, and who knows how much intelligence he gleaned from Kostaki before he killed him."

"*Alive*, is he?" replied Von Bork. "I thought your people referred to your condition as being *Undead*?"

"Do not mock me, German. You seem somewhat unconcerned as to events," she replied.

"Not at all! I am always concerned over events," Von Bork responded. "However, the reality is that the Whites are on the run. Even Churchill has started to tentatively talk to Moscow. The loss of Kostaki is unfortunate, as is those of a number of my troops; however, it is clear that victory is in our grasp. Liatoukine has nowhere to go. Soon, we will crush the Whites here in Southern Russia, and the war will be won. As for intelligence, well, Kostaki had no real link to Selene, let alone any knowledge of our little alliance. And even if he did, what could Liatoukine do with it? If we were being defeated, yes, he could cause some trouble for us, but it is too late for that. Our victory is assured. The presence of his accomplice was certainly a surprise, but we will be ready for him next time."

The reports from the Chekists who had fought Liatoukine's doppelganger were rather garbled; neither Polly Bird nor Von Bork had understood the true nature of what had really occurred.

The German spymaster may have appeared untroubled to Polly Bird, but secretly, he was not pleased with the turn of events, having underestimated Liatoukine. This failure could easily be concealed from his superiors, who were not too informed about vampire matters.

"Of course," continued Von Bork, "Liatoukine may now come after me. But if he does, he will face considerably more opposition than he did with Kostaki. And even if he does not, the defeat of the Whites will render him powerless. He is too proud to return to your city, or maybe too cautious, given that his complete lack of a power base leaves him open to his enemies in Selene. You are operating in Novorossiysk. I think it is prudent to set another trap for him, through information I can make sure he receives. He will no doubt suspect a trap. If he had any common sense, he would avoid me. However, I think he will come for me. He will have no idea about you, although, of course, he must be looking for the 'White Lady'."

"I would favor that option," Polly Bird responded. "I would find it most reassuring to see that Liatoukine is liquidated one and for all. There are minor factions in Selene who are against our alliance with you. We cannot rule out his causing some trouble."

With that, matters were then set in motion.

Things went pretty much as Von Bork had predicted. The Whites were on the run. Boris Liatoukine walked through the streets of Novorossiysk. The town was teeming with people trying to leave. Evacuations had already begun to get everyone out. The military was headed to Crimea to make their last stand. The streets stank. Typhus was everywhere.

Liatoukine could have got to Crimea earlier, but he wished to follow various leads as to Von Bork's precise location, as well as dealing with the White Lady. She had continued her activities: a number of unwary lower orders had been murdered, causing more terror. She never killed military officers, or aristocrats, or even the middle class. Always the poor. For whom, of course, he cared nothing. However, it did cause more resentment against his side, given that the White Lady was considered an aristocrat.

The White Lady was portrayed as a provocation by the Reds in White propaganda. And indeed, Liatoukine considered this to be probably real. After his encounter with Kostaki, he suspected that the White Lady did work for Von Bork. He wondered if he knew who she was. There seemed to be something personal in her activities. It seemed as if her recent murder had gotten closer and closer to his base in Novorossiysk. Likely or not, this was just harrying them. The Red advance and the typhus were enough reasons for panic.

However, a murder had taken place just streets away from his headquarters, and he had to investigate. He approached the scene. A crowd had gathered around the corpse. They made way for him. There was a corpse on the ground: a young woman, her throat ripped out.

Kneeling next to her was a young man—her husband it transpired. He had been by her side when the attack had happened. He had been gibbering earlier about what had happened; but was now in some kind of shock.

Liatoukine had already heard the story from others, but he wanted to hear it from the husband. He grabbed him by the chin and pulled his head up to face his own.

"What happened?" he asked.

The man answered. They had been out last night in search of a doctor; his wife was ill. *Typhus no doubt*, thought Liatoukine. The man started to look fearful, saying:

"She appeared out of nowhere… She grabbed my wife and ripped out her throat with her teeth. I tried to stop her, but I could not move. She lifted a hand towards me and I still could not move!"

"Coward!" one of the crowd shouted—from well behind some others.

Liatoukine glared at the crowd. There were no more interruptions. The Vampire Captain was known by some as an officer not to cross. And the others who did not know him could sense that he was a dangerous man.

As he left, an old woman stepped in his way and held a cross up to him. He simply smiled. Seeing it had no effect, she moved away from him.

Liatoukine didn't like crosses, but it did not have the same effect on him as on so many other vampires. He would hardly have lasted so long in Russian society if they had.

Back at his headquarters, he considered the matter. The husband gave the usual description of the White Lady—a white dress, most likely a wedding one, black hair. It could be anyone. Was it someone he knew? He idly considered that it might be the Countess Marcian Gregoryi—an old foe. Then again, it could just have been a Russian aristocratic woman. The revolution had resulted in the deaths of many of the aristocracy. It was entirely possible that, in the chaos, one woman had been turned into a vampire. One missing aristocrat would hardly be considered odd at this time.

One thing he was certain of, the White Lady was a Red provocation, no doubt controlled by Von Bork in some way. She had used her mesmerism powers in order to stop the husband, but left him alive in order to relate what he had seen in order to spread terror. There had been an assumption that she left people alive in order to make a quick escape. Now, he knew otherwise.

He had also received information that Von Bork was somewhere north of Crimea, in Ukraine. He wondered about this. Was it a trap? Did Von Bork expect a visit from him? Perhaps. Liatoukine knew that, for his own safety, he had to eliminate the Bolshevik spymaster. However, he would take precautions.

Liatoukine used a secure line to get hold of Squadron Leader Raymond Collishaw, commander of the Royal Air Force's Crimean Group. The RAF had done excellent work in fighting the Bolsheviks. They—and other British units—had done much to destroy Red troops and equipment. It was unfortunate indeed, thought Liatoukine, that the just ousted General Denikin had bungled things so badly. His troops had committed atrocities, especially against the Jews. The Vampire Captain's only concern with this was that it detracted from military objectives. A lot of supplies the British had provided had even fallen into the hands of the enemy. Now, however, the British were due to pull out imminently.

Liatoukine was aware that there were some last attacks planned. Collishaw himself was involved. It was worth seeing what was scheduled. The Vampire Captain was well regarded as an "efficient" soldier by the British, due not only to his being an intelligence liaison, but his known battle skills.

Collishaw was forthcoming. He did indeed have an attack planned for the next day, the 26th of March. Conveniently, it would be on the encampment of Von Bork, in southern Ukraine.

Liatoukine was pleased with his good fortune. He could not rely on the bombing, but if anything went wrong, it may prove a useful diversion. He did believe himself invulnerable, but he certainly was more likely to survive a bombing than the humans. Time, however, was against him.

He gave orders to his remaining staff to immediately evacuate and retreat to Crimea. He himself had a mission to carry out and would join them there.

As Liatoukine started to leave, a lieutenant came up to him.

"Sir," he said, "I would just like to convey the men's appreciation for your staying to the end here."

"It is not required; we all do our duty," Liatoukine replied.

The Vampire Captain did not care about staying with the last troops until the final evacuation. He had only stayed due to the vampire situation, for it was very much in his own interest to find the truth.

Liatoukine left the town on horseback and went into the nearby countryside. There he walked into a field, which had a dilapidated barn in its center. But only the Vampire Captain could see it; there was a device he had appropriated from the Sepulchre that disguised it. It did not make it invisible exactly, but rather something not to be noticed. Further, it caused either feelings of foreboding or disinterest in those who came near it. If an entire army came past it, it might well notice it; but with smaller units, locals, looters, etc, the device ensured that it remained undisturbed.

Liatoukine let his horse go. He proceeded into the barn where there was an aircraft waiting for him—his Russky Vityaz. He had made certain modifications to it and it had served him well in the past.

The Vampire Captain had established the whereabouts of Von Bork. Perhaps a little too easily? A trap, he wondered? He had to deal with Von Bork—he just would have to be cautious.

Liatoukine landed his plane, with little trouble, a few miles away from where he knew Von Bork's train was. He walked the rest of the way on foot, eluding Red troops easily. Aside from his powers, he had dressed himself in Cheka style to help him get through. He had a low opinion of their fashion; it reminded him of the less than joyous style of the Sepulchre.

He had landed at night. By the time he reached the train, it was morning. If the raid was coming, he had timed it well. He was allowed to proceed towards the carriage. The Red troops made no attempt to stop him— either through orders, or fear of the Cheka uniform.

The Vampire Captain took note of the surroundings and the disposition of enemy forces. Once he had eliminated Von Bork, he felt he could elude them at speed, using his power—whether or not the bombing raid took place. This was arrogance on his part. That had been a failing of his in the past—but that attitude had also helped him many times.

Liatoukine noticed some green on the windows of the train. Clearly, the White Lady was present— presumably a vampire who, like him, could operate to a greater or lesser extent during the day.

One of the doors on a carriage opened. A Chekist beckoned to him. A trap then.

The Vampire Captain should have attempted a retreat at that point, but his arrogance prevented him. He did not wish to lose face. He entered, contemptuously tossing a kopek at the guard for his trouble.

He took in his surroundings in a split second. The usual comforts top Bolsheviks enjoyed, the overconfident Von Bork sitting behind an elaborate desk in an ornate chair, and, finally, the White Lady, who was indeed an old acquaintance—and ally—Polly Bird.

He was stunned by her presence, but did not show it. He also noted a rack of swords on the wall. Silver blades.

Deliberately ignoring Von Bork, who was merely human after all, he spoke to Polly Bird.

"It seems you have fallen low to work with such as these," he said, gesturing to Von Bork contemptuously.

"You were once on the Vampire Council—what transgression have you made that has led you here?"

"My dear Boris," she replied, smiling at him, "you are so naive..."

No one had ever called him naive before!

"...I still am on the Council. I am here with their knowledge."

Now the Vampire Captain did show incredulity. But Von Bork spoke first:

"Selene has decided that an alliance with the proletariat of Russia—and the world—would be most beneficial. We, Bolsheviks, are the future."

Liatoukine could hardly ignore him now.

"Vampires have no interest in the workers—aside from that of nutrition, of course. A bit like you Bolsheviks."

*Antagonism would do no harm now*, the Vampire Captain thought.

Von Bork looked annoyed. Polly Bird laughed loudly.

"How has this come about?" Liatoukine asked. "The Bolsheviks are barbarians. They would reduce the world to a dull level, claiming equality, but providing the best only for themselves."

"Von Bork approached us with a proposition," replied Polly Bird.

*That made sense*, thought Liatoukine. The German spymaster, when he was working with the Kaiser, would certainly have come across organizations that dealt with the supernatural. The Austrians had the best one. Very likely, he had found much out about the Sepulchre from them. The war, however, had been devastating.

Unconsciously echoing Von Bork's own thoughts, he wondered if these organizations had been swept away by war? He did not know. In fact, he did not even know what had been happening in the Sepulchre of late. Until now.

"I offered autonomy to Selene," said Von Bork, "in return for certain services. We, Bolsheviks, seek only world peace."

Liatoukine could barely believe what he was hearing. He was also surprised that they were stupid enough to be discussing all this with him now instead of just killing him. And people thought he was arrogant!

"These people will simply destroy the Sepulchre when they can—or take it over and use vampires for their own ends," he said to Polly Bird, gesturing to Von Bork. "Their revolution has not even taken place in Serbia, where it is based."

"Boris Liatoukine," she replied, "you promised us that Russia would win the war against Germany and Austro-Hungary, that it would dominate Europe, with you effectively leading it. Our future, you said, would be secure. Instead, the Tsarist government was overthrown, and the Bolsheviks achieved peace with Germany by giving up large parts of their territory. Agreements can be found with the Reds. Furthermore, we can foresee a future where their power will extend beyond their borders. Peace with them now is acceptable to us and to them; as opposed to a conflict that would cost both sides dearly."

Polly Bird's words contained much truth. Almost too much for Liatoukine. Almost.

"That agreement has hardly been a huge success," he responded. "Far from allying with them, Selene should be devoting resources to destroying them—to restore the status quo."

"Why would we wish to do that, Boris?" She laughed again. "More to the point, why should *you*?"

"You wish to let these people have power?" he asked her.

"Who was it who kept saying we must not provoke the empires into attacking us? It was you. Furthermore, you seem rather, er, comfortable with them. Or at least, with the Russian one, which has not gone unnoticed. They all seem to have a great respect for God and the Church—even when the secular state is in charge. The Bolsheviks however, don't respect God, and neither do we vampires. Frankly, Red power is preferable to us. The fewer crucifixes around, the better."

Such a line of thought had not really occurred to him. Liatoukine had always managed to get away with minimal contact with the Church. However, whilst his first loyalty was to himself, it was true to say that he was a proud Russian. He regarded the Sepulchre as simply a source of potential extra power to him.

"They will not tolerate rivals," he said evenly.

"Not rivals—allies," said Von Bork, slightly impatiently. "Let us get on with business. Your fellow vampires do not think you would ever come around to our way of thinking. Given that you have been quite a nuisance for my comrades and I, liquidating you is the best way forward. And your accomplice too, if you brought him along this time."

Liatoukine said nothing regarding his "accomplice."

"Your liquidation is a task for me," continued the German. "It seems the Vampire Council do not quite want to be seen directly dealing with you. Perhaps there are still some Liatoukinites about?"

Von Bork laughed, then brought out a pistol.

*Silver bullets, no doubt*, thought the Vampire Captain. Perhaps with ashes of burnt vampire hearts inside them, too? The silver would hurt, but the ashes may well destroy him instantly. He decided to play for time, sensing something, literally, in the air.

"What was the point of the White Lady?" he asked.

"To create terror and anti-White feeling amongst the populace as well as discreetly keep an eye on you," Von Bork replied succinctly.

Polly Bird suddenly jumped up.

High above, Squadron Leader Collishaw flew his Airco DH9 bomber towards his target. This was likely to be to be his last bit of active service against the Reds. British personnel were being recalled. They had made a strong contribution, but the Whites were not likely to win. Given their conduct, this was not surprising. Still, at least this would be a good target—trains were strategically important.

He dropped his payload.

The bombs hit with perfect timing. Von Bork's carriage was not directly hit, but it was flung off the tracks. All inside were thrown about. Outside, the locomotive was a write off; the other carriages were strewn around and many of their occupants dead.

There was silence for a moment—then, some moans and shouting from Red troops.

Liatoukine had heard the bombs falling; Polly Bird had done so seconds later. Their enhanced senses worked well for them. Von Bork only realized anything was wrong when Polly had jumped up. For vampires, having explosives dropped on you was not a good thing; physical damage sustained could take a while to regenerate. Liatoukine knew this from experience. He had reasoned that the raid may be able to help him out of a tight spot—he had been right, but this was too close. If Von Bork had just shot him rather than indulge in a conversation, the outcome may have been different.

In the mess of the carriage, Liatoukine threw off Von Bork's table, which had smashed into him, breaking many bones. The bones were already regenerating. He looked over to Polly Bird. She, too, was on her feet, shaken, but with fewer injuries. They made eye contact. In that moment, she knew that he was going to kill her. She did not fancy her chances in sole combat with him. Then, there was a moan—Von Bork was still alive.

In that split section of distraction, Polly Bird jumped upwards through the shattered carriage window, now above her, and ran away at inhuman speed—almost a blur to the still dazed troops outside. Her fear of Liatoukine must have been considerable, for she had escaped with a broken leg.

Back in the carriage, Von Bork got to his feet. His face was bloodied, he was dazed and probably could hear little—but ironically, he was less injured that his opponent, whose rib cage had been crushed.

The Vampire Captain could feel his bones regenerating, but not quickly enough! He could move, ignore the pain, but not much faster—if at all— than the German spymaster. This would be a fairer fight than he would have wished. Then, he saw what Von Bork had in his hand—a silver sword from the rack he had seen earlier. He saw another one—now, on the floor—beside him. He scooped it up and lunged at the German. Von Bork fought the attack off, almost a little too easily. He was known to be an excellent fencer.

They fought in the carriage; the clashing of the swords was all that could be heard. Neither combatant had the inclination for pointless prattle while they tried to kill each other. The vampire was not able to use his powers—although he could sense them coming back slowly. He needed time—a minute even. Then Von Bork slashed his face with his sword. Energy trickled into the air, before the wound healed. Such was the effect of silver.

The Vampire Captain could not believe that a mere human was starting to best him. The cut, though minor, held back his healing. They fought on, jumping and leaping over the wreckage of the carriage, their swords clashing all the while.

Outside, the Red troops had started to gather their wits. One was peering over the window.

Liatoukine realized his time was running out. If those troops entered the fray, he did not believe he could escape. A small amount of energy was returning. He summoned his double. It appeared next to him without a sword, and lunged at Von Bork, who thrust his sword into thin air. The double had vanished—the Vampire Captain did not have enough energy to sustain it. But the distraction had been enough. He exited in the same way Polly Bird had done, using up his energy for the leap. On the way up, he shoved the curious Red trooper down into the carriage—on top of Von Bork.

"Quickly!" he shouted to the soldiers. "Get inside and assist Von Bork"

He leapt of the carriage and ran off. Some soldiers obeyed him, the smarter ones pursued Liatoukine. But they soon lost him.

Liatoukine ran. His body regenerating, he began to pick up speed—but he still feared it was not enough. He ignored the pain. The fight, the leap, now the running. Was this the end for Boris Liatoukine?

Von Bork was not pleased at how things had gone. However, he knew that victory was now a matter of time—and not too long—for the Bolsheviks. Liatoukine would keep.

Later, the Cheka found a trail leading to a clearing where some locals had seen an aircraft taking off. Liatoukine had survived, of course. He ended up in Crimea with the last of the White Russian forces, now under the more capable command of Baron Wrangel. Despite a spirited attempt to fight back, the Whites were defeated. The Vampire Captain fled his own homeland on a French ship bound for Constantinople.

*Paris, 1928*

Boris Liatoukine returned to his fashionable Paris apartment from a pleasant night on the town—although not so pleasant for the unfortunate man he had drained for energy earlier on.

Before entering his apartment, he had noticed a tint of green through the windows. Further, there were a number of figures in the street. It would seem that Von Bork had finally caught up with him. He was surprised it had taken him this long. Whilst Liatoukine had taken an assumed identity, he could not—and did not want to—pretend that he was not Russian. And so he led the life of a White Russian exile in Paris. He did not mix too much with other exiles, but even so, he could not keep too low a profile—his ego prevented that. Clearly some clues about him had reached Moscow. After all, were there not Bolsheviks in France?

He could see that his opponents were a mix of humans and vampires—the Soviet/Sepulchre alliance still held in some form, it seemed. It would be difficult to elude them. He would go to his apartment and face whatever was there.

Inside, sitting on his expensive couch, was Von Bork. Did the man ever stand when someone entered? A number of others stood in the room, in the shadows. Only one lamp was on, illuminating Von Bork. Standing behind him was Polly Bird—in a clearly subordinate role.

*Things have changed*, Liatoukine thought.

In the Bolshevik's hand, held downwards as if it were a walking stick, was a stake built of silver—complete with a hammer and sickle engraved on it. Von Bork beckoned Liatoukine to sit down. The Vampire Captain did so; he was not confident against such a weapon. He would not attempt a last stand. He sensed that his destruction was not what Von Bork was after.

Von Bork got straight down to it.

"As you can see, we have finally caught up with you. Before you ask how, let us say that we are aware that, in the past, you have married wealth, and that your wives, rather unfortunately, were all mysteriously murdered soon after. Imagine our interest when we heard through our local comrades that a Russian exile's wealthy wife had died suddenly here."

Liatoukine knew exactly what he meant. He enjoyed an expensive lifestyle, which his recently deceased wife had paid for. He found wives an encumbrance; and so he had murdered his latest one by draining enough energy only to induce a seizure. His arrogance had overridden his concern for his safety.

Von Bork waved the silver stake at him.

"Incidentally, I think this could destroy you if plunged into your heart, so you should reconsider if you think you can escape."

Liatoukine did not wish to test if he could. However, he did want to get onto what Von Bork was really here for.

'What do you want from me?' he asked.

"I offer you the opportunity to serve world revolution, Comrade Liatoukine!" replied the German, smiling. "As you can see, I use a number of your kind to further the aims of the proletariat. Many former bourgeois oppressors have been successfully rehabilitated into our cause."

Liatoukine wondered if Von Bork actually believed in all that.

"You would employ me? Even under the laws of 'bourgeois' society, I am a murderer—a monster."

"Of course!" Von Bork beamed at him. "The revolution needs such people to further its aims!"

Liatoukine wondered briefly if the German was insane. Regardless, he better find out the terms that were being offered. The sullen-looking Polly Bird was clearly in a position he did not want.

"What would be my place?" he asked.

"You would work directly to me," Von Bork replied immediately. "Your powers and military knowledge would be used to their full extent. Your, er, dietary requirements would be seen to—we have many prisoners who cannot be reconciled to living in the worker's paradise. You would even have rank, above these certainly," he waved at the various figures in the room. "We are the future. Your Russia has gone. And soon, we will control the world. The only place you could have is with us."

Liatoukine's mind raced. Once, he would not have contemplated any such agreement. Yet, here was an opportunity, was there not? Von Bork would no doubt have methods of control other than the threat of a silver stake. And yet, the Vampire Captain was immortal, and Von Bork was not—and perhaps did not even wish to be. Soviet society could cover his true nature most effectively. Over time—perhaps even decades—he could change his position into something rather more congenial and more powerful. And if there was one thing he missed in his present situation, it was power.

*Let there be no further delay then*, he thought. He gave his answer.

"Your terms are reasonable. I accept... Comrade Von Bork."

## The Berlin Vampire

*Berlin, Soviet Sector, 16 June 1953*

He had been killing Germans soldiers the last time he was here, thought Boris Liatoukine. Now he was back in Berlin—the Eastern part—where he expected to kill more Germans. Previously this had to do with the struggle against Hitler—and, of course, taking control of a chunk of Germany.

At the moment, the Germans seemed to be less than grateful for their induction into the glorious workers' paradise enjoyed by the people of the Soviet Union and elsewhere. The workers were striking—they seemed displeased with the rule of the local communists, the *Sozialistische Einheitspartei Deutschlands* (SED), and thus must be taught the error of their thinking. With the assistance of Russian tanks, of course—the power of which the locals would be aware.

Not that the Russian MVD[4] vampire Boris Liatoukine entirely blamed them. Communist rule was, indeed, rather dull. All very ordinary and low grade— how he longed for the imperial courts of old, the genial atmosphere and the privileges of his then-high rank. Still, the Germans should know their place.

He looked at his newspaper—from the decadent

_____

[4] The Soviet Union's Ministry of Internal Affairs. The intelligence service MGB had been merged inot the MVD earlier in the year, and in 1954 would be moved back out as the KGB.

West Berlin he enjoyed visiting.

It appeared that there had been some murders. Three people had been found largely drained of their blood. The "Berlin Vampire," they called the perpetrator.

What the newspaper did not report—because it had been kept secret by the SED—was that a number of such murders had also happened in the East. Liatoukine had no doubt that this was the work of a vampire, the primary reason he and his superior, Von Bork, were in Berlin.

A knock on the door distracted him.

"Come in," said Liatoukine.

A burly guard shoved in a handcuffed prisoner and sat him in front of the MVD officer and then left. The man in front of him had been arrested a few days ago. He was a trade unionist who had demanded better living conditions. He had little family, just a wife. This was why he had been brought to him. Liatoukine was not interested in this man's case. He simply looked at him.

The unfortunate trade unionist looked back at him. Why the silence, he thought. Why is he staring at me? He looked at this man—clearly a Russian. He had a pale face and black beard, but the eyes—they were like a cat's.

He could not take his eyes off him. He felt himself start shaking. His vision started to blur—his head seemed to move down, giving some sight of his hands—which were flaking away? He saw his hands as bones, and then saw no more.

There was no more to him but ash.

Liatoukine looked down at his handiwork. Liatoukine was a vampire—but living energy was what he took, not blood. He had feasted well. Not for nothing was he called "Captain Vampire" by some—despite now having the rank of Major.

He rang the buzzer. The guard came back in and was unsurprised by what he saw. Liatoukine said to him, "I have executed this man. As you can see, I have also cremated him—thus saving his widow some expense. Let it not be said the proletariat are not cared for!"

They both laughed.

Later that day, Liatoukine called on his superior, Von Bork. Their specialty was supernatural matters—dealing with any threats of that nature, but also using dark powers in the furtherance of Soviet aims, both at home and abroad.

He entered the spymaster's office, which, of course, was rather larger than his own. They were in an old German military building, taken over for Soviet purposes. It still bore the marks of war damage, despite some rebuilding to make it habitable.

Von Bork beckoned him to be seated. A man advancing in years, he had operated a spy ring in Britain for Imperial Germany just prior to the of outbreak of the first world war. He had been undone by the detective Sherlock Holmes and returned to Germany in disgrace. The communists there found use for his skills. He never looked back, and was now senior in the MVD. He had accumulated a number of supernatural operatives, Liatoukine included.

Liatoukine did wonder how, despite his advanced years, Von Bork managed to seem so fit and energetic. The German gestured to Liatoukine to sit down, which he did.

"Major Liatoukine, you have eaten, I understand?" he said.

"Yes, Berlin cuisine was better than I expected," the

Russian vampire replied.

Von Bork smiled. "Good," he replied. "Moscow now wants us to assist more with the anti-state activities of local subversives. Still, we must not lose sight of this 'Berlin Vampire.' We have had information that these killings are directed by the West—the British MI6. The aim is to further destabilize the situation here. So far, they have failed. However, we must still capture the perpetrator."

Liatoukine considered this for a moment. This was not MI6's style, to use a vampire in such a manner. It was known that their equivalents there considered them too unreliable for such work. However, he was aware that the MVP had excellent sources from within the British security agency, and this was not likely to be bad information, unless Von Bork was not being entirely truthful. Liatoukine stroked his beard and said: "From newspaper reports in Berlin, the vampire has struck at least three times in allied sectors. That is less than the seven times we know of here, but why would they have their own vampire commit murders in the Western sectors?"

Von Bork seemed to have been ready for this question, and responded: "We think it is possible her blood-lust has taken over. "

"*Her?*" asked the Russian vampire.

Von Bork smiled. "The vampire is Countess Marcian Gregoryi."

Gregoryi! Liatoukine's mind raced. She was an old foe of Liatoukine's, once participating in a plan to eliminate his influence in the Sepulchre, the vampire city known as Selene to the humans. She had fled when that plan had failed. That was in 1913. He had not encountered her since. This was not unusual. The two world wars, whilst providing much death, also wiped out many vampires and, indeed, many humans who had opposed them. There were far fewer vampires and other supernatural beings now than there were in 1913. Where had she been all these years? There had been reports, sightings from his own sources and those of the MVD unit he worked for, but nothing confirmed.

"Has there been any information from the Sepulchre?" Liatoukine asked.

"Nothing. However, as she is working for MI6, she may well be avoiding the Sepulchre."

Liatoukine bristled. It was not for humans to refer to the city as such; he could not care less if they called it Selene or whatever. It was an affront, but it was a way for Von Bork to exercise his power over him. Liatoukine had tried to fight these communists and failed; they later found him and made him work for them. Liatoukine was playing a long game, waiting for circumstances to change.

"We have not heard from the city for a while," he said.

The German spymaster ignored the comment. "Find Gregoryi. Our superiors have much to question her about."

Back in his own office, Liatoukine pondered the situation. Did he detect a reluctance to discuss the Sepulchre? And why did their superiors want to talk to the Countess? They usually left such matters to them. He would have to question her first.

However, how would he capture her? She seemed to be moving between Eastern and Western sectors. He had issued a description of the Countess to checkpoints. This was hardly infallible; she may have made some cosmetic changes, and he certainly didn't what clothes she was wearing. He simply hoped that the guards would pay more attention to a beautiful woman crossing the checkpoints. However, she may not be moving around in a conventional manner. A vampire with her powers could cross borders without being detected.

Liatoukine considered the problem further. As a vampire, she could well be disguised as a human; as far as he could recall, she was one of those—like himself—who could, to a greater or lesser degree, operate in the sunlight. Then again, she could simply be holed up in various places. With her powers, it would be much easier to hide in various places—there were enough ruined buildings in both parts of Berlin left over since the war for her to hide in.

Liatoukine had looked at the police reports of the vampire murders. All most informative, and yet there were no reports of anything unusual, bar the killings themselves. There was always the possibility that there were details not included in the reports—matters so odd that the policemen writing them up would not wish to mention them in case it might cast doubt on their own competence. It would do no harm to go out on the ground and speak to the police directly. However, he knew he had to move fast. The political situation was decaying rapidly. He knew very well that Soviet tanks were to deployed to crush this German uprising—and that he himself may have to assist, regardless of the high priority of the current mission. The Countess would no doubt exploit the chaotic situation. As perhaps he could.

The Russian vampire made his way to the scene of the latest killing, not too far from the Brandenburg Gate. Naturally, some of the locals knew what had happened, but not the whole of the city, due to the information blackout—some word was spreading through subversive lines, but generally the public in East Berlin was unaware. The killings in West Berlin were more publicized due to the free press there. The RIAS—Radio in the American Sector—had not broadcast anything about the killings in what they called the Soviet Zone of Occupation.

Liatoukine went to see the policeman supervising the investigation locally. A Sergeant Schmidt. He was not in overall charge, but was the man who knew the area. Liatoukine met with him, not in an office, but in a local bar. This had not gone down well with East German higher ups, but they kept their objections to themselves. Now was not the time to stand in the way of the MVD.

"My dear Sergeant," Liatoukine began, having bought the policeman some schnapps, "I have read your notes on this murder. They are most efficiently presented."

Schultz nodded his head in a way that denoted his thanks for the compliment—although this was not the first time he had been commended on his efficiency by a Russian. Was it a genuine compliment or some sly remark on his being a German, he wondered.

Liatoukine gave nothing away on this. "The victim was a young woman, an Andrea Gruber, aged 20. You believe that she knew her attacker, perhaps?"

"Yes," Schultz replied. "Despite her throat being ripped out, there seemed to be no other resistance. She was unharmed in any other way. Her body was discovered in the morning. No one heard anything during the night either."

"You have spoken to her friends?"

118

"Friends, acquaintances, her comrades at work, they all seem to have alibis of one kind of the other, and we can't seem to find a motive. However, we are probing deeper. Naturally, we are seeing if any of them had any links with the other victims." He then added hurriedly "Of course, we are simply trying to eliminate all possibilities—we are aware of the view that the criminal is an agent of the imperialist West."

Liatoukine could see that this policeman thought little of the Western agent theory. He wondered how much coordination had gone into this investigation, given the secrecy involved. It was perfectly likely that only he and a few others had had full access to all the police reports. The Countess, of course, had mesmeric powers of seduction. Her victims would naturally put up little resistance. Male or female. He continued his questioning:

"Sergeant, aside from this murder, has there been any other strange occurrences? Matters that appear a little odd? We live in unsettled times—oddities may be a clue to subversive activities."

So that was it, thought Schultz—this was political. Like a number of regular police, his sympathies lay with the workers, and not with the SED and their quota mentality. Nevertheless, political or not, murders were being committed, and it would certainly not do to hold back.

The Sergeant looked at the Russian vampire. "There were..." he paused, his face clearly displaying some concern as to what he should say next.

Liatoukine made a gesture with his hand—suggestive of asking the Sergeant to continue. Which he did.

"...This may seem foolish, but some of the locals reported a green tint on their windows for the previous couple of nights—they could not detect the source. This came to us from the housing officials. But we could see no connection with the murder."

But Liatoukine did! Although he did not display any emotion, his mind was racing again. Some vampire's presence could be detected by strange green lights in the vicinity. They were often those who had strong connections with the Sepulchre—and Gregoryi certainly had that in the past. He himself had managed to master this embarrassing problem of late, but clearly the Countess had not. He now had a way of anticipating her next move.

Whatever the reason for her killing frenzy, she was still familiarizing herself with the local area before striking—still operating with some degree of caution.

Liatoukine moved fast. He sent a message to all police stations and through various channels asking for reports of such green lights. The request made vague mentions of them coming from Western spies using special cameras. It was nonsense, but no one queried it. Liatoukine wondered if those hunting the Countess in the Western sectors where using the same method. There could be no way of knowing where she would strike next—it could well be in the West.

He received a few reports; the witnessing of the lights coincided with the killings in the East, except for one, the previous night, 15 June. That could mean that, tonight, on 16 June, she might strike. He had to be ready. However, today was not the best day to lay a trap for a vampire...

Liatoukine was summoned to his superior's office.
"Have you not seen this?"
Von Bork waved a newspaper at his subordinate.

He had. It was a copy of the day's *Die Tribune*. An article about compulsory work quotas had caused protests from construction workers building the Stalin-Allee boulevard. RIAS broadcasts were not helping either.

Von Bork was clearly feeling a little harassed. "It is likely we may have to intervene on some level. I cannot give you the men you require to trap Gregoryi. I have been explicitly told that the hunt for her now takes second place to the current political situation. Those SED fools seem to have been taken by surprise and have little idea what to do. All our personnel, including our more specialized ones, are to be put on stand-by to deal with matters as they arise."

Liatoukine knew that "specialized" was a euphemism by those higher up the chain of command for operatives such as himself—used to maintain secrecy, and as a form of mental denial of the reality of the supernatural.

Liatoukine leant forward across his superior's desk. "The Countess can cause further trouble by more killings—creating lack of confidence in the authorities here. She is a priority on that level."

"Quite so, my dear Major. That is why I can spare you six operatives. Not what you want, but all that can be spared. If any questions arise, then of course we are hunting for a western agent provocateur. See to it that no such questions arise if you do not capture her tonight."

With that, the Russian vampire took his leave. He found it quite interesting that Von Bork was keen enough to give him six people at this time of crisis. It could be his natural desire to capture the Countess as part of his duties, but Liatoukine sensed it could be something more. Perhaps Von Bork would also like to talk to her before handing her over to their superiors?

Liatoukine took his specialists to the streets around Bernauer Strasse. It was here that green tints had been reported on people's windows. There was a problem in that the area was next to the French sector. The Russian had already made up his mind that, if necessary, they would cross into it. They already had, whilst scouting the area earlier. It occurred to Liatoukine that, perhaps, the Countess had more recently targeted the Soviet sector due to secrecy; the killings in the Western sector had created some media interest—and thus pressure to find the culprit. Here, in the Soviet sector, there was a press blackout and people would not be so on guard.

It was now shortly past midnight. Liatoukine's operatives were well versed in secreting themselves in such urban areas. The day had proved eventful, politically. Whilst looking out for any signs of Gregoryi, he and his team had observed various workers protesting against the government. The Russian vampire was well aware that many of the factories had been dismantled and parts taken back to the Soviet Union. Liatoukine was no real communist, but he did approve of looting in foreign lands. However, he did wonder if things had gone too far. After all, if the Germans were allowed to create a bit more wealth, there would be more for Russia to take.

Liatoukine doubted that the Countess would make any kind of move during the day, with so many people milling about due to the political situation. The protests against the regime appeared to have petered out late in the evening. Liatoukine did not believe that would be the end of it—he was certainly aware that his Soviet comrades had moved tanks and men to areas of strategic value in the whole of East Germany.

In the last couple of hours, things had been quiet.

His team had kept an eye on the few people who walked past. Such people were suspicious and should be questioned as to why they were about at this hour—but he did not want to scare away the Countess. Further, they served as useful, albeit unwitting, bait. However, the specialists were taking it in turns to venture out—observed by at least one other colleague. They were all in radio contact.

Liatoukine himself was atop a building, from where he could see more. A crackle on the radio and one of the specialists voices—a man called Ageykin—came over, "One of the street lights near the church is glowing green," he said.

This must be it! And yet, so close to the church? This was the neo-gothic Church of Reconciliation on the strasse. Vampires had difficulties with consecrated ground. Perhaps she was thinking of escaping to the French sector, reasoning that any pursuer would not follow her there? An error if so.

He ordered Ageykin to go onto the street and walk towards the street lamp but not beyond the church—and told everyone else to converge swiftly and as covertly as possible to him. His specialist would be used as bait—a duty the man understood and was well armed for.

Liatoukine had expected to get to the scene in but a couple of minutes—but then heard the radio again:

"Contact! Contact!" the specialist was screaming.

The Countess must have struck the moment the man broke cover. He scaled down the building he was on and ran to the scene. He was there a minute later.

In that minute, much appeared to have happened. With his enhanced abilities, he took in what had happened. Ageykin's weapon had been discarded but he could see no empty shells. One part of Liatoukine's mind considered this—the enemy had been able to deal with the specialist before he could use his weapon. However, his mind was mostly focused on what was happening on the steps of the Church. The specialist had been making his way up them, fleeing what was behind him.

And what was behind him was not the beautiful form of the Countess Gregoryi. No—this was some decaying creature in barely human form. The head was little more than a blackened skull with eyes, with putrid fluids dripping from the eye sockets. It seemed to be clad in some kind of military fatigues.

Steam was coming off the creature—as if it were burning? Perhaps due to proximity to the church? The specialist had not been able to deal with it and had run towards the church—a good strategy, but not enough. The creature was upon him. It had fangs and bit deep into Ageykin's throat.

Liatoukine bounded up to them and grabbed the thing. It dropped the unfortunate specialist and smashed its fist in the Liatoukine's face. The Russian dropped onto the ground, but picked himself back up quickly. As he did so, he saw the creature change. The blackened skull with fangs regenerated, white flesh appearing, and growing and long healthy hair flowing. It was the face of the Countess Gregoryi!

As her flesh grew back, she hissed in pain—the church was clearly causing her much agony. Before the Russian vampire had gathered his wits, she ran past him, kicking him savagely in the head and knocking him firmly back down. By this point, another specialist was present, with the others converging. The one in front brought out a crucifix rather than fire his weapon—mindful of the original instruction to capture if possible.

The Countess simply broke his arm, but clearly winced in pain at the cross, which fell to the ground. She grabbed the man, flew upwards and swiftly disappeared.

Liatoukine did not have that power. The Countess had eluded him. The specialist she took would soon be dead. However, Ageykin was still alive. He may be able to shed some light in the matter. His team gathered the wounded up and disappeared. It had not been a good night.

Liatoukine and his men had returned to their base. Von Bork was less than pleased with the night's events. In his office, he asked Liatoukine to give him the full details.

"Major Liatoukine, are you finally getting old? You and six top specialists were unable to deal with a single vampire?"

The Russian defended himself:

"The circumstances were not quite so simple. As I have already related, Countess Gregoryi has appeared to have changed into something else—or appears to be cursed. It gave her some new-found strength."

Liatoukine knew that this was not quite true. Her strength and powers were much the same as previously. She had always been formidable, but he had underestimated her—his pride coming before his strategic intelligence. And he had indeed been taken by surprise by her horrific new form. What lay behind that, he didn't yet know, but guessed that it was important.

The phone rang. Von Bork took the call and relayed to Liatoukine what he was told:

"The body of the specialist has been found. His remains were thrown into the Graf Spree. He appears to have been drained of blood, of course. He is in our sick bay. Perhaps this is an opportune time to look on Ageykin?"

Like most members of Von Bork's organization, Ageykin was Russian—very few human members were not, unless they had some extra skill. Von Bork considered non-Russians untrustworthy, and was especially careful about his supernatural workers, who had usually been forcibly recruited. However, it was inadvisable for any underling to point out Von Bork's German origins.

They found the Doctor just outside the sick bay. Liatoukine recognized him—Sitnikov. In his 40s, he was experienced as a combat medic having fought during the Great Patriotic War. He was also used to handling sensitive matters. He could keep his mouth shut, which is why Von Bork had recruited him. Still, Liatoukine was surprised to see him here. Was he not stationed elsewhere?

"Comrade Doctor, how is Ageykin? " asked Von Bork.

"Dead," Sitnikov replied.

Liatoukine was surprised to hear this.

"The man's wounds were severe, but I did not expect him to die so soon; he should have survived."

"Yes, he may have pulled through, but there appeared to be complications. He seemed to be suffering from some curious after-effects, causing some blistering on his face. It appeared that the Countess infected him with something. I have some more tests to run; come back in an hour or so. I should have some more answers then."

Von Bork nodded. "Very well. In the meantime, current events must be attended to."

He strode off back to his office, no doubt preparing to set some of his forces against the local German protestors—early indications had suggested that the previous day's unrest would continue. The Soviet army may be busy today. The Russian vampire had noted that Von Bork seemed strangely lacking in questions. The doctor closed the door of sick bay behind in a manner suggesting he did not want Liatoukine to see what was in there just yet. Swiftly, the Russian put a hand on the door before it closed, pushing it open a little to ensure the Doctor's head popped around to see what was happening.

"Doctor Sitnikov, I am surprised to see you here," said the vampire. "I thought you were stationed in our outpost in Kazakhstan?"

"I was. Comrade Von Bork summoned me here to help in the event of any political problems that may arise here, in addition to this business with your 'Berlin Vampire.'"

Liatoukine let the door go. "Thank you, comrade, I was simply curious."

And he was now even more curious. He would spend the next hour looking at Doctor Sitnikov's file—to which, of course, he had access.

The file did not yield much: honorable war service, and then some work with their department, treating those wounded by the supernatural, and researching the biology of such creatures. He had spent some time recently in Kurchatov in Kazakhstan, attached to the military there, whilst also being a liaison officer for their unit in the region. There was nothing obvious as to why Von Bork would have summoned the man. Liatoukine closed the file and got up to head to the sick bay. The hour was already up.

The Russian vampire was not surprised to see Von Bork already there—no doubt, already briefed. The German stood near to the door, almost blocking

Liatoukine's way as he entered.

The room was small, but not so much that Von Bork would have had to stand back so far from the beds. Liatoukine understood the reason why in a split second. On two of the beds were the corpses of the specialists. In front of both beds was the doctor, clearly wearing a protective suit of some kind, complete with mask. He held some form of instrument in one hand and, with the other, he was motioning Liatoukine back. He took off his mask and spoke:

"Ah, Major, there you are. Let me show you what I have just demonstrated to Comrade Von Bork." He put the mask back on and waved the instrument at the first corpse—Ageykin. There was a ticking sound. He then moved over to the other one. The noise became louder. He turned back to the MVD men, taking off his mask again. "That was radiation. These men have been in contact with something radioactive. Do not be alarmed—there is not enough here to damage any of us provided we are careful. Indeed, Ageykin may have survived the dose had it not been for his other injuries. As to what this radioactive source is, I can only speculate that it was something on Gregoryi's person—or herself."

"This radiation may have caused Gregoryi's change in form," speculated Von Bork. "Perhaps a process akin to what we know as a mutation? She may have been subject to radioactive experiments by the West. We must find her and get the truth from her."

Liatoukine nodded his agreement. "The problem remains as to how to locate her," he said.

"That should be less of a problem now," the doctor said. "You have been tracking your target with sightings of reflection on window. Now you can track her with radiation detectors."

"Excellent," said Von Bork. "Major, you will be in charge of this operation. Send our men around the city— have them dressed as civilians. Their cover to the German authorities will be that of spying on the counter-revolutionaries. Indeed, they may as well file reports on such activity as well. Kill or capture the Countess, Liatoukine, but try not to get too close to her."

Von Bork strode off, leaving any double meaning to his last phrase in the air. The Russian vampire swiftly realized why the doctor was there; his file said he had previously been stationed in Kurchatov, the base for the Soviet atom bomb testing site of Semipalatinsk. He had been involved in studying the medical effects of radiation. It was also convenient that a number of radiation detectors were so readily available. Von Bork knew more than he had been telling...

Liatoukine planned swiftly. As they were to provide intelligence on the subversive events of the day, as well as hunt for the Countess, he could use more specialists, and could even bring in some regular Soviet Army on the pretext of finding 'Western saboteurs.' Red Army tanks were already starting to move on the streets— Moscow had no confidence in the SED and its police to deal with the political situation. They believed the German authorities had no firm grasp on the matter.

Liatoukine could only concur. A procession of workers was already heading out to confront SED party leaders. News of the uprising had spread throughout East Germany; people were coming out on the streets in Bitterfeld, Halle Leipzig, and elsewhere. A radio car had even been taken over with comments such as "Goatee's got to go"—a reference to the SED leader Walter Ulbrecht's beard. Liatoukine cared nothing for the German leadership. He was annoyed, however, by disobedience of subject peoples to Russia, no matter what their grievance. Such people should be firmly dealt with—and the Red Army was going to do it. They had crushed Germans before, after all.

His priority now, however, was to find the Countess. He would help repress the Germans later. A number of supernatural operatives could not be used due to their inability to work in the daytime. Even his own powers were reduced.

As the day wore on, unrest continued. Liatoukine observed with pleasure Soviet tanks move against protesting crowds, breaking them up.

Strong traces of radiation had been found in the area around the Church of Reconciliation—it was important to find similar traces. The matter was compounded by the fact that, the previous night, the Countess had flown away. Liatoukine's main concern was, what if she had gone back to the West? If this had happened, his resources would be limited; he could hardly lead Soviet tanks in there—no matter as much as he wished to do so.

But never became necessary. There had been major clashes with protestors at Unter der Linden and in Potsdamer Platz. Now, his operatives detected some radiation at Potsdamer Platz. These had been larger readings. Presumably, the Countess was hiding amongst the protestors—perhaps in plain sight, Was it a deliberate ploy? Liatoukine doubted that she was aware of their new tracking methods, but would she stay in the area after the disturbances had been dealt with?

Suddenly, his phone rang. Von Bork wanted to see him immediately.

"Major Liatoukine, there have been new developments," Von Bork said as soon as the Russian vampire entered his office. He was standing and made no intimation that they should sit.

"One of our tank crews sent out to deal with the subversives returned to its barracks. Its crew is dead, except for the driver who it seems had been ordered under hypnosis to return unobtrusively. He is of little use of us; he is not responding to our questions. The inside of the tank is full of radioactive traces. Countess Gregoryi must have somehow gotten inside and took her fill before leaving. We have no witnesses of a woman doing this—but however she did it, the situation has now changed. Our superiors are demanding that she be destroyed. Not only does this represent an attack on the Soviet Union, but, given the current situation, this can only create greater problems."

"Destroyed?" asked Liatoukine. "We still need to find out how she got into the state in which she is. Draining so much blood means that whatever is afflicting her is also draining her own energy at a rapid rate. We need to know how she came into contact with radioactive material."

"Liatoukine, that no longer matters," Von Bork impatiently responded. "Senior command want this problem dealt with right away. They do not care at the moment about the origin of the Countess' present condition. It has been made clear to me that, if we do not deal with it soon, others will be given the task of doing so. I would say that we have about 24 hours—if even that. How do you intend to find her?"

The Russian vampire paused before answering. Did their superiors really not care about how the Countess had suddenly become radioactive? Or Von Bork? This was surely important on so many levels—not least, the effect that radiation was clearly having on a vampire. Their superiors and Von Bork had obviously some idea of what had happened—and now urgently wanted her liquidated rather than have her complicate the situation in Berlin. It was he who had been kept unaware of what had really been going on.

The trouble at Potsdamer Platz had died down by late evening. Soviet tanks had done their work in crushing the protestors. Indeed, the German uprising throughout the country had been largely put down.

Aside from members of the security forces, the only people around were Liatoukine's own specialist staff—dressed in plain clothes.

Had the Countess left the area? This would surely be the logical thing to do, unless she was thinking of hiding somewhere where she thought she she would not look? Did she suspect they could find her via radiation traces? Then again, perhaps her condition caused her to behave erratically?

The Russian looked around the square. Nothing suspicious, his own men taking further radiation readings, a patch of mist, bored Soviet troops, the drab buildings, the—

Mist?

A patch of mist was drifting towards a stationary T-72 tank. Of course! Some vampires had the ability to turn into mist. It was a rare skill. Count Dracula himself had been said to have possessed such awesome power. This was no doubt how the Countess had been able to enter the previous tank. Now she was using the same trick again.

Why was she acting in such a fashion. though? As if she wanted to be caught? She could use this formidable power—albeit one that was said to take up much energy—to enter people's homes. Why tanks?

Liatoukine let the mist enter the tank. Then he rushed to it—clambering on top of it. He swiftly instructed his specialists not to interfere. He wanted to deal with the Countess alone. The tank crew was exiting, already in a panic. He jumped inside, a stake in his hand, confident he could deal with the Countess.

Too confident! He received a bullet between the eyes. His regenerative ability kicked in—but he was confused, his brain functions being impaired. He sensed, but did not fully comprehend, that he was under attack. Then he felt a pair of fangs penetrate deep into his throat.

He heard a scream, and, for a few moments, he felt nothing. It was enough time for his brain to regain some senses. In front of him, he could see the Countess vomiting blood and observe what seemed to be some kind of energy flashing around her face. A dead soldier was slumped at some controls—she had managed to kill him and drink some blood in the time it had taken him to get inside the tank. Her frenzy suddenly calmed. They looked at each other. Her appearance looked young and beautiful—as he remembered her from long in the past—but then he could see some patches of burnt blackness starting to form on her face and neck.

He recognized the energy flashes. They came from his body—he saw them sometimes, when he was injured. Then he understood her behavior. She had lured him into a trap—to get his energy presumably in the hope of curing whatever was ailing her. She confirmed this immediately.

"You were my last hope," she said bitterly.

Liatoukine could feel his head regenerating—she

could no doubt see that, providing a contrast to her own lack of healing. She dropped the gun she had used against him. Liatoukine could see she had virtually given up.

"It seems my type of blood is not to your taste," he said, "if indeed you can call the energy that courses through my veins blood. More immediately, you are of course, surrounded. And I suspect your mist trick has already left you weakened—otherwise, you would have already employed it again to make your escape."

She nodded and said, "And so, you intend to destroy me. One day, your masters will come for you, given that humans have destroyed most of our kind."

Something in the Russian Vampire's expression gave away the fact that he may not quite know exactly what she was talking about.

"Oh, Boris, how it is that you have been kept in the dark? Do you not know of *Operation Tropic*?"

He looked at her levelly. "Perhaps you would care to enlighten me?" he said. He was not in the best of moods; not only was he not being fully informed of what was going on, but he had walked into a trap—not dissimilar to the ones set for him in the past.

She smiled—although that must have caused her slight pain, given that her face seemed to be gradually blackening with burns. "I can give you a memory of everything—as we vampires can."

Vampire had certain psychic powers, and could transfer memories to each other. Liatoukine realized that she could leave some matters out. Nevertheless, he would have the knowledge of this '*Operation Tropic*' within a moment, and given that time was not on his side, it seemed to present an excellent solution.

"Very well. Communion!" he said.

"Communion!" she replied.

And, in a moment, he had the memory. The memory was naturally edited, and entirely from her point of view.

*London, January 1953 (Six Months Earlier)*

The Countess stared across the table at her superior. He was an Englishmen simply called Control. Not his real name, but a code-name. She was a bit fed up with every other spymaster in the British secret services calling themselves "Control," "M," "Hunter" and the like. Was it some English humor thing?

"This is not a course of action that I find credible," she said.

Control leaned forward to her. "Not at all. It seems to suit everyone, my dear Countess."

His use of her title was not intended to display any respect. Rather, he used it to emphasis her powerlessness. She had worked for the wrong side during the humans' last World War. The British had captured her, and, utilizing certain mystical techniques at their disposal to ensure her loyalty, had more or less recruited her to serve their MI6. This was not to her taste—she had hoped to flee Europe for a while. Still, it was better than working for the Soviets, whom she detested even more than the Western Allies.

"How so?" she asked.

"The atomic bombing of the Vampire City, or The Sepulchre, or Selene, whatever the bloody hell people call it, will remove a terrible threat to all humanity."

The Hungarian vampire rolled her eyes.

Control grinned. "Oh, very well. Stalin tells us that is why he wants to do it. Of course, we know that he thinks the city can't be trusted. He believes it colludes with us now, and probably did so with the Germans during the War."

The Countess groaned inwardly. For all she knew, the allies did deal with the Sepulchre. However, the fascists—and she had worked with them—were largely clueless about such matters, despite having access to territories, people and information involved with the supernatural. They followed their own lunatic mysticism. After the war, the West and the communists had gathered up what remained of Central Europe's supernatural heritage that hadn't been destroyed by two world wars, including her, of course.

Control continued. "We and the Cousins don't want the Soviets having any further access to the Vampire City—we would certainly enjoy the secrets of that place, but that does not seem feasible at the moment. Better it is wiped out rather than possibly offer the Reds anything useful at this time."

The Countess was not going to let this go too easily. "They do have secrets; the Sepulchre could still be useful to us if we could persuade the Russians to stay their hand, and open our own lines to it, perhaps via Tito?"

Tito was the communist dictator of Yugoslavia, on whose territory the Vampire City was situated. He was not on the best of terms with Stalin.

"Countess, this city has provided little of use to the Soviets, bar a few operatives. One of our own citizens in the late 1700s managed to create havoc there. The most recent national security threat from such creatures came in 1893, from Count Dracula, and that was seen off by a group of civilians.

"As for Tito, he is going along with it. He does not want Stalin finding some pretext to roll his tanks into

Yugoslavia. What's more, Tito is as much a strongman as Stalin. He wants no opposition of any kind, and he will be happy to see the Vampire City gone. Of course, if they'd done a deal with him, that might be different, but their deal is with Moscow—a rather more powerful political center than Belgrade. One of the reasons this is a joint operation is that it makes Tito feel better about it. Another, incidentally, is that Stalin wants to show us that he is capable of using atomic weapons. He will hardly listen to us, even if we were inclined to prevent it. Politics aside, you will be on the mission representing us. Don't even think about arguing. This can't go wrong—and on our side, you are the asset we have who has the most experience with Selene."

This was not something she had wanted to hear. She did not care much for the Sepulchre—their collusion with communists did not sit well with her—being against God was one thing, but taking her rights and properties for their own personal enrichment was another. Nonetheless, she was aware that humanity's wars had smashed the supernatural, especially in Central Europe. Indeed, the humans had seen that part of Europe effectively and simply divided between East and West. Was the end of the Vampire City in her long-term interest? For her, being immortal and dead, the long term was something that she could appreciate. However, there was perhaps a way to turn matters to her advantage...

*Yugoslavia, March 1953 (Three Months Earlier)*

The Countess found herself in Tito's Yugoslavia. The Sepulchre was in the Vojvodina area, and sealed off. It was meant to be a military site—but, in reality, it was sealed off to keep people away from the Vampire City.

There was plenty of vegetation around it. Keeping the secret thus far, since the emergence of cameras, had been something of feat. Of course, the existence of the City had had been rumored, and indeed a number of perfectly authentic photographs had managed to appear over the years. The Countess had seen them—and also the many other obviously fake pictures with different depictions of the City which the Yugoslav secret service and its Serbian predecessor had given to the gutter press to create confusion and disbelief.

The Countess looked around at her group, all dressed in Soviet military fatigues. Most were Russian, but some were not. She was there for the British—an MI6 officer was also there with her.

She recalled the recent briefing. Supposedly, under the long-standing Soviet-Selene Accord, the Russians were delivering books and documents that had originated from Dracula's castle and the library of the Scholomance—the school of dark arts the Count had attended. Vampires would study them and pass on their insights to Moscow. However, the large sealed casket on the lorry did not carry any such materials. It carried an atomic bomb.

It had to be done by land—dropping it from the air might run afoul of the various defenses the City employed against aircraft. Such defenses may not be of much use, but certainty was required, even if that involved risking people on the ground.

"Apparently, it's God's will that the City appears for but an hour a day. Presumably as warning to us humans. Do you believe that, Countess?" the voice came from her MI6 colleague, breaking her chain of thought. He was called David and was part of the MI6 team that dealt with the supernatural—a department of low importance staffed only by enthusiasts. She knew David had a view on beings like her—and that this act was something he almost certainly had no problems with.

"God is not an area I consider much. Why it materializes for an hour a day is mystery. Some vampires consider it does so to absorb energy from the Earth to power it," she responded.

"We'll certainly be giving it a lot of energy today," he said laughing.

She looked at him. It was a look that had struck terror into many people over the centuries—often the last thing most of them ever saw.

He laughed again. "Don't look at me like that. The actual material that Selene thinks it's getting provided us with the control we have over you—we can make you stake yourself if we want to."

Ah, so that was how they had control over her. Information gleaned from the great Count or his old school. Her will was often her own, but she was unable to flee or to disobey orders. Still, the power MI6 had was not absolute. She could not mesmerize David or look into his mind. However, she could sense things. Yes, he hated her, but deep down he desired her. She was beautiful—she knew this, of course. And he wanted her very badly. Perhaps these mixed feelings were to do with his bloodline? She had heard him been referred to as Harker—a slip by Control, who perhaps thought she was out of his hearing. She had little doubt he was related to the couple who participated in the murder of Dracula. Had the Count not had a certain hold over the woman Mina Harker?

Yes, a tiny weakness for vampires there. She would one day take great pleasure in giving him his desire. She would seduce him, turn him into a vampire and make him serve her forever. If he somehow survived the day that is. Whatever the precise nature of MI6's control over her will, she did not think it would extend into the Sepulchre. She had not been there for decades, but she had been in its vicinity in the course of her duties, and she had felt the spy's hold lessen. What would happen if she entered it? MI6 kept her well away from entering the City, or indeed any centers of supernatural activity. They believed she would fail as an infiltrator. Her talents were sparingly used against human enemies of England, and the occasional mystical nuisance.

The City started to materialize at 11 a.m. as it did every day. The strange, abstract shapes of the Vampire City formed out of thin air.

"We are on," David said.

The carrying of the collection into the City had involved much negotiation. It would not be given over at the gate. It would be transported by the military into the heart of the City, at which point they would be given a receipt for it and leave. The vampires were used to Soviet bureaucracy.

The City fully materialized and its dark, sinister gates opened. The small convoy—a Soviet military car with she and David sitting in the back, an armored personnel carrier carrying the load, and another military car—moved slowly forward. Then the APC came to halt, breaking down. This was planned—after 30 minutes, the convoy would resume. The vampires would see nothing suspicious in this. They also expected that sort of thing from the Soviets.

After the "repairs," the convoy moved forward. It would take about ten minutes to get to the center of the City. The bomb was timed to go off a few seconds after it dematerialized back into whatever dimension it spent most of its time. Control had said the atomic explosion would have no effect on Earth whatsoever. The Countess recalled the void outside the City—there seemed to be nothing there. And vampires who had ventured too far into it had never returned.

The convoy moved into the City. Suddenly, the Countess could feel her freedom return. MI6's mystical hold had no longer any effect here—the real reason they kept her away from the Sepulchre. She instinctively gasped in pleasure. David noticed the change in her and brought up a stake. Should she kill him and warn the City? She leapt out of the car and flew upwards and to-wards the City center. She looked backwards briefly—the convoy was speeding up.

She flew down into the heart of the Vampire City, to its version of City Hall. A small delegation was there. She recognized the one who was in charge—Baroness Phryne.

She landed gracefully in front of her—looking odd in her Soviet military fatigues. Phryne recognized her immediately. "Countess! how good to see you after..."

She cut him off. "Baroness, we have little time. The humans are betraying you. They are delivering not a col-lection of books and documents—but an atomic bomb. All the great powers have agreed to destroy you. You must get it away from the City—it is timed to detonate almost immediately after dematerialization"

"Don't be absurd—we have had an alliance with the Russians for decades now. We have heard, Countess, that you now work for the British? It would be in their interests for to create discord."

There was no time for this, thought Gregoryi. "If I am lying, then there will be no atomic explosion when you get it out of our city, and I will be your prisoner."

The Baroness looked at her warily. The convoy was arriving swiftly, and stopped. David got out of his car.

He went straight up to them. In perfect Russian he said: "This is a British agent—she is here to get you to reject the collection, claiming it's an atom bomb. Their operatives outside the gate are now being arrested."

Baroness Phryne looked at him warily also—although she knew a couple of the officers with him, she did not know this man. One of the officers she recognized waved a radio and said: "It's true—our comrades have had to subdue them."

David said: "We have to get back to help—and your city is leaving in a few minutes." He pointed to the Countess, "Her, we're happy to leave to your justice."

With that, he and the others headed back to their cars and drove off.

There was no time to unravel any of this. Baroness Phryne motioned to her minions to take hold of the Countess. But she smashed them away and lunged for the cab of the lorry. She got in and tried to start the vehicle—but all that happened was a loud bang. The wheels had collapsed. The lorry was immobilized. Phryne's servants grabbed her and pulled her out.

She flung them aside with ease, and said to the Baroness. "Look—they have immobilized their own vehicle! Why would they do this? Why? We must physically move the bomb ourselves."

The Baroness was frozen in indecisiveness. Gregoryi ran to the back of the lorry and leaped in—and was then repelled backwards. On the large casket containing the bomb was a silver cross. A number of them had been strewn around the lorry. Along with garlic and bottles of holy water. Such tools were standard weapons carried by the Soviets in the vehicles they used when entering the Vampire City. They were no doubt hung there the moment she had escaped.

The Countess staggered back in and knocked the cross off the casket, burning her hand. She screamed out in agony.

"Help me, you fools!" she commanded the vampires.

They tried to get in but were repelled. Even Baroness Phryne could not seem to get in.

She realized then there was no hope. They could perhaps move it in time, but they could not face the pain and fear of dealing with the crosses and holy water. The water had even been splashed on the casket. Her will was far stronger—she could, but was unable to move the bomb alone.

Survival was now the objective. She flung herself out of the lorry and flew down the road. She could see the convoy ahead, still not out of the City. They had been slowed by attacking vampires. Someone in Phryne's entourage had presumably taken her seriously and got word out to stop them. Much good that would do. The humans were giving a good account of themselves—with silver bullets and weapons firing stakes. She could see their vehicles smash through the gates and out. She was flying hard and fast to catch up—she would be back under MI6 control and they may very destroy her, but she faced certain death if she stayed.

The Vampire City was already starting to dematerialize! She flew down to the damaged gate which had had been closed, but, due to the damage sustained by the convoy smashing out, was not locked. She wrenched it open with all the strength in her possession.

She later saw an image drawn of what the Soviet troops outside saw at that moment. A black skeletal silhouette of her—unrecognizable—against a blinding white flash. They had to describe it, for their eyesight had been damaged.

The bomb had gone off slightly early. It was not known why. However, the blast took place after most of the City had already dematerialized. It was not widely known if opening the gate would provide entrance and exit for a few seconds more. The flash out of the gate-way was momentary—and not even completed. It was enough to leave behind some radiation, but easily covered up.

She had been vaporized, but her dust had been blasted out. After a few days, she somehow reformed. First, she appeared as mist, and then floated away from the area—this ensured she was not noticed by the observation team left to see if the City would return. Her survival had been achieved by sheer force of will; the Countess refused to die. Only when she was safe did she change back to a solid form—a blackened skeletal form. She came across a peasant later and drained him of his blood and reformed back into the beautiful woman she had once been.

However, soon she deteriorated back into a blackened husk, requiring ever more blood to regenerate. She killed her way back to London. Her condition horrified her, but the atomic blast had one positive effect—it had severed the mystical hold MI6 had held over her.

She found David Harker, seduced him, and brought him under her control—but she did not turn him into a vampire. She did not wish to trip any of the supernatural alarms MI6 employed. Those alarms were not much use in any event. MI6 were lax in such matters and she wouldn't have been surprised to learn that the MVD had compromised the entire spy agency.

David revealed much to her. Selene, it seems, had been obliterated. It had not manifested itself in weeks. He also told her of the existence of Von Bork's little MVD operation. A group, it seems, that had played no part in what the British had called *Operation Tropic*. Other Russians had led this attack. Von Bork was believed to have valued the agreement with the Sepulchre too much. David further mentioned the existence of the energy vampire, Boris Liatoukine, who worked for Von Bork.

The Countess knew she was deteriorating; she could not absorb enough blood from her victims to heal completely and defeat the radiation that had damaged her so. Perhaps she could absorb Liatoukine's special energy? Surely that may work. David certainly thought so.

They knew Von Bork had a major outpost in the Berlin sector of the Soviet Occupation Zone, which he and his top people visited regularly. It was a simple matter for David to go to West Berlin on a pretext, providing support for the Countess. She would kill people to draw Liatoukine into a trap. This was supposed to happen only in the Soviet sector, but her needs drove her to kill in West Berlin. David let it be known through various lines that it was the Countess who may be responsible for the killings to further entice Von Bork's group to take an interest—especially Major Boris Liatoukine.

*Berlin, 17 June*

The MVD vampire was finished with the memories the Countess had imparted to him. He looked at her for a moment, feeling as near to shock over the destruction of the Sepulchre as he would ever get.

"That information is most useful to me. Presumably you think you will get a bit of revenge in some way if I use it?" he said.

She nodded her head. The burns were rapidly taking her over now. "It is over for me, Liatoukine. I do not have the energy now to turn into mist. Whatever is in you has accelerated the process. I only have hours left. Kill me."

Liatoukine considered this. It might be useful to take her in, to see how she died from radiation. Much information could be obtained on radiation's effect on vampire physiognomy. However, did he really want Von Bork to have such knowledge? No. He had no intention of absorbing her energy due to the radiation. Somehow, he still had his stake in his hand. She braced herself, and he smashed the stake into her heart. She held his gaze even whilst turning into radioactive dust. He regretted her passing. She had been a formidable foe.

Soon, he met again with Von Bork. The German was pleased with the turn of events. "The subversives have been crushed and we have eliminated the Countess. Did she tell you about the Sepulchre?"

"Yes," the Major replied. "Why did you not tell me of this *Operation Tropic*?"

"Major Liatoukine, as you know, we are not entirely appreciated by some. I was informed of the plan. Stalin was still alive then and I made no objection, of course, although our superiors knew full well I valued the Accord with the Sepulchre. Stalin apparently believed we had no agreement with the City. 'You cannot have a binding legal agreement with those who are already dead,' he reportedly said. Legally, I suspect that is actually quite true.

"I was strictly informed not to pass on the information about the bombing to my operatives. I certainly did not want to draw any further attention to us—we may have faced another purge."

Liatoukine could hardly disagree—Stalin's era had seen a number of attempts at liquidating them. However, those who had tried to instigate such proceedings were often found dead from "natural causes." Yet, there had been some close calls. They had only pretended to mourn Stalin's death.

"However, our liquidating of this radioactive Countess when others failed will prove our usefulness again," Von Bork continued. "Her escape from the City was not something anyone knew about, and it is good we have cleaned up the mess of others. Incidentally, I am pleased to see that your regenerative powers were able to deal with your exposure to her radiation."

Neither man mentioned anything about informing the Germans of the radioactive traces now around Berlin—such a thought did not even cross their minds. The Russian vampire still had more to say:

"The destruction of Selene was foolish; we could still have learned much. The Accord had been useful over the years."

"Major Liatoukine, if you have some grievance, perhaps you would like to take it up with the leadership in Moscow. You can see how they deal with problems." He pointed at the outside world beyond the window, where the Germans had been crushed by Soviet tanks.

Liatoukine, of course, would not be taking the matter further. He had long wanted to control the Sepulchre, and, in due course, he had expected to do so. The bombing had taken place on 5 March, the day of Stalin's death - his last gasp an atomic blast. The communists had cheated him. Still, he always knew it was possible the

147

humans would destroy the Vampire City in time, with the help of their superior weapons. It was a setback to his ambitions.

Nonetheless, he had certain knowledge that he had not known previously. He now knew that the MI6 officer David Harker was no doubt still susceptible to vampire influence; perhaps he could be manipulated again one day. He also knew that the British had artifacts taken from Count Dracula and the Scholomance, no doubt looted after the War. It would be useful to eventually get hold of them at some point. As an immortal, he had time.

# The Death of Von Bork

*August 1979*

In her catsuit, the intruder effortlessly clambered back out of the window of the French Riviera mansion she had just robbed. Bag slung across her back, she paused to ensure that the security camera would have a picture of her. She pretended to fumble with her mask; she let the outside camera take a shot of her face. She jumped to the ground—a feat that would have broken the legs of any normal human—and bounded out of the drive. She could hear the alarms going off. Splendid! She could have robbed the wealthy family of their precious jewels without setting off any alarms. However, she wanted to make sure that she was seen. She bounded off down the drive, and merrily jogged down the road, startling some passers-by. Turning a corner she climbed up a wall—seemingly effortlessly—and onto a roof and was seen no more.

Just a few minutes later, a rather elegant black-haired lady carrying a couple of shopping bags got into a nearby black Lotus Esprit and drove off, heading towards Monaco. At the wheel, she laughed and laughed. She enjoyed driving. She often used her private chauffeur to drive her around. However, for this work, that was inadvisable. And she did rather enjoy these night rides. Tonight, she was going a bit fast. A police motorcyclist waved her down. The policeman strolled up to the car window.

"Good morning Madame. You understand that you were breaking the speed limit just now?"

"Was I?"

She had intended that to be charming, but unsurprisingly the policeman was not amused.

"Please step out of the car," he said.

Now here was a thing. Should she kill him for his impertinence? No, of course not. Killings would bring a lot of unnecessary attention to the area—any linkage with the theft of the family jewels last night would not be good. Not that she would be recognized as the thief, she had a different face on right now, but nothing should be left to chance. Her other talents would have to be used.

"Officer, everything is in order surely?" she smiled her most winning smile and showed her license.

The young policeman looked at it, and back at her, and was suddenly overwhelmed. He would do anything for this woman.

"Of course, Mrs. Adler, I just wanted to make sure you were having no problems."

"Thank you for your concern, officer, but I am fine. I must go now."

And then she drove off, taking care to not to speed again. Best not to push her luck. The policeman himself stood dazed for a moment. He shook his head, and got back on his motorcycle to resume his patrol.

The next day, she was in her own mansion in Monaco, her booty laid out on a coffee table in front her. She also had the late editions of the newspapers. They had held the presses for this story. *France-Soir* had the banner headline *Irma Vep strikes again!* And there was a picture of her from last night. At that moment, she did not look like the picture. She could do that. She was delighted with all the coverage—even more so than the actual robbery. She looked up at the TV news. They, too, were discussing the robbery in fevered terms. They were pondering how could Irma Vep be committing such robberies in 1979? Had the once-famous criminal gang of the Vampires reformed? Could this be some descendent of Irma Vep, its most notorious female member?

She knew the answers to all of these questions: No. Not least because Irma Vep had died in 1916. Her being like the original was no more real than the identity of wealthy young widow, Mrs. Adler, she used for everyday purposes.

She looked at a copy of the *International Herald-Tribune*. Too late to cover the robbery. She turned to the arts pages and was delighted to read about the opening of the new Soviet-French Cultural Center to be opened in Nice in a couple of weeks' time with an exhibition of Russian historical treasures. Would the security be strong enough, given the robberies committed by Irma Vep, it asked.

The so-called "Mrs. Adler" smiled. Yes, this would be her next, irresistible target. She had some Russian business that needed attending to, and she was very much looking forward to taking care of it.

At a cafe on Dubrovnik's Stradun, the Adriatic city's popular main street, Boris Liatoukine was reading the same edition of the *International Herald-Tribune*— but focusing on an article about the situation in Afghanistan. The place was clearly not very stable. As a KGB colonel, Liatoukine was, of course, more aware than most of that fact. His superior, the notorious spymaster Von Bork, was especially keen to get involved there.

151

Von Bork was old, dreaming of more glories. He was keen, in particular, to send Liatoukine there, with a couple of specialists to assist the communist government. The higher ups—KGB Chairman Yuri Andropov in particular—were convinced of the need for full, military intervention, and were prevailing upon General Secretary Leonid Brezhnev to agree to it. Brezhnev was no longer the man he had been, so might be persuaded to do it. These were the machinations of old men, whose time was passing. Even in this state—Yugoslavia—dictator Tito was not in the best of health.

This Afghanistan thing made Liatoukine uneasy, however. The Soviet Union had happily invaded other countries, and he had participated. He had helped crush anti-Soviet elements in East Germany, Hungary, Czechoslovakia... He was all in favor of subjugating other peoples. He himself was older than all of the rulers in Moscow put together. However, his body was young and thus his mind was as sharp as ever, with the benefit of experience. Such was the advantage of being a vampire. His mind went to the past. He had been to this Croatian city before, in 1806 when Russia and Montenegro savagely besieged the city during the war against Napoleon. Despite the damage wrought, in particular outside the city walls, the fortifications of the city did their job and remained to this day. The city in many ways looked the same now as it did then.

His thoughts moved back to the reason why he was here. He had an excellent view of the café opposite. He had been watching a British diplomat drinking coffee there. Liatoukine knew that someone else would be joining him soon; he was that person he wanted to know about. The evening was starting to draw in. Like a number of vampires, Liatoukine was able to exist in daylight, albeit with reduced supernatural powers. The twilight would help his heightened senses.

Within minutes, another man joined the British diplomat. He was in his early 30s and looked, in fact, rather like a younger version of his superior, Von Bork. Which is what Liatoukine had expected. He was aware that Von Bork had grandchildren, with a grandson in the military. Von Bork was always discreet about his family, but Liatoukine had made sure he knew about all of them, including their appearances. Despite his resemblance to his superior, however, this man was not one of Von Bork's relatives.

The two men sat together for a few minutes, discussing the delights of Dubrovnik in German, including its impending UNESCO recognition as a World Heritage Site. The diplomat then bade him good night and left, leaving behind some papers under a discarded copy of *The Times*. All a bit obvious, and Liatoukine wondered if MI6, or possibly Tito's notorious UDBA[5], were behind this.

However, looking around, the vampire could not detect any surveillance, and, with his senses and experience, it was probable he would have detected any if there were. He strolled over to his target.

"May I?" he asked.

The man looked surprised, casting a glance at the empty table next to him, essentially saying, "Why can't you sit over there?" The Russian vampire ignored that and simply said, "Thank you," and sat down. It was fortunate that it was the diplomat who had left rather than this fellow. It made things a bit easier, despite it being rather public.

---

[5] The Yugoslav State Security Administration

Liatoukine spoke in Russian. "Good evening, Comrade." The other man sat bolt upright at that. Very poor, thought Liatoukine. "Guten Abend" his interlocutor said, in German. That was even poorer. He should have feigned complete lack of understanding rather than answer in German. Liatoukine continued, "Comrade, I believe we work for the same employer."

The man started making his excuses and clearly was about to go. It was time, Liatoukine thought, to use one of his special talents. He fixed his eyes on the man. "Please," said Liatoukine, "stay... have a drink with me." The man looked into the eyes of the Russian vampire. They were like a cat's. He then decided, that yes, he would have a drink with this charming fellow. "Of course, it would be my pleasure," he replied—in Russian.

Liatoukine summoned the waiter and ordered a slivovitz for both himself and his guest.

"Tell me, what is your name and who do you work for?" asked Liatoukine.

"My name is Pyotr Suvorin. I work for the KGB."

"What is your current mission?" Liatoukine asked.

"I am working here in our embassy here under the assumed name of Von Bork."

Von Bork! This was certainly not Von Bork, and Liatoukine had a good idea what was going on. The rest of the conversation informed Liatoukine that this "Von Bork" was an officer of no real connections suddenly deployed in a new role under the assumed name. At this point, he was handling a mole in the UK embassy in Belgrade, meeting in this Adriatic city. Liatoukine looked over the photocopied papers the diplomat had given Suvorin, much of which seemed to be routine diplomatic material.

Liatoukine told Suvorin to go away, and to simply think he had had a pleasant drink with a tourist after his rendezvous. Then he sat a while. There was much to consider. What he had seen was familiar. As an immortal vampire, he had had to replace himself in Russian society with a fake son, or occasionally another 'relative', after faking his own death. The fake would then effectively replace him, looking younger. Sometimes he used others for those purposes, under mesmerism, and discarded them just prior to his "death." However, he had a splendid ability—albeit one he barely understood—to create a duplicate of himself, which appear as a "younger" version of himself prior to his "death." Naturally, this was not foolproof, but those who were suspicious would either be no longer so after a spot of mesmerism, and the more difficult ones would simply die of the usual "natural causes" or have an accident of some kind.

Clearly, Von Bork was preparing the same ground—if a little crudely, given that this Suvorin had only a resemblance. Any inquiries as to who this relative taking over Von Bork's post would find a trail of sorts, and further inquiry would probably lead to the death of the curious. Suvorin would either be liquidated, or reassigned to somewhere like Siberia.

But Von Bork was not a vampire. He was an old man who had refused the *dark kiss*, which would have meant to be under the thrall of another vampire. That was something he would never countenance, and he had made it clear many times that he would die a human. So something had changed, and this did not suit Liatoukine at all. He intended to take over the control of the KGB's supernatural division after Von Bork passed.

He finished his slivovitz and decided he had to re-turn to Moscow at once.

A few days later in Nice, "Mrs. Adler" had the opening of the Soviet-French Cultural Center to attend to. She drove to the entrance and someone took her ve-hicle to the car park. The banners around the Cultural Center were large and clear, heralding *The Treasures of Russia*. This would be the first exhibition at the Center and consisted of various jewels and treasures that had belonged to the Tsars and the wealthy noble class. The Soviet state had appropriated the items after their takeo-ver.

Security was tight. Everyone was concerned. Would this new Irma Vep strike again? It was thought that the exhibition was too high profile for her. "Mrs. Adler" smiled inwardly at that. That might be true, but she had certain inside knowledge to help her. She had every in-tention of robbing the exhibition, albeit not today. Today was for her to be seen at a major society event. And yes, a spot of early reconnaissance. She walked up the steps to the entrance. There seemed to be a commotion in front of her. A tall, haughty redhead with that American sounding accent that some Europeans have whilst speak-ing English was arguing with the doormen, with a couple of plainclothes guards hovering nervously nearby.

They may well be nervous, "Mrs. Adler" thought. This lady was none other than the Polish Countess Irina Petrovski. She would have received no invitation what-soever.

"No, I am not on your invitation list," she was say-ing, waving her arm at the guards who were as likely as not French police.. "But I have every right to come inside. The Petrovski Cameo is here. It belongs to my family not these... communists!"

"Mrs. Adler" stood patiently behind. She knew Petrovski, but the Countess would not recognize her. Indeed, she had met her only a few weeks before—as Irma Vep—in order to discuss her next theft. The Countess was a sort of neighbor; she lived in Monaco as she could hardly do so in communist Poland.

The Countess continued with her tirade. "That cameo belonged to my grandmother. She lost it in a rail disaster in 1906 in your country. It was retrieved years later by godless communists and has since been held onto by them rather than being given back to my family!"

A couple of other staff came out to see to the other guests. "Mrs. Adler" went into the Center. Yes, The Petrovski cameo was one of the smaller attractions of this exhibition. But her stealing it for the Countess, for a suitably agreed-upon sum, would have the excellent effect of showing Irma Vep as being not merely a thief but a restitutor of property back to its rightful owner. Her legend would grow, she would make profit—and there was still another certain aspect to consider, too...

Liatoukine left his Moscow office for a meeting with Von Bork. He had to play this very carefully. What was Von Bork up to? Outside his superior's office, Von Bork's secretary buzzed him. No reply. She buzzed again. Again, no reply. This was happening with more frequency of late. The secretary got up and went to the door. She knocked loudly and went in. Presently, she came back out. "He will see you now," she said to Liatoukine.

As Liatoukine went in, he took a look at the photographs on the wall: mostly, his superior pictured with various Soviet notables. There was one with Lenin, one with Khrushchev. There was a recent one—Brezhnev. The Trotsky and Stalin pictures had, of course, long gone. Von Bork had kept a low profile in the past when necessary, but, at this point, the photographs produced the desired effect on some visitors that he was not without some degree of influence. Von Bork had wanted advancement, but being in charge of this supernatural division—officially titled the Special Logistics Directorate—had certain disadvantages due to the distrust some felt towards it. They had dodged various purges by ensuring that anyone wishing them harm would be dissuaded or simply liquidated. The powers at their disposal—they employed a number of supernatural beings as agents—gave them an advantage in survival that millions of others had not. However, whilst effectively autonomous, they were unable to exert the influence that they wanted.

Liatoukine then looked at the figure behind the desk. An old, bald man slouched in his chair. Advanced in years—was he approaching one hundred? He had likely been dozing when his secretary had buzzed him. He remembered the young, proud man of old. Von Bork had created this division out of nothing. It had served the Soviet Union well. Guarded itself against Stalin, against all odds. And yes, Von Bork had defeated him, the great Boris Liatoukine, and made him work for him. Von Bork gestured him to sit.

"How was Prague?" asked the German spymaster.

Liatoukine had officially not been to Dubrovnik at all. His cover was that he spent those couple of days in the capital of Czechoslovakia.

"It went very well. The local StB [6] afforded me every help. The reports we had of Golem activity turned out to be nothing, let alone the thing's sighting. We did however, find a West German—a private citizen—looking into the same reports. We were unable to capture him for interrogation, and he spirited himself out of the country with the help of the BND [7] the moment he realized he was under observation. It is possible that the man was part of some private network in West, working with their secret service. It's all in the report," he pointed to a file on the desk. He wondered if Von Bork had even read it. It was all true, however. Liatoukine had the power—which Von Bork knew about—to create duplicates of himself. That was what Liatoukine had sent to Prague. In the past, this technique could only be used at short distances, with a limited lifespan. Over the years, however, the Russian vampire had worked hard on developing this unusual skill. His duplicates could now operate for days, with autonomy, and at greater distance. It did require, however, a considerable intake of energy from Liatoukine. He had carefully ensured that Von Bork knew nothing of these improvements.

"Germans?" asked Von Bork.

"Yes," said Liatoukine. "It appears that the BND are continuing their limited interest in supernatural matters. We have always suspected that they took over the Austro-Hungarians' resources decades ago. Their continued interest perhaps indicates that they didn't all fall into the hands of the British and the Americans at the end of the war."

---

[6] Czechoslovakian state security service.
[77] The West German Federal Intelligence Service.

Von Bork snorted. "The BND need Prussians to do the job. Only we have the right mentality. But we were not appreciated." He paused. "*I* was not appreciated," he said bitterly.

Liatoukine was slightly startled by this. Von Bork would not deny being a German *per se*, but it had been decades since he had heard him refer to himself as a Prussian.

"*They* appreciated me," Von Bork, continued, pointing to a picture of Lenin on his wall. The Russian knew what he meant. Von Bork had been unmasked as a German spy in Britain in 1914 by the private detective Sherlock Holmes, later even blamed by British propaganda for starting the First World War. He returned to Germany in disgrace and was rejected by the Kaiser's government, whereupon the Communists lost no time in recruiting this embittered man. He had since served them rather well, despite being German.

Von Bork looked at the file. "No, my old friend. Let us not think of those to whom we have already brought socialism. We must think of the future, as Lenin did. Kabul, old friend, Kabul! Our comrades there need our help."

Again, he speaks of Afghanistan, thought Liatoukine. He decided to try and dissuade him from thinking about this. "Comrade Von Bork, there is not much for us to do there. Our reports of supernatural activity are somewhat scant and..."

In a surprising burst of energy, Von Bork cut him off. "Supernatural activity has been scant since the Great Patriotic War, and especially since Stalin destroyed the Vampire City with an Atom bomb!"

Liatoukine remembered that well. It had been kept from him for a time.

"We have a role in using the talents of this directorate to further the liberation of the working classes around the world," the spymaster continued, "and to defend the Soviet Union and her allies from threats at home and abroad." He pointed at the Russian vampire. "Never forget, Liatoukine, that we bested you in the end, and your sudden conversion to communism has always been closely monitored by me."

That was true. Von Bork had found in him in Paris in 1928 and gave him a choice: work for Moscow or taste a silver stake. Liatoukine had a surge of resentment against this impertinent German addressing him—a former Imperial high Russian—in such a manner. But he suppressed his annoyance. He was playing a long game, intending to take over when Von Bork died. However, things were coming to the surface. A conclusion was perhaps coming into view?

The Russian vampire decided to soothe Von Bork. "I have served the cause well, Comrade. You are correct; I will send Comrade Ivanov to Kabul to assess how we can be of assistance to our fellow KGB officers already there. Perhaps we can run an assassination program against reactionaries and counter-revolutionaries?"

Von Bork looked pleased. "An excellent idea; however I would like to make a small change. It would be best if you were to lead the group. The KGB has a formidable presence there already, but I believe that soon we will be sending much greater assistance. General Secretary Brezhnev has been listening to the wise counsel of Comrade Andropov. We will save Afghanistan as we saved the German Democratic Republic, Hungary, and Czechoslovakia! We will normalize the situation, and the world will see our strength. Sending you, my top aide, will be a clear signal that our Directorate fully intends to play a powerful role in Afghanistan. If only I were younger, I would join you, but I have other duties."

Liatoukine was about to say something, but Von Bork was waving him away with his hand and clicked on the intercom. "Colonel Liatoukine is just leaving." His secretary came in and gently ushered Liatoukine out. Glancing back, he could see that Von Bork appeared to be dozing again.

In his own office, the Russian vampire considered the situation. Something was clearly going on. Von Bork was setting up a replacement for himself. Further, he was sending him well out of the way to Afghanistan. It could only mean that Von Bork was intending immortality for himself. What had changed? Perhaps Von Bork had somehow changed his mind on the matter? Had he found a way, some method of immortality, that did not involve vampirism?

The Vampire colonel had a way of finding out. The KGB Special Logistics Directorate Von Bork commanded had many defenses against the supernatural built into its facilities and indeed upon individuals themselves. One would have to be very foolish to try to mesmerize Von Bork, even in his advanced years. Such defenses extended elsewhere of course, to protect the Soviet Union. Quite deliberately, such defense responsibilities were not given to Liatoukine. However, over the years, he had quietly probed them. He could not overcome them, but had found a weakness or two.

Later, he boarded a train on the Metro and walked past a young lady sitting down. He stopped and spoke to her. "Good evening Elena!" She was a typist, whom he knew worked for Von Bork's secretary.

She seemed taken aback. "Good evening Comrade. I did not know that you took this route home."

She was entirely correct, he did not. However, they had met like this a number of times before, not that she would remember. "I am on the way to see a friend," he lied, sitting next to her.

There were no people around them, which was fortunate, as it meant he did not have to waste time walking with her out of the station to where there might be fewer people. He gazed at her intently, draining her very slightly of energy. This was merely to weaken her will. He turned on his mesmerism facilities, at a low level. "How are things in the typing pool? Von Bork keeping you all busy? He certainly does me!"

They both laughed. "Well, we are typing up the orders for your going to Afghanistan in a couple of days' time." She was not supposed to discuss such matters in public, but it was hardly a secret and no one was in earshot. Where was the harm?

Liatoukine laughed again, "Yes, I look forward to that! What else is he up to to make our lives a misery?"

Elena leaned forward conspiratorially. "He is off to Nice for a few days—as part of a cultural trip."

"A cultural trip?" asked the vampire. He knew that Von Bork did go on a number of these, to examine the "decadent" West at close quarters.

"Yes, he is due to attend a reception connected to an exhibition of some of our precious artifacts— probably a lot of drinks are involved!"

They laughed again. Liatoukine had heard enough—he would find out the rest. It was best not to probe too much, in order to leave only minimal psychic traces. "This is my stop Elena. You look tired, please forget you saw me tonight and sleep a little until your stop." Which she did.

The next day, in his office, Liatoukine mapped a strategy. He had heard of the Soviet-French Cultural Center being established in Nice, but had no idea that his superior was planning to go there. This was unusual— Von Bork was usually not secretive on such matters. He was to leave for France the very next day after Liatoukine was due to go Kabul, which was tomorrow. Nice was clearly the key.

Upon further research, he discovered that the Petrovski cameo was part of the exhibition. This could well be part of it. There was a notorious incident in 1906, an "accident" involving the Trans-Siberian express. But it was not an accident. There had been a creature from beyond this world running amok on board. Indeed, it had been Liatoukine in Moscow who had given the orders to destroy the train. The locals had not wanted to go anywhere near the wreckage which had been difficult to retrieve, having gone over a sheer incline. It was the Army, under Von Bork's direction, who had retrieved what lay below, several years later. Amongst what was retrieved from a safe that had survived were the valuables belonging to two passengers— Count and Countess Petrovski. This included a cameo of the Countess herself. It was going on display in Nice, as a property of the Soviet state, much to the chagrin of her descendent. However, Von Bork had access to the Cameo if he wanted, and indeed it was he who had ordered the release of such items from the KGB vaults.

There was another more intriguing possibility. Across Europe, in the Côte d'Azur in particular, there had been a recent number of high level thefts, paintings and jewelry. The perpetrator was referred to by the press as "Irma Vep." The original Vep had been part of a notorious French gang that had called itself The Vampires, and which had terrorized the country in the early part of the 20th century. They had committed quite a few strange and ingenious crimes, killing a number of people along the way. They were not actual vampires, however. Liatoukine recalled that a number of true vampires in the Sepulchre had thought them impertinent and sworn that they should be dealt with. None had tried, however. This criminal gang was not be trifled with, even by the undead. They were brought down by humans in 1916, with Irma Vep being shot and killed in the process.

Liatoukine looked at the feature on this new Irma Vep in a recent copy of the *International Herald-Tribune*. The original had been known to occasionally dress in a black catsuit, exactly as the current one did. More relevantly, a picture or two of the thief showed her exact likeness to that of the original. She clearly had been posing; she wanted her picture taken. And the same with a video at another theft. Plastic surgery by a current woman thief was a popular press theory to explain this "resurrection."

But could the original Irma Vep have achieved immortality in some way in 1916? The third leader of the gang of the Vampires had been a master-chemist named Venenos. Could he have created some immortality formula? The press—most of it, anyway—would not entertain that theory, but the Russian vampire knew that such things were not necessarily far-fetched. If Irma Vep had become a real vampire, she would have long been exposed at some point. An immortal human, however, may not have come to the attention of those such as he—if they were being careful enough.

Liatoukine's strategy was clear. He would quietly go to Nice and find out what exactly Von Bork was up to. He would also send his double to Kabul—it would have full autonomy.

"Mrs. Adler" returned home early from the opening ceremony of the exhibition. She had seen enough. Security was too tight to risk a theft, but she had a certain advantage. She got to her door and hesitated, to make sure the man who had followed her all the way from the exhibition was still doing so. She entered, leaving the door open for him. Stupidly, he just walked in after her.

She whirled around and picked him up by the neck. She took him into an adjacent room. Glaring into him, she used her power of mesmerism to the fullest. "Who sent you, and for what reason?" she demanded, although she had a pretty good idea.

He was struggling not to speak, and succeeded. As one of Von Bork's agents, he had been well trained in such resistance. She repeated the question two more times, and then broke through. "I was sent here by Von Bork," he gasped, "with instructions to locate Irma Vep to see if the elixir of life she claimed to have was real—and to steal it if possible."

Having established control, she put him down. "How did you locate me?" she then asked.

He faltered slightly, still resisting control, but spoke again. "The methods you set up to communicate with us were not as secure as you thought. We determined that one of your messages had been sent from this neighborhood. Of all the local residents, we found out that only you were scheduled to attend tonight's opening. We decided to follow you and see what connection, if any, you had with Irma Vep."

She nodded and asked, "Von Bork did not think to send a vampire or some other supernatural agent of his?"

"No, such resources are few at the moment, and many are earmarked for Afghanistan."

That made sense to her. The destruction of the Sepulchre in 1953 had reduced the vampire population somewhat. Things were clearer now. She—as Irma Vep—and Von Bork had been discussing the exhibition, its security arrangements in particular. They had a deal—one which Von Bork had clearly reneged on.

She got a few more details from the man. Then, she walked him back to his car, where she ordered him to drive to a secluded spot out of town, with her following him. There, she left her car a little way off, and walked over to where he was parked. He was still sitting in the driver's seat. She shot him in the head with a pistol through the window. She peered through the shattered glass to make sure he was quite dead, then went back to her own car. The body would be soon discovered, but having been killed in a human fashion. Let Von Bork continue to think he was dealing with a human, albeit an immortal one. His little gambit had failed. He would have to give her what she wanted in return for immortality. Which she would give him, and which would be her greatest prize.

The flight out of Moscow towards Kabul was uneventful. The duplicate of Liatoukine was seated on in the hold of the Antonov-12 with a number of troops. These were human Spetznaz—Soviet Special Forces troops—especially trained to work with the Supernatural division. There had been some discussion of what was to happen in Kabul. A headquarters for them had been set up, with the cover for the troops being that they would guard Soviet facilities. Their real objective would be to assassinate targeted rebels, investigate anything super-natural threats, and even liquidate the local communists who were seemed less than reliable. Although this Liatoukine was a duplicate—albeit one without the full powers of the original—somehow, he was still part of the same consciousness.

He looked over to the soldiers; they were examining their weapons and the crates. Aside from regular weapons, Kalashnikov weapons and so on, there were the usual special weapons, such as silver bullets, stake guns, gallons of holy water, etc. The soldiers finished what they were doing and broke open a bottle of vodka, taking swigs from it, laughing and joking. The officer in charge came over to him with the bottle. "Join us, comrade colonel!" he said, offering the bottle to him. It would not do to refuse. Over the many years, Liatoukine had re-mained a true soldier and knew that it was a good idea for an officer to be seen as one of the men from time to time. And he could not refuse a drink from a brother of-ficer.

The vampire took a swig from the bottle. His mouth burned! He spat it out. Holy water! They had given him holy water! Something smashed into his shoulder. A wooden stake—they had fired a wooden stake into him! But it had missed his heart—an error that would cost them dearly. He was splashed with what seemed to him like acid, but was simply more holy water. He ignored the agony, effortlessly snapping the neck of the soldier who had gotten too close with the bucket of the water.

Liatoukine knew he was trapped. There was only way out—he would have to jump out of the aircraft. Un-like some other vampires, he could not fly. However, he may be able to survive the fall. He lunged towards the door. And then he saw something protruding from his chest. It was a silver spike. It was the same silver stake that Von Bork had made years ago. It had been used effectively on others many times even though Liatoukine knew that it had really been constructed especially for him. He was not dead yet, though! He grabbed the stake and tried to push it backwards and out. Perhaps, if he succeeded, his heart might regenerate...

"Die, damn you!" he heard the officer who gave him the drink shout. It was clear he was holding the stake in place. Liatoukine twisted, and then lunged forward. He was splashed all the while with holy water, burning him all over. He was free, but others grabbed him again. His arms flailing, he grabbed with one hand a pistol that had been secured on the bulkhead. With what remained of his strength and speed, he somehow got the safety off and started firing wildly. The Antonov lurched - the bullets had hit something important. That was the last thing he felt. He was now a burnt creature, and he disintegrated, strange energy dissipating with skull and bones falling to the aircraft floor. He was dead. The officer grabbed the skull as it rolled with the lurch of the aircraft, before realizing the aircraft's trouble was quite serious.

In Nice, the original Liatoukine was in an apartment with a good view of the sea. It was not a KGB one, but simply a private one that he had rented out through his own means, that he had covertly developed over the decades. It was well that he was in it, for the attack on his duplicate self on the Antonov suddenly took over his thoughts. He felt the moment of his double's death, feeling the same agony that the other had felt.

Suddenly, it was over and Liatoukine had all the memories of his duplicate. He collapsed on his bed, drained of energy. Von Bork wanted him dead; this could make sense, if the spymaster were to gain immortality. The German had correctly reasoned that he, the legendary "Captain Vampire," would not accept working for him forever. Von Bork was old and had become careless. Now, Liatoukine was no doubt already officially "dead," as well as being undead. This gave him a supreme advantage; Von Bork would hardly be expecting him when the vampire liquidated him.

Also in Nice, at a fashionable café on the rue Saint François de Paule, Countess Irina Petrovski was sitting and chatting with Irma Vep. They were two beautiful, sophisticated women, hardly out of place on the French Riviera.

"You are taking a bit of a chance sitting out here in the open, aren't you?" asked the Countess.

"Not really," her companion replied. "As you can see, I am differently attired from the pictures you may have seen in the press." She pointed to her flowing white dress. "And I don't have my 'silent film' look. People are not expecting to see Irma Vep sipping coffee!" What she did not say was that her low-level mesmeric powers pushed the curious away. It was a risk; but one of many she enjoyed at this time.

"You will soon retrieve my family's cameo?" asked the Countess.

"Yes," replied Vep. "Your fee is most adequate, and, of course, I shall be pleased to be seen to have retrieved the rightful property from the hands of communists. But how will you deal with all the legal implications of how the cameo got back to you? Surely the police will be wanting to speak to you?"

"The established chain of how it got back to me will have no direct connections... Certain anti-communist groups will announce they have procured it by underground means and returned it to me as a gift. The French have come to an agreement with the Soviets about dealing with such items for their little cultural Center—owners cannot claim back their property from such displays. But the cameo will find its way to the United States, which do not recognize such laws. There, it will be returned to my family—not here or in Monaco. I will have had nothing to do with the robbery itself, and the cameo does, after all, belong to me, as US law recognizes"

"And this Center will have taken a great blow to its prestige, having only just opened," Vep said.

She knew very well about the Countess's crusade against communism, being determined to free her Polish homeland from it. The Countess nodded her head agreeably, observing Vep. Was she just a jewel thief with an uncanny resemblance to a legendary criminal, or something more? She and others had a private interest in such matters, which had begun with the 1906 incident her grandmother had been involved in. Not a matter for just now, however.

During the day, Boris Liatoukine was busy in Nice. As an energy vampire, he took the living essence from people. Sudden deaths and complete disintegration were possible in this process, but might have attracted some notice, and he could not afford any undue attention. The death of his duplicate had left him drained. Consequently, he needed human energy. He visited many places in the city, the Place Massena, the Place Garibaldi, the Naval Museum and Galerie des Ponchettes among others. He grabbed small bits of energy off as many people as he could. They would only feel weak for short while. This would hardly be the amount of energy he really needed, but it would see him through the next 24 hours, which he knew would be crucial. However, it would not be enough to create a new duplicate of himself, which was a disadvantage.

He had to get to Von Bork and liquidate him. He knew he would be at one of the receptions organized to celebrate the opening of the Soviet-French Cultural Center, off Place Massena. He needed more information though. And this proved simpler than he had thought. He went to where he knew the KGB had rented an apartment. He entered easily, and found one of Von Bork's personal guards, a vampire called Ivan. He was one of those who had great difficulty with daylight, and he found him asleep on a bed. Ivan had been a low-level dissident marked for death. Instead, he had been forcibly given the *dark kiss* by one of Von Bork's vampires and thus came under her control. Then, she had disappeared, and Ivan had been confined for some years. It was assumed that she had been killed in the destruction of the Sepulchre. Ivan was purposefully created weak, so that he could pose no threat. Von Bork only had a few such vampires created, and by different vampires, lest they be used against him someday.

With the one who turned him dead, Ivan was susceptible to the power of Liatoukine. He woke him up. The weakened vampire started in terror at Liatoukine. "Captain Vampire!" he said.

Liatoukine was amused by the use of his old nickname. "Colonel Vampire now, my dear Ivan, surely?

Now, please, tell me all about Von Bork's plans here in Nice."

Which he did. Liatoukine had guessed correctly. Irma Vep did have some elixir of life to sell to Von Bork. He was to make it easier for her to rob the museum of its most valuable items, much of which had belonged to the Tsars such as Faberge eggs, and so on. They had tried to double-cross her, but she had killed their agent and upped the amount of material she was to steal. This would all take place at 10 p.m. tonight, at the Center.

It all seemed a bit risky for both sides, thought Liatoukine. Still, the rewards would be high. However, he would be there to deal with matters. "Go back to sleep now, Ivan, and forget this conversation," he told him.

There was much back slapping at the reception at the Cultural Center that evening, with all the guests being permitted a view of the exhibits—the controversial Petrovski Cameo being of particular interest. This was a largely diplomatic affair, Liatoukine noted, when he saw people start to file out at around 9 p.m. He had mesmerized Ivan into leaving a ground-floor window open for him.

In her catsuit, Irma Vep entered the building though an open skylight, which had also been left open on purpose. Soon, she was in the main hall. There, next to the Petrovski cameo, was Von Bork, Ivan standing a few feet away.

She took her mask off, revealing her face. Not her true one, but the Irma Vep one. For now. "Well, Comrade Von Bork, we finally meet. I do hope you are not going to try and kill me again." She waved a glass phial at him. "Otherwise this will get smashed for a start."

"Your Russian is excellent," said Von Bork.

"Oh yes, I've had plenty of time to learn languages. All thanks to Venenos, the leader of our gang back in the 1910s. He was a genius. Sadly, he was killed before he could test on it on himself. So I took it. I've always had a bit more." She had a rather large bag, which she dropped on the floor. "I take it your man here means me no harm?" she asked.

"None whatsoever," said Von Bork.

She looked at Ivan. "You won't harm me, will you?" Ivan made no response.

She gave him the spymaster the phial. "Just drink it. It will take only a short while."

He gulped the phial down. "Tastes like water," he said.

She nodded. "It is water."

Von Bork looked confused.

She was pleased, it was going well. "Don't worry, Comrade. You are going to become immortal. Just not quite as you thought."

"Ivan!" he snapped and pointed to her. But Ivan did not move.

She laughed. "He won't harm me. I was the one that turned him." She smiled at Von Bork, who was gazing at her in both confusion and fear.

Her face started to change. And some of her teeth grew to become vampire teeth. Now, Von Bork recognized her.

She grabbed his head, pushed it back, sunk her fangs into her neck and drank deeply. She then let him go. He staggered around, and then he started to change. He straightened up. And there was not the aged KGB official of 1979, but the German spymaster of 1914, young and vigorous again. He opened his mouth to reveal fangs. Dead—yet undead!

He stood up, now straightening to his full height—the first time in years!—stretching out his arms, testing his rejuvenated body. He laughed.

Irma Vep laughed too. "I have given you immortality as promised."

"Yes," he said, "but under vampiric control. Not part of my plan. However, I know who you are now."

She smiled at him. "I am your master now. Do not fear, Von Bork. I intend that you carry out your ambitions for power and influence in the Soviet Union in the way you see fit—unless I disagree, which may happen now and again. I will always be the one whom you will obey, but you will simply be an asset I may wish to use from time to time. Let us begin at once with our plan. Ivan, will you please activate the video cameras."

He dutifully moved to do so, whilst her face returned to that of Irma Vep. He was an excellent servant, she thought. He had already purged all evidence pertaining to her "Mrs. Adler" alter ego from the KGB files, and only Von Bork and he knew about her.

Then followed a staged presentation of Irma Vep entering the hall, masked in her catsuit, delicately opening the cabinet with the Petrovski cameo. She took it out, pulled off her mask, held the cameo up to the camera and then walked off. She enjoyed the notoriety of being 'Irma Vep'—as important to her as obtaining wealth and influence.

Von Bork and Ivan returned to the gallery. Von Bork seemed puzzled. "Is that all you are taking?" he asked.

"Of course," she replied. "To steal more would ensure even more police resources coming after me. And stealing this item—whose ownership is in legal doubt—enhances my reputation rather than making me look greedy. Furthermore, the real target was always you, Von Bork. Now, you must see to it swiftly that the video of this evening's events is edited properly."

It was at this point that Boris Liatoukine entered the proceedings, appearing in the gallery in a leather jacket and jeans with two stakes in his hand, and a bulge in his jacket.

"Ah, Boris!" exclaimed Irma Vep, "I am so glad you are able to join us. Von Bork, you look surprised. I think what happened is that you managed to kill his duplicate—presumably Boris has improved his skills in that area. Boris made contact with Ivan here," she gestured to the vampire guard, "completely unaware that I, who had given Ivan the *dark kiss*, was still alive. Ivan told Boris only what I told him to."

Liatoukine then realized who he was actually dealing with.

"Polly Bird!" he said.

"Yes," she replied.

Her features blurred, and there she was—Polly Bird. They had worked together once. She had later joined forces with Von Bork, and then fallen under his control. She had chafed under him, as had Liatoukine, but he had used that opportunity to consolidate his position within the KGB, whereas she had not. He had not seen her for decades. She had gone missing during World War II. In that chaos, a number of those working for Von Bork had simply disappeared. Most had been destroyed by the Germans or the Allies, but some had simply used the chaos to circumvent the supernatural bonds that had kept them in servitude to Moscow.

"We thought you had been obliterated in the destruction of the Sepulchre," Liatoukine said.

She smiled. "Not at all, my dear Boris. I kept a rather low profile after the war, but I did put about some rumors that I was in hiding there, which of course the Sepulchre denied for the good reason that it wasn't true."

Damn himself for a fool! He and Von Bork had never fully believed that she had perished in the Great Patriotic War. They even had imprisoned those like Ivan, whom she had turned, just to be on the safe side. With the destruction of the Sepulchre, and her subsequent non-appearance, they had assumed she had indeed perished there. They had let Ivan out to serve them in the 1960s, driven by a shortage of supernatural operatives. They had been complacent and careless. He noticed no green tints on the glass exhibit casing—such tints being a giveaway for certain vampires. She clearly had learnt to control that.

Polly Bird changed her features back to Irma Vep's. "I enjoy the lifestyle and fame I have. The Irma Vep guise has done me good. However, with the opportunity to steal from here, I thought of trying to gain control of Von Bork and eliminating you in the bargain. That would end any KGB threat to me. Von Bork, Ivan, please eliminate Boris. And this time, check if he is a duplicate."

Liatoukine reacted quickly. He pulled a gun from his jacket and fired three shots in rapid succession— silver bullets, of course. One hit Ivan in the shoulder, sending him reeling in agony. Von Bork moved fast out of the way of the bullet, adapting to vampire speed very swiftly. Polly Bird just stood there. She caught the silver bullet in her teeth.

"Ow," she said, removing the bullet and tossing it back at Liatoukine before it could burn her.

Liatoukine moved swiftly, running up a wall and firing again, missing both his targets. He flung a stake with inhuman power at Polly Bird. It smashed into her rib cage, causing her pain, but missing the heart. The silver fragments inside it made it more painful. Von Bork bounded to her and pulled out the stake. Now he was armed and prepared to kill the threat to his new master.

"It is time for you to be destroyed, Liatoukine," said the spymaster. "You always were a counter-revolutionary."

Why was Von Bork indulging in political banter? thought Liatoukine. He decided against using his gun again. Best to get close with the stake.

Von Bork clearly thought much the same as he ran up the wall. Liatoukine jumped back onto the ceiling, thinking this would disorientate the newly-made vampire, but Von Bork took this in his stride. Soon, they were lunging at each with their stakes, gravity seemingly meaningless. Now was the time for the gun! Liatoukine got off one shot which went wide. The German grabbed the Russian's wrists and twisted hard. He dropped the gun and it fell to the floor. Von Bork was adjusting to being a vampire far too quickly for the Russian's liking. However, Liatoukine was well aware that he had more combat experience than the German. Centuries more.

He leapt off the ceiling and somersaulted back onto the floor. There were the Tsarist scepters he had seen in the hands of those long-dead monarchs. Scepters which contained some silver...

Von Bork had also come down. "Yes, look around you, Liatoukine. Look at the remnants of your Tsarist masters, the regime you served so faithfully, if for your own ends. And now, I will destroy the last of their ranks. It takes the death of Von Bork to do so--reborn in my new form!"

He came towards Liatoukine. The Russian smashed the cabinet near him and grabbed the scepter inside, dropping his stake. It caused him pain, but he was able to bear it.

Von Bork laughed. He dropped his weapon and gestured towards another exhibit case. "Ah!" he said, "the one once held by Nicholas II. My comrades dealt with him." He smashed the cabinet and grabbed it. And then screamed with pain. He thought he could deal with the pain as Liatoukine had, but he couldn't. He dropped the scepter.

Liatoukine was onto him, smashing his head with the royal artifact. Von Bork reeled and hit the floor. Liatoukine then drove his scepter into Von Bork's heart, pushing down so hard that it went right through the German and onto the floor. Von Bork was clearly in rage and agony.

Liatoukine glared into his eyes. "For Imperial Russia!" he hissed at him in contempt. Then, he started to drain the spymaster of his power. Von Bork disintegrated into bones, with the skull seemingly staring at the Russian, and then, that too turned to dust.

Von Bork was finally dead. Liatoukine was now full of energy. He had handled silver before—painful as it was—and had accumulated a certain tolerance to it for a very short time. Von Bork had not, and had suffered the consequences for his Prussian arrogance. Now for Polly Bird...

She had already regenerated somewhat and was crouching on the floor, aiming his own pistol at him. Out of the corner of his eye, Liatoukine could see Ivan staggering to his feet. He appeared to have dug out the bullet that had gone inside his body. But neither would be able to defeat him. Polly Bird leapt, but not at Liatoukine. She went for the wall, smashing the glass on a fire alarm, which duly went off.

"I suggest a truce, Boris," she said. "This alarm will not go unnoticed, and we can fight until others arrive—or leave. Go now, let Ivan clear up. We have no real argument now."

Liatoukine was not sure about any of that. He thought that Von Bork had cleared the building. Nevertheless, it would be best not to complicate matters with the arrival of any police or even regular KGB agents. He simply nodded and swiftly left. He had achieved much tonight, and had something of a journey ahead of him.

Liatoukine sat at his desk in his Moscow office. He had a decision to make. Things had gone rather well in the months since August. It was now December—and he had taken charge of the Special Logistics Directorate.

The official report by two surviving Spetsnaz operatives stated that the Antonov had suffered a major technical fault. They had been picked up fairly swiftly by the Russian Army. They hadn't seen Liatoukine bailing out after them, but he must have, and it had taken several days for him to heroically walk all the way to Kabul, killing some rebels along the way.

He had been given the Order of Lenin for his remarkable survival and endurance from a plane crash. The Spetsnaz troops were delighted to see him, of course. Liatoukine had to return to Moscow urgently due to Von Bork dying in a botched kidnapping scheme in Southern France.

Liatoukine allowed himself a smile at the story. All nonsense of course. It had been a bit of journey to get to the outskirts of Kabul from Nice, but the authorities had not questioned his survival. The two terrified Spetsnaz survivors had raised no questions. He had assured them of no hard feelings—they had to obey Von Bork, who was now dead. They would be staying in Afghanistan, which they were happy to do, as he was returning to Moscow. If they were not killed there, he would organize something later.

Ivan had cleaned up the situation in Nice. The KGB was told that Von Bork had tried to defect to the West. Liatoukine had investigated the matter personally, and reported that his former superior might have defected but may also have been kidnapped, and that he had learned from their own moles in Germany that, either way, he had died soon afterward. The story was accepted—nobody much cared to look into this too deeply—and the German was posthumously awarded the Order of Lenin too. It was thought best to keep quiet, in case the West produced evidence of his defection. Ivan himself disappeared soon after, no doubt going back to serve Polly Bird, who, as "Irma Vep," had been celebrated for her "liberation" of the Petrovski Cameo, now beyond Soviet reach in America. Liatoukine knew that he would have to deal with her at some point. But for now, let her enjoy her notoriety.

Now he had an important meeting to take. His secretary showed in a party official who worked directly for Andropov. Andropov had convinced the ailing Brezhnev of the need to invade Afghanistan. That was imminent.

The official sat down in front of Liatoukine. "Well, Comrade, what will be the contribution of the Special Logistics Directorate to helping our friends in Kabul?"

Liatoukine was all in favor of empire building and repressing others. He had done much of it himself. However, unlike these communists, he did not look at such matters through Marxist-Leninist eyes. His age gave him a sense of history. He knew how the British had had problems in Afghanistan for decades, leading to them to leave. He knew the power of religion there. And he knew the country was five times the size of Vietnam, where the Americans had failed. He did not want his division sucked into a similar quagmire. But he also knew how invested the KGB were in this operation. He had to play things carefully.

"Comrade," he said, "I propose to send a special team of operatives to assist there. We consider there are few, if any, threats that require our specialist skills. However, we will assist regardless, in whatever ways are required." He did not say that he would be sending those he considered easily expendable or that he wanted to be rid of.

"Merely a team? Von Bork was thinking of the majority of your division going?" asked the official, clearly not impressed, no doubt expecting a much fuller commitment.

"A team which may be increased if the need arises," added Liatoukine, starting to emit a low-level mesmerism. "There are a number of threats that may require out attention in Europe. I have heard of Golem sightings in Prague and an increase in strange incidents reported from here in the Soviet Union. I have also heard that Countess Petrovski may be part of a private network operating in this Directorate's field of interest against us, and that she may have had something to do with Von Bork's disappearance."

"That decadent Countess?" asked the official. Mesmerism was hardly needed. The theft of the Petrovski cameo was a sore point. Liatoukine pushed things home. "And I would certainly like to look into the activities of the criminal Irma Vep. Please, comrade, take this file on the matter. I am sure you will find it most informative."

"I am sure I will," the official said, picking up the file. "These are enemies of the Soviet Union. I am pleased you are taking the matter so seriously. Proceed as you have outlined; I am sure I will be able to confirm matters after I have had read your file and consulted with Comrade Andropov."

He left, clearly satisfied with the way the meeting had gone.

Liatoukine, too, was delighted. He had placed his department in a good position—and himself of course. Von Bork was gone and the rest of his generation was going too. Change could well be on its way. Boris Liatoukine was going to make sure he would be on the right side of whatever the future held.

## The Skull of Boris Liatoukine

*Moscow, July 1998*

The luxury helicopter shook with the force of the rocket-propelled grenade hitting it. The pilot had some-how maneuvered the aircraft to take a glancing blow. However, it was still going down, hard. The helicopter's sole passenger—and owner—was pleased that his in-vestment into onboard security measures, including hir-ing a top ex-military pilot, had been worthwhile. He was less pleased that the ground was coming up fast.

The pilot struggled with the controls. The helicopter crashed and skidded along a road by the Moskva River. The passenger dragged himself out of the wreckage and collapsed. Most of his bones were broken, but he could feel them regenerating already. He looked behind him—the pilot was dead, no doubt about that. Probably instan-taneously. Most unfortunate. Such skilled operatives were much in demand. It would be easier to replace the helicopter—an augmented Eurocopter Dauphin. The road they had crashed on was closed for works. Whether the pilot had realized that or not, he did not know.

The passenger lay waiting. He could see half a doz-en members of the public running down towards the wreckage and himself. The emergency services would soon be here. However, he was waiting for neither them, or the members of the public. Sure enough, a group of three burly men came from nowhere, armed with pistols. The assassination team had come to finish the job. The few members of the public who had reached the scene backed away swiftly—they did not want to be involved in any mafia business.

The three assassins ran toward the body of the passenger. He got up. All three men fired their pistols—Soviet Makarovs, the passenger noted—into him and looked dumbfounded when their target simply jerked around but remained standing. He grabbed the nearest attacker by the throat and took his weapon; then, he shot the other two in the legs, disabling them.

"Who sent you?" he asked of the first man.

The assassin swiftly replied with a name. More bullets slammed into the passenger—the injured men on the ground had resumed firing. Then their bullets ran out.

"You seek my attention?" their target said in mock delight. "Then you have it!"

He broke the arm of the man he was holding and threw him to the ground. He went over to the terrified men and stared at them.

"Are you all there is? One of you fired the grenade?"

One nodded and then pointed at the first man. Boris Liatoukine promptly shot the man who had not responded in the heart. He then resumed his questioning, as if nothing had occurred.

"Please also tell me who supplied the weapons, my movements, and so on."

He got the answers he wanted and shot the man dead. He went over to the first man—who, by now, was under no illusions as to his fate. Liatoukine gazed into the eyes of the assassin. This man was terrified—he knew he was dealing with the very devil himself. He felt as if all his energy was being sucked out of him—which in fact it was. And the last thing he thought was how like the eyes of a cat his killer's were.

Liatoukine did not take all his victim's energy. Just enough to help him regenerate further. He then stood back and shot the dead man in the heart. For appearances.

He could hear sirens. Within seconds, Moscow's finest were surrounding him. It was fortunate he had already dropped the weapon.

"On the ground, now!" one of them shouted.

"Officers, I am so grateful you have arrived!" he responded. "I am Boris Liatoukine, a businessman of some repute and a friend to many of your superiors. I was forced to defend myself against criminals who killed my pilot and tried to murder me. Truly, it is a miracle I live!"

Liatoukine could see that the officers knew well enough not to make him kneel down with his hands behind his head. How much had they seen? It mattered not. He had enough wealth and FSB[8] influence to ensure that a heroic story of surviving an assassination attempt and killing his would-be assassins would prevail. The publicity would be unwelcome. Perhaps his old nickname—whispered during his time in the KGB and far further back in time—would be used again? Yes, references to *Captain Vampire* could well instill fear into his enemies.

The caretaker closed up the museum. It was a small place in Moscow, linked with a similar establishment in St. Petersburg with a number of items of not much interest to the populace. It had been open for a number of

[8] Federal Security Service of the Russian Federation, the main successor of the KGB.

years, even during the communist era, but then it had been billed as a "museum of the bizarre." It did not do good business, on account of its artifacts being clearly fake and uninteresting. It had been too insignificant for the Communists to close it. The caretaker was grateful, however, because it had provided him with a steady job, and was close to his home. Since the end of communism, it had been privatized and rebranded as a "museum of the supernatural." It had duly taken a few more paying visitors—not that the caretaker cared. He had not been paid in months now. He preferred the old regime. He did not care much for this capitalism. The Gulags did not affect him, so he did not care about such things. Increasingly, he could not be bothered to lock the doors properly. And tonight was one such night.

After he had gone, a slim, feminine figure bounded up to the doors. Dressed in a black catsuit, she walked in. She was unmasked, and was clearly a beautiful woman of Chinese origin. She looked around the small hall. That is all it was—the front door led straight into a hall. She was here to steal something and wanted to be seen doing so. But there were no cameras.

Irritated, she went straight over to an exhibit marked "Facsimile of Vampire Skull" in Cyrillic. It would have to be fake—a place like this would not be permitted to contain real human remains.

"Are you real then?" she asked it.

*Indeed I am, Irma Vep*, said a voice in her head. *Permit me to introduce myself. I am Boris Liatoukine.*

In Surrey, England, a full-bodied Boris Liatoukine had just concluded a business agreement with a notorious Russian oligarch who had made England his home. The vampire and his solicitor looked out of window of the mansion they were in, overlooking the large grounds, complete with helipad and Liatoukine's helicopter on it.

"A fine agreement, sir," the solicitor said. "All the outstanding business issues have been dealt with in your favor—and it was good of him to accept your suggestion to come back to his home to celebrate."

"Yes," replied Liatoukine, smiling. "I suspect the elimination of every single person involved in the attempt to liquidate me—from the assassins to those who supplied the weapons—helped him in being reasonable. I must thank you, Mr. Tepes, for your discretion and skill in this matter."

"My firm has been dealing with your people for generations, sir. Count Dracula was one of our first clients."

Liatoukine and the Count were not the same nationality, but that was not what Mr. Tepes meant. He also knew that the lawyer's firm—despite effectively taking Vlad the Impaler's name—never had Dracula as a client. Even now, there were those who sought a link with Dracula's name for commercial gain.

The Russian vampire pondered for a moment. The Count had seen something in this country, but had been undone by a few determined individuals. Often, in dealing with vampires, that is simply what it took. Over the years, Liatoukine had learned not to underestimate the living. He had learned from his own mistakes—and more especially those of others. Despite this country's record in firmly dealing with the supernatural, there were still those who would serve vampires—for the appropriate financial recompense. Using mesmerism, he had discerned from the solicitor that, barring torture, the man would be discreet. Providing, of course, he was handsomely paid.

"I think I would like to have residency here in this country. Many of my countrymen have moved their money here, and I would like to do the same," Liatoukine said to the solicitor.

Mr. Tepes was eager for further commission. "There is a scheme which the previous government instituted. Such rights are given for an appropriate financial investment in the UK. The current New Labor government is keenly carrying on with the same policy."

"What about my previous record with the KGB?" the vampire asked.

"A matter of little interest, sir. It is the financial benefit to this country that is important. As to the publicity you have recently received, due to the attempt on your life and your conflict with our late friend here, I see few barriers being erected—none that cannot be dealt with by investing a bit extra."

They looked down to where their *late friend* was. A pile of white dust they were standing in.

"Most fascinating sir, to see you drain him of energy like that—I understand it is usually blood with your people."

"Yes," Liatoukine said. "My way is more energy efficient. And it certainly helps with the cleaning bills—provided I don't get too much of the dust on me. We should leave soon. We can leave his maid to deal with this." He knocked over an ashtray. "Perhaps they will think he knocked over his ashtray?" They laughed uproariously. "I could have killed him in London, I suppose, but I did want to see where he lived. Everything was set up well—he left our meeting and no one knows where he went. My powers and your employees have done well."

Mr. Tepes bowed slightly. Yes, Liatoukine thought, a foothold in London would greatly help in his business affairs, provided he did not overreach himself.

Back in her Monaco mansion, Irma Vep sat down in her luxury chair and looked at the Skull on the table before her. It looked human, with two fake fangs stuck on. She snapped them off. The real Liatoukine did not manifest fangs—not having much need for them. She addressed the Skull:

"So, 'Boris Liatoukine,' now that we have arrived back safely, perhaps you can finally explain to me why you wanted me to steal you. The messages put about to my contacts of a genuine vampire skull—with great powers—were clearly directed at me rather than just general rumor."

*I see little gets past you, Polly Bird*, the Skull replied in her head.

Vep's posture moved a little bit more upright. How could it know that? She had her fake public identity as one Mrs. Irene Adler, a wealthy Monaco widow, and then she had her favorite fake identity as the criminal Irma Vep—the cat-suited thief who had stolen so many valuables over the years.

*Of course, I know who you are, although I know you much prefer to use the Irma Vep identity much of the time. You are vampire, like myself. Although blood is more your thing. Surely you remember our adventures— remember all that business of the trial of Van Helsing in the Vampire City?*

"How..." she started.

*I was one of the duplicates of Boris Liatoukine. Of course, you know of his power to create short-lived du-*

*plicates of himself? It helped confuse many of his ene-
mies.*

Polly was indeed aware of this.

*He created me almost twenty years ago, sending me
to Afghanistan to confuse those in the KGB who were
trying to eliminate him. Spetnaz troops managed to destroy me, and I disintegrated—but my skull remained
intact. One of the soldiers took it as a trophy. It would
appear that the circumstances of what happened to me
permits my consciousness to live on inside it. Such are
the ways of the supernatural. I was able to influence the
soldier a little and got myself sold to more interesting
parties. Liatoukine has no awareness of me—or rather,
the times he has been nearby, he has sensed something,
but never considered it could be me.*

"Why were you in that museum in Moscow, and the
other one in St. Petersburg for years before that?" Polly
asked.

*I see you are well informed. I have been gathering
information—from the local aether, shall we say? It
helps me to calculate what—or who—may be important
in the future. I tend to travel sometimes to find out.*

She sensed she would get little more from the Skull
on that.

"Why did you want me to steal you? The messages
you placed on the grapevine indicated you were valuable—but I know very well that they were directed at
me."

*Indeed, indeed. We have a common interest. It is
but a matter of time before Boris Liatoukine destroys
you. Or worse, place you under his control. He has not
forgotten his last encounter with you, in which you were
enemies. Your being a former ally only makes things
worse. I want him dead also—but only in the sense that I*

*should have developed enough power to integrate myself into him—taking over his body and destroying his mind, rather than the opposite, when his duplicates have no more function.*

"How can I trust you? You can still be a threat to me yourself?"

*I have all his memories, but I am not him. He created me simply to do his bidding, and I was expendable. He may effectively be my creator, but believe me, I feel I owe him nothing, and see no reason to carry his grudges. I have felt his displeasure towards you, but you and I have no quarrel. Help me to take over his body—which will give me all his wealth and power—and I will be grateful. You are an international thief, and provided you do not steal from me, I have no interest in you.*

The fake Irma Vep pondered for a moment. She did not trust this Skull. However, the elimination of Boris Liatoukine would certainly benefit her. In 1979, she had told him that they had no real quarrel left after the death of his superior, KGB spymaster Von Bork. However, only minutes earlier, she had turned Von Bork into a vampire in order to kill Liatoukine, and the Russian Vampire was not likely to have forgotten that. He would come for her at some point. If the Skull were to become an enemy, then she would not be worse off than before. The risk was worth taking, and she would take whatever precautions she could.

"Very well. What do you have in mind?"

*Excellent. As Irma Vep, you have made one or two thefts in London. That experience will be useful. It seems that Liatoukine is establishing a base for himself in that city.*

A few days later, Boris Liatoukine was dining at one of London's finer establishments. He was pleased with how things were going. He had purchased a home in central London. His young wife, Magda, was especially pleased—she had been keen to see many of her friends in London and was delighted to be in close proximity to them—and to Harrods. Boris liked Magda. She was unconcerned regarding the mysteries around him and did not care about his various lovers. Liatoukine had been married many times before, murdering a number of his wives in order to obtain their wealth. That would not be necessary with Magda. He was the wealthy one, and she would most likely be amenable to an amicable divorce when the time came for her to leave his side.

His dinner companion arrived. This was an Englishman in his late 50s. He sat in front of Liatoukine. Harker was a former MI6 officer. He had been suborned by another a vampire in the 1950s. After she'd died, Liatoukine had been able to mesmerize him easily, given that he was already susceptible to vampiric influence. He used him as a private asset, rather than KGB one —the Russian vampire had told no one about him, and kept no records. He was only interested in information of direct interest. He did not ask Harker for major information regarding spy matters. In this way, the Englishman was never suspected of anything, and thus never caught. He'd left MI6 after a successful career and established a private security firm for wealthy clients. Liatoukine made himself one of them. This was rather ironic, thought the Russian vampire. This man was the descendent of those who had destroyed Dracula, and his family may yet be unamused to find out about David Harker's treachery.

"Good evening, Mr. Harker. I understand you have something for me. Please order whatever you desire."

Harker ordered his meal, and then reported to the vampire.

"I have some information for you. The woman you wished my firm to keep an eye on, Mrs. Adler? She arrived in London earlier today. She is staying in a hotel in Kensington. My sources at Heathrow Airport were able to X-ray her baggage. This one is of great interest."

He handed Liatoukine a small palm held computer. The central feature of what appeared to be a hatbox was not what one would usually expect to see. It was a skull. Liatoukine felt like he was looking into a mirror—an unusual sensation for a vampire, even one that was able to create artificial reflections to avoid detection such as he.

"We have no idea how she was able to get through security at Nice and Heathrow Airports. We can only surmise that the agents were bribed," Harker added.

Liatoukine knew better. Polly Bird would have used her vampiric powers of influence to get through all the security checks. But why had she come to London? And what was the significance of that skull, which evoked such strange feelings in him? He had every intention of finding out. Besides, it was past time to deal with Polly Bird—or Irma Vep, since that seemed to be her favorite identity.

"We need to intercept her," he told Harker. "As you know, I consider her to be part of the Vampires gang. The current Irma Vep—the one of Chinese appearance—also needs to be intercepted if she appears, as she well might."

He, of course, knew very well that Vep, Adler and Polly Bird were one and the same, but no need to tell

Harker that. Liatoukine proceeded to outline to Harker what he required of his company. However, he was not the only one with an interest in Mrs. Adler.

The Countess Irina Petrovski looked across the London skyline from her hired office in one of London's newest office buildings. She could see St. Paul's Cathedral, and various other skyscrapers in the process of being erected. She liked London. She had many friends and contacts here. She caught a reflection of herself in the window. She was nearing 50, but looked still in her 30s. Her long, luxurious red hair looked as healthy as ever. She knew she was fortunate—her wealth, being from an old aristocratic Polish family, did her no harm. However, she felt that her life as an adventurer had helped keep her young. The battles against communism had gone rather well. As indeed had her sideline as part of a network dealing with the threat of the supernatural. However, there was more work to be done.

Her mobile rang. Such instruments were still relatively new. She liked technology and made sure she had the latest model.

"Ah, Karl, you have arrived? Just introduce yourself at reception, and you will be shown up."

A couple of minutes later, a short bald man entered dressed in a smart suit.

"Karl!" beamed the Countess. "It is so good to see you my friend. Please sit down."

"And you are as beautiful as ever—moreso," he replied.

He came to her, took her hand and kissed it. She was delighted.

"It is good to see old courtesies observed," she replied.

"And I like to practice them," he replied.

They laughed and sat down.

"Well, Countess, it seems something is indeed going on. Boris Liatoukine and Irma Vep are both in London. Not a coincidence, I think."

"The messages on the international criminal grapevine to Irma Vep telling her to steal a skull in Moscow were clearly directed to her—but of course, we have our sources listening out for such things."

"Quite," responded Karl. "My superiors at the BND[9] are only interested, and to a limited extent, in the possible political aspects of Vep's criminal activity—international incidents and so on. The supernatural aspects would be disbelieved, and I would be soon out of a job. But you know all this."

"To think, there used to be whole departments and government organizations that dealt with vampires and so on," sighed the Countess. "Now, with most of the supernatural gone with the modern age, the forces against them have dissipated and it's barely believed they exist. Only a few years ago, you would not have had to be so circumspect with your employer. Even what remains in the archives do not seem to be persuasive." It was an old conversation, and the Countess turned to current matters. "Do you have some information on Boris Liatoukine's wealth for me?"

Karl smiled and produced a folder from his briefcase.

"There, I can produce a lot more that my superiors are interested in. We know he is a former KGB officer. From what we can ascertain, his department went the way all supernatural departments did. With the collapse

---

[9] The German Federal Intelligence Service.

of communism, seeing where things were going, he wrapped up his own Special Logistics Directorate and left the KGB—or FSB as it would be now—taking some personnel with him. We also suspect he moved his archives, or at least copies of them, into his own custody.

"To build his wealth, he had his own cooperative based on Gorbachev's reforms—these included restaurants and kiosks selling chocolates. Then he took full advantage of the government's voucher scheme. Like the other oligarchs, he manipulated it to gain stakes in state assets. He was one of those who helped Yeltsin get re-elected in 1994 by the 'loans for shares' scheme. This involved a loan to help plug the government's deficit in return for shares in export firms. The loans were not repaid and these people took control of these firms for next to nothing. And, of course, money went into Yeltsin's re-election campaign. He is certainly what we would now call an oligarch. He did all this through middlemen, more than the others. Politically, we think he would prefer someone who deals more strongly with the West, for his support for Yeltsin is based purely on his self-interest and holding onto his money."

"Yes," interjected the Countess. "I certainly think his long life and the changes of government in Russia have made him cautious and indeed flexible. He was a Tsarist at some point, fighting the Reds as a White Army officer."

"He must meet with your approval on that point," interrupted Karl smiling.

She wagged a finger at him playfully and then continued:

"…and then, he switched to working for the Communists when they hunted him down in Paris in the 1920s. He eventually took over the department that had tracked him down. Now, he appears to have adjusted rather well to post-Communism. Too well, in fact. He may well be the wealthiest vampire in the world—and thus a threat. Although perhaps someone else has tried to get to him before us?"

Karl nodded and produced another a file and gave it to the Countess.

"As a known ally—albeit in the private sector—of the BND, you can have sight of this material."

The Countess could see it was in regards to the oligarch who had recently vanished off the face of the Earth, after allegedly trying to assassinate Liatoukine.

"The intelligence community believed he tried to kill Liatoukine over some dispute on the selling of shares in an energy company," Karl went on. "Liatoukine appears to have had everyone involved killed, and there is little doubt he is behind the disappearance. There is no hard proof however. He does seem to have taken a liking to London, and unfortunately, it does seem that the British authorities are going to indulge him—not least due to his apparent intent to provide significant investment here."

The Countess shook her head in near disbelief.

"It looks like we need to deal with him then."

Karl smiled and gave her something else from his briefcase. Again, the Countess was delighted with him.

"A Walter P5 Compact pistol—with silver bullets! How considerate of you!" Then her face hardened and she touched the large silver crucifix around her neck. "Vep and Liatoukine are amongst the last remnants of an old threat to humanity. God will guide us in putting an end to their activities."

Night was falling over London. In her hotel room, booked under yet another false identity, Irma Vep was having a conversation with the Skull. She had changed her form into the current iteration of Irma Vep and was sitting in a luxury chair, dressed in her catsuit, with only her head uncovered. She was expecting action that night.

*Tell me*, the Skull asked, *Why have you taken the form of a Chinese woman?*

"To confuse the police looking for me," she replied. "For some years I used the form of the original Irma Vep. They now think that this version of Irma Vep appearing means there is a gang, which the press have dubbed *The Vampires*, after the original criminal group from 1916. All quite effective."

She thought it best not to mention that she enjoyed watching Hong Kong action films that had actually given her the inspiration. Liatoukine was a snob, and no doubt that went for his duplicate Skull.

*Most ingenious. Little wonder no one has failed to capture you. Now, we must move. I am aware that Liatoukine is in London. This hotel was selected as it is close to his Kensington apartment. I sense he is nearby. He must be at home. The plan is very simple. Simply get me into his home, and I will do the rest. Within the hour Liatoukine will be eliminated and I will take all that he has.*

"You will get your revenge for Afghanistan and I will be rid of an enemy."

*Yes, but please, do be careful in your carrying of me.*

Vep picked up the Skull and placed it into a dark, padded shoulder bag. She proceeded towards the window. London was busy at night; she might be seen at some point, although her garb was probably more acceptable in public than it would have been in previous years. She opened a window to the back streets.

"I look forward to seeing how you re-absorb yourself back into dear Boris's body," she said.

"*I look forward to seeing how you re-absorb yourself back into dear Boris's body*," said the voice over the speaker.

"She's mad," said Harker, "she is talking to herself."

Sitting next to him in the back of the private surveillance van was Boris Liatoukine. The references to Afghanistan and reabsorption and his familiarity with the Skull all came together. He did not how this could happen, or the full details of it, but the Skull had to be dealt with at once, regardless of any embarrassment.

"Send your men in now, Harker. Kill her and smash the skull. The ammunition I have provided them will be sufficient."

Ordinarily, Harker would not have done anything like this, but Liatoukine held a mystical hold over him—and the rather large personal commission from the Russian also helped him move beyond his split second of doubt.

In her hotel room, Irma Vep tensed. She could hear footsteps outside.

The door was smashed open and three men with silencers burst in. One took direct aim at her at fired. The bullet flew out of the weapon and towards the vampire. But Vep was already moving. The bullet missed her—silver, she noted—and smashed into the wall.

She grabbed the shooter and broke his neck effortlessly, using him as a shield against the others. She then grabbed a dagger she kept in her boot for such eventualities. She threw the body against one of the other two assailants. He fell back, but regained his balance, and raised his gun.

In a split second it took for him to fire, however, Vep had slit the throat of the other man and he saw something coming towards his head. Her knife embedded itself hard in his forehead and he fell back on the floor, dead.

Vep moved fast. She hurled the bodies fully into the room, grabbed the bag and was out of the window and scaling down the wall into an alley. She always ensured a room with such a view. What was key to getting away was to physically escape before other assailants—or the authorities—came to confront her.

Out of the gloom of the alley appeared two figures.

"Hello again, Polly. Or should that be Irma Vep or Mrs. Adler, or..?" asked Boris Liatoukine, Harker next to him.

Both had pistols aimed at her. She dived, rolled and fired at them. Liatoukine moved swiftly out of the way, but one of the bullets hit Harker and he was flung back down, his bulletproof vest, however, saving his life. Without pausing, Vep was on her feet and out of the alley.

Parked right outside was a Porsche. She made eye contact with the driver and recognized her—Countess Petrovski. They knew each other of old, and even had worked together once, in a fashion. She smashed the passenger window, opened the door and leaped into the car.

"Drive!" she ordered, pointing the gun at the Countess.

The Polish aristocrat turned towards Vep—her silver crucifix seemingly blazing. Instinctively, Vep recoiled, and the Countess shoved her back. Vep fell out of the car and on the road. And she saw her holdall in the outstretched hand of the Countess.

The car sped off. Vep chased it at speed—witnesses be damned! —but despite her efforts, could not keep up with the car. She slowed down and wandered swiftly into a street side.

Boris Liatoukine was less than pleased with the night's events. He had failed to eliminate the threat of the Skull, or indeed deal with Vep. His bravado in talking to her—rather than just shooting her with silver bullets immediately—could have cost him the opportunity to deal with matters at once. Furthermore, Special Branch had become involved. They wanted to know his whereabouts. Vep had no doubt tipped them off. He cursed himself again—he had hesitated to go after Vep due to fear of being recognized by the public, or spotted by cameras. The CCTV that had picked him and Harker up were too indistinct. The others, Harker had deactivated through various means. He was able to give the police an explanation of course—he had one of his duplicates be seen at a public event at the same time. However, the attention was unwelcome, and could damage his presence in London.

A bleep went off. This was his satellite phone with a secure link to Moscow. He picked it up.

"Good morning" said a voice on the other end, in French. It was one of his trusted contacts in the FSB. "We know of the events in London, and that you are perhaps somehow connected. The Kremlin is not pleased. There is an important meeting in London taking place today. The International Monetary Fund is discussing our country."

Liatoukine knew this very well. Russia had been suffering severe financial problems.

"I am aware of this. This incident you speak of saw three British mercenaries killed, not Russians."

The voice at the other end cut him off.

"The international media have been tipped off that this was an incident in which Irma Vep was involved in a deal with Russians which went wrong—and their hired British mercenaries paid the price. The last thing the Kremlin wants is Russian-related violence in London at this moment. What is more, you know that we are not the power we once were. And Yeltsin may even be appointing a new FSB head. Our position is sensitive. The view here is that you should return at once to Moscow— or at least leave the United Kingdom."

Liatoukine understood the sensitivities. It was in his interest that Russia was bailed out and that the new FSB head not be someone who would work against him. However, it was more in his interest to stay in London and destroy the Skull.

"Very well. I will return to Moscow today."

"Excellent," said the voice at the other end, and the call was terminated.

Liatoukine turned around. A figure materialized in front of him. A duplicate of himself. He had reabsorbed the duplicate he had used the previous night, and this was a new one. Given what he had learnt about the Skull, this one had less consciousness than previous versions. He ordered it to go to Moscow and stand in for him. He would stay in London and deal with the Skull.

In her London residence, the Countess had the Skull on a table. She walked around it. Karl was with her.

"Were the police satisfied with your explanation?" he asked.

"Yes," she replied. "I told them that I was looking out for Irma Vep—which was completely true—when everything happened. They know me of old, and we still have one or two contacts in Scotland Yard. They don't like 'vigilantes,' but they had no reason to hold me. It helped that I went to them at once, rather than waiting for them to spot my car's license plate on CCTV. Of course, I gave them Vep's holdall that had some burglary tools in, but I retained our friend here. Our contacts would not be in a position to deal with their colleagues if I did hand it over."

The Skull listened to the conversation. He was also able to absorb some of what these people were about. He knew that they would want to destroy him. They—especially the Countess—were resourceful. It would only be a matter of time before they worked out what he was, of that he was sure. And then, they would destroy him. He had plans for the future—his powers had developed to be able to not quite predict the future, but to know what would become important, and he would not let this Countess stop that. He had to act immediately. A risk, but it had to be taken.

*Permit me to introduce myself*, the Skull said, startling the Countess and Karl. *I am Boris Liatoukine.*

The Countess reflected later on what the Skull had said. He had been a duplicate of Boris Liatoukine, and been destroyed in his service, only his Skull remaining. Such an existence tormented it, and it wanted to die, but only along with Boris Liatoukine. The Skull wanted revenge. That was why he was here with Irma Vep. Separated from Vep, he now offered the Countess the opportunity. She did not believe the Skull. However, it was too good a chance to destroy the notorious "Captain Vampire." She started to make plans.

Irma Vep left Scotland Yard and was out into the sun. She despised the daylight; it sapped much of her power. She rarely used her original Polly Bird form these days, but it was not likely to be recognized by anyone in the Metropolitan Police. She was tall, raven-haired and, of course, beautiful. It always felt like a special treat to wear this form. She had gained the power of shape-changing decades ago. Suddenly, she gave a start. Next to the revolving New Scotland Yard sign outside the building stood Boris Liatoukine. She could sense that there were others—no doubt, British mercenaries. Would he really make a scene here? He must know he would surely be on a camera. But he put up his hands.

"Peace, my dear Polly. A truce. I am hardly likely to attempt anything here, am I? Let us walk, and discuss matters. Surely we can come to some... arrangement?"

They turned a corner and walked together down Victoria Street, towards the Houses of Parliament.

"How did you know where I was?" Polly asked.

"My servants retain certain connections with the authorities," he replied. "It suddenly came up that someone was inquiring with the police about the whereabouts of Countess Petrovski. We were on the look out for any such inquiries. No doubt you had simply walked in and used your powers of mesmerism. Quite a feat, given our limited powers during the day."

She nodded. He was indeed correct.

"What now?" she asked.

"Tell me about the Skull's plans. Then we shall see."

She thought she could run—she could probably escape. However, there may be something here she had not accounted for. Things had already gone wrong. There may yet be a way to turn things to her advantage. So she explained the Skull's plan. They had reached Parliament Square by this point. They came to a halt by the statue of Winston Churchill. Liatoukine looked over at the Palace of Westminster, and up at St. Stephen's tower that housed the bell of Big Ben.

"Dracula himself came here, you know," he said.

"Much good it did him," Polly replied. "Van Helsing, Mina Harker and the others chased him out from here across Europe and destroyed him in his own homeland."

"Indeed," replied the Russian, "He did effectively try to invade this country. Had he kept a low profile—and spent a lot of money at the same time—perhaps he would still alive today. I often consider that he was the first real casualty of the forces of modernity. Rather than swim inconspicuously with the new age, he thought he could dominate it. We certainly had power before, but we never had total control. Humanity determined its own history, and now their science and intelligence have reduced our numbers. The decline of religion in the West has not helped in the way one might have thought. Worse, the revival of religion in Russia and in the ex-communist sphere has aggravated matters."

Polly was not that concerned about Liatoukine's musings, but thought it best to humor him.

"Yes, perhaps that is why the few of us that remain should stick together."

Liatoukine could see that she may be open to a deal.

"This Skull is not one of us really. It is an upstart entity, nothing more. Help me destroy it and I offer you the same deal: a permanent truce providing you stay out of my affairs. To help you decide, please bear in mind how long I have lived and how I have survived even communism. This Skull is not likely to get the better of me."

That made sense to Polly.

"Very well," she said.

"Excellent," he replied. "We know the Countess's whereabouts, and we should pay her a visit. She will be expecting us, of course. Just as I have contacts here, so does she. It may not be an easy task dealing with her, especially if she has made some kind of alliance with the Skull." Something else occurred to the Russian vampire. "One thing. Why did the Skull stay in St. Petersburg for so long?"

Polly thought for a moment.

"It said it was monitoring something. It claimed it could sense where power would be in the future and wanted to absorb as much information as possible. It claimed it was a slow process, but that this ability eventually told him where power would lie, but could not specifically predict the future. The Skull could be quite boastful, but it did not reveal any details. My personal suspicion is that St. Petersburg will become the capital again, or that some long-lost descendent of the Romanoffs will be found and the throne restored. I put that to the Skull, but it did not confirm or deny it."

"How interesting," said Liatoukine, intrigued. "There are no Romanoffs left with a claim to the throne. Lenin and his barbarian Bolsheviks made sure of that. However, I think that St. Petersburg could be made the capital instead of Moscow. With that drunkard Yeltsin, such things are certainly possible."

At that point, Liatoukine's mobile phone started ringing. He answered it, and spoke briefly. When the call finished he turned to Polly.

"That was Countess Petrovski. She wants to meet us tonight. St. Paul's Cathedral. Midnight."

Polly looked surprised.

"She has friends in the Church of England, it seems," he continued. "She says she wants to destroy the Skull, but it is impervious to her efforts, even on church grounds. She thinks only I can deal with it by reabsorbing it, which may be true, but I think that physical destruction is best. I do not believe her claim of imperviousness. Our time in the Cathedral will be limited; our powers will be reduced and to stay too long would result in our deaths. During the Tsarist era, I was able to enter churches for long enough to ensure the 'Captain Vampire' stories remained just rumors. I assume you can do the same?"

"I can," she replied.

"It is a trap. We will reconnoiter the area as best we can with my hirelings. We can always not enter. However, if the Skull is there, and we can see what the trap is, we will destroy it—and the Countess."

It was approaching midnight. Liatoukine and Irma Vep were approaching the steps of St. Paul's Cathedral. They came to a halt at the foot of the steps.

"We've reconnoitered and found nothing," he said to Vep. "One of Harker's men was able to stay behind in the Cathedral after it had closed. He was found by a man with a German accent and politely asked to leave. He reported that the only people there was this German and the Countess. Not even any security staff. And outside, there appears to be no threat. The City of London police are simply doing their routine patrols, although, of course, they could approach in significant armed numbers at very short notice."

"I've been scaling along the rooftops," said Vep. "I, too, detected nothing."

The Russian vampire gave her a glance.

"Oh, don't worry Boris. I know very well how to elude security cameras—when I want to."

Liatoukine knew that she liked to be caught on camera occasionally. Her guises as Irma Vep—looking like the original French criminal and now as a Chinese woman—not only confused the police, but also provided her with the entertainment of seeing herself all over the media.

"Or perhaps the police have been told not to respond to any sightings?" he said. "Harker says they are patrolling slightly less tonight. The Countess and her network have their own contacts."

They both looked around. Just a few people out late, mostly tourists, including a couple sitting on the steps. Their enhanced vampiric powers could see no giveaways that any of them were anything but what they appeared to be. Not impossible that they were undercover agents working for the Countess, but they would certainly have to be very good, thought Liatoukine. He looked at his companion's garments.

"Did you have to dress like that? I know you like attention, but…" Liatoukine was referring to Vep's catsuit, which covered her body bar her face.

"Dear Boris, it is my trademark, and I find it rather practical. Which is more than what can be said for your cheap suit."

The Russian did not rise to that. His suit was a rather expensive affair from Saville Row. Vep was originally an English farmer's daughter with a ridiculous name—little more than a peasant in his view. Despite her minor wealth, what would she know of matters of taste and style?

"It's a minute to midnight. I suggest we enter."

They went up the steps and knocked on the doors. They felt tired just going up them. Churches were not conducive to vampires. Prolonged exposure led to death. Neither wished to show or mention the effects of the consecrated ground to their enemies—and more especially each other.

A short bald man opened the door. Liatoukine sensed this was the German Harker's man had seen earlier. He gestured for them to walk down the aisle. They did so. Liatoukine walked down, feeling weaker with every step. The Countess was no fool, making them come here. However, he was confident that he would be able to have enough strength to deal with both her and the Skull. The Skull itself would presumably also be underpowered.

The two vampires could see ahead of them. In the center of the Cathedral, under its iconic dome, stood the Countess, Walther P5 Compact in hand. And next to her, on a stool, was the Skull.

They stopped a couple of feet from them, in front of the chairs that surrounded the inner circle under the dome. Quite apart from the power of the Cathedral, the Countess was wearing her silver crucifix. Some distance was necessary.

*Greetings, Captain Vampire*, the Skull announced in their heads.

Liatoukine ignored the Skull; it was clearly trying to unsettle him by using his nickname. He spoke to the Countess, pointing at the Skull.

"May I do what apparently you cannot, and destroy this thing?"

"Please proceed," the Countess said, smiling.

He looked at the Skull and began the process of re-absorption. Nothing happened. The Skull laughed manically.

*You are too weak, Captain Vampire—this cathedral is taking its toll.*

The Countess had expected things would go wrong. She swung her revolver straight over to the Skull and fired. Eliminate the Skull and she and Karl would deal with the vampires themselves. Silver bullets came out of the gun and simply hovered in the air in front of the Skull. Then they fell to the ground.

The Skull rose up from its stool and hovered mid-air. Vep, Liatoukine and the Countess could feel pressure on their minds. They were in agony. The Countess's firearm was flung by the Skull's power well out of anyone's reach. By the doors, Karl, too, was under attack. The Skull ranted in their minds.

*Fools! Over the years, I have acquired great power simply by absorbing the psychic powers of people who came to see me in the various museums where I was on display. There were even some genuine supernatural artifacts from which I was able to draw psychic strength. A strange vampiric variant—not blood or energy, but psychic power in my case. How little you know of your own biology, Captain Vampire, and what it has begat. I will now absorb myself into you, take your body and happily crush your mind. These others will be my first meal—if they survive my restraining of them.*

*You lack ambition, Captain Vampire. You merely wish for power and influence—but on human terms. I will use your position to create new vampires. Many, many of them. I will restore the supernatural. And I will use that to control the world. Finally, vampires will control history, not humanity!*

Liatoukine decided to play for time.

"The humans cannot be defeated. Their science and numbers will see to that," he gasped.

He was about to go on, but stopped. Why was the Skull spilling out its ridiculous plans? Why not just get on with destroying him? Reabsorption takes seconds—and if the Skull was that powerful, why had it not done so? Of course! The Cathedral was affecting it as well! There was huge power there—the power of the British nation, its people, its warriors. Was not Wellington and Nelson buried beneath it? This nation had seen off Dracula, after all... His theory was correct; it was what the Skull was thinking as well. There was still a link between them.

Liatoukine sensed fear from the Skull. However, time was short. The Skull was still crushing them down. He was the main focus of its efforts. He looked at Vep. She was on her knees, struggling simply to stand. He looked at the Countess. She was on her feet, her face full of anger and fury, her hands on her crucifix raising it towards the Skull. Her will was stronger than Vep's! She was the answer. The Russian vampire concentrated on the Skull, trying again to reabsorb it. He knew he could not do it, but just a minor effort could be enough to relieve some of the pressure from the others, and the Countess might be able to attack.

They made eye contact. She understood he was trying something. He concentrated what was left of his energy into the attempt. He knew this act itself could destroy him.

*Too late, Captain Vampire! Too late!* the Skull screamed.

However, both Vep and the Countess felt a slight lessening of pressure. Vep simply fell forward. Seizing the moment, the Countess ripped the crucifix off her neck and smashed it down on top of the Skull fracturing it.

"In the name of God!" she shouted, "I expel you from this Earth!"

She smashed the crucifix down again and again, pushing the Skull back onto the stool it had been on. It started to scream—a disturbing, unearthly sound. Bits of it flew around under the assault, bone and teeth crashing to the floor. Its power was shattered. And then, the power of the Cathedral exerted its full wrath—what was left of it disintegrated into powder.

The Countess stared at her handiwork. She looked at her hand, a little bruised and bloodied from where it had hit the Skull, but still gripping the crucifix. Some of it had broken off—it was fortunate that she had it constructed with steel reinforcement within.

She turned to the vampires. Now it as their turn. She saw Vep already halfway down the aisle, holding up Liatoukine. She shoved a disorientated Karl out of the way, a shot from his firearm going off wildly. And then they were out.

The Countess was too weak to chase them. She looked back at what remained of the Skull. Its powdered remains were blowing away in the mysterious wind that traditionally disposed of many vampire remains. She liked tradition. Vep and Liatoukine would keep for now. Karl staggered up to her.

"They've gone," he said. "Disappeared."

"They'll keep," the Countess replied. "We have scored a victory for God and humanity this night. The Skull had intended to unleash vampirism on a scale not seen before. I shall pray to thank the Lord for His help this night."

She promptly went to her knees. Karl would have preferred to leave at once and do the praying later. However, he knew it would be unwise to suggest this. He sat down on one of the chairs and waited for her to finish.

Liatoukine and Vep had been picked up by Harker in one of his company's vehicles and swiftly spirited away. Both vampires started to feel some energy returning, having left the Cathedral behind.

"I take it we are now on good terms?" Vep asked.

"Yes," said Liatoukine. "Provided you stay out of my way, you have nothing to fear from me."

Liatoukine was in any event too weak for another fight. Regardless, he wanted to be seen as someone who kept his word—to serious people at least—and there was always the possibility he may need her again as an ally.

"Very well. Drop me off here," she said to Harker.

He complied and she disappeared into the night.

It took Boris Liatoukine a few days to regain much of his energy. It had gone well. The threat of the Skull had gone. He was already being more cautious with the creation of new duplicates. Nothing had come out of the incident in the Cathedral. The Countess and her network clearly still had some influence, but not enough for the authorities to come after him. The current disbelief in vampires was working in his favor. He would still need to tread carefully. The power of the Cathedral was a reminder that he, too, could be vulnerable.

He turned to the newspapers. He was catching up with world affairs, and went to his favorite first, the *International Herald-Tribune*.

And there was an article that effectively revealed what—or rather who—the Skull had been monitoring for years in St. Petersburg—a person it believed would be important in the future.

Boris Yeltsin had sacked the current head of the FSB, Nikolai Kovalev, and replaced him with someone who, until two years ago, was an official in St. Petersburg, and before that, a KGB man—the very organization the Russian vampire had worked for himself.

Like the Skull, he intuited that more change was on the way.

*Yes*, thought Boris Liatoukine. *This Vladimir Putin would be a man to watch.*

## The Vampire President

*Moscow, 8 March 2024*

Boris Liatoukine always felt uncomfortable in church. Given that he was a vampire, this was unsurprising. He occasionally attended church for the sake of appearances. He could not stay for too long sustained exposure could be fatal. He was in a church office, but it was still on the grounds. Still holy.

The man sitting opposite him was a priest. They had made some small talk, but now it was time to get to the reasons they were here.

"Father Joseph, I am honored to be invited here to your church. However, spiritual matters aside, I believe you wish to discuss with me political topics?"

Father Joseph stroked his long beard.

"Of course, but all in connection with the church. You are a candidate in these elections to become President. I wish to know more about you and your attitude to the church. Although you are seen as a nationalist, a number of people consider you a liberal, and more inclined towards the European Union than Bezukhov—a man who respects the church. It must be said that you are hardly a frequent visitor to the church."

Liatoukine understood that he had to be careful in what he said.

"My belief in God is in my soul; I appreciate I should attend church more often, but many pressures mean I work long hours—my businesses continue to be successful because of this and thus keeps many Russians in work and taxes paid to the government which benefits all. In this way I believe I carry out the work of God."

Liatoukine took momentary pleasure in having said that with a straight face. Father Joseph looked incredulous, but the Russian vampire pressed on before he could recover.

"As for being a liberal? Yes, perhaps I am. I believe in democracy, just as Vladimir Putin does, a man I take great inspiration from. As for the European Union, I would certainly like a closer relationship; it would be good for our industry. Certainly it should be easier for Russians to visit the EU."

*That was more truthful*, thought Liatoukine; freedom of movement in the EU had been most convenient in order to conduct his affairs—both legitimate and otherwise.

Father Joseph had managed to compose himself. It was clear to the Russian vampire that the priest had not bought into anything he said—and he sensed that this went beyond the usual cynicism about politicians. What was going on here?

Father Joseph spoke. "This is most interesting. Let us have some vodka in order to deepen our conversation."

Liatoukine could detect the man's heartbeat—it was going fast.

From a bottle already on the table, he poured out to the drink into two tumblers and gave one to Liatoukine.

"*Za zdorovye!*" they both said and drank the vodka.

The priest drank it down straight and looked back at Liatoukine. The man had frozen, his tumbler in his raised hand, but not quite near his mouth. He stared at the priest, and the priest suddenly noticed that his eyes appeared to resemble those of a cat. Father Joseph felt fear—fear, as he had not felt before.

He knew it was over.

Liatoukine put his tumbler back down.

"Why is this vodka so warm? I can feel it through the tumbler?"

He touched the top of the liquid with his finger. He sucked his breath, smiling at the priest and then showed him his finger. It looked burnt, with steam coming off it. The priest said nothing. The Russian vampire then resumed speaking.

"Holy water mixed with vodka. An old trick to poison vampires. It would have burnt my throat severely, incapacitating me somewhat. However, whatever made you think I would not detect it before it got to my lips? Ah, perhaps you believe that in this church my powers would be blunted enough to not notice? Yes, my powers are blunted—but not to that extent."

Liatoukine rose. *Time for a quick interrogation*, he thought. In that moment, the priest regained his wits and courage. He leaped over to nearby cabinet and out of it grabbed a Heckler and Koch MP5 machine gun.

Before he could raise the weapon to fire, the Russian vampire's hand was around his neck and he was lifted aloft. The machine gun fell harmlessly to the floor.

"Silver bullets?" he asked.

The priest said nothing; he just stared at the vampire—terrified, but also defiant.

"Who provided you with this weapon? Someone in the West?" Liatoukine asked the priest.

Again, the same look of defiance.

"Hell awaits you!" he managed to say.

Liatoukine nodded. "Yes, Yes. I know that—in fact, I expect to be given a position of some authority when I get there."

The vampire laughed. Father Joseph did not.

Liatoukine realized that time was not on his side. He could break the man, but his powers were lessening the longer he stayed in this church. It would not look good to leave here with a dead priest left behind. Letting him live would be risky, but who would be believe this man? However, it was now clear why Father Joseph had insisted on such secrecy; Liatoukine would just have disappeared with no trace back to this church. That secrecy would now seal the priest's fate.

He stared into his eyes, and drained him of energy—which the vampire needed right now—but stopped short of complete absorption. He dropped the body of the priest onto the floor.

He opened the door to the main church. Sitting a short way away was a layman of the church, entirely oblivious to what had happened. He walked over to him and they man stood up. Before he could say anything, the vampire had fixed him with a glare. They layman could only see the cat-like eyes of Liatoukine. The vampires started to speak:

"You will go to see Father Joseph in ten minutes. You will find him dead, and then you will contact the authorities. You will forget any memories of me or Father Joseph meeting anyone. He was simply working in his office."

The layman sat back down.

Liatoukine left unobserved with his head bowed. He walked over to his car and got in the back. The car moved off. Next to him in the car, was a raven-haired woman wearing a smart business suit.

"We used electronic jamming to catch any recording devices we have missed," she said, "as well as making sure the security cameras were scrambled, in addition to those we already disabled. How did it go?"

"Very well, Natasha," Liatoukine replied "He wanted to kill me; so I killed him. One less threat. I assume he had intended to record my death. Given the secrecy, perhaps it was a recording for a select audience to prove my death, or it could be he wanted to release it to the public if he felt it was convincing enough. No doubt this is linked that network around the Countess Petrovski."

"We should certainly retaliate," said Natasha.

She was fully aware of Petrovski's network—as a vampire herself, she could not afford not to. Her original, true name was Polly Bird. She has taken many names, forms and identities since, including that of the notorious criminal Irma Vep when she herself spent many years as a famous jewel thief. Now she was Natasha Rostova—a name suggested by Liatoukine, based on someone he vaguely remembered meeting in the 19th century. Her role was that of a well paid political advisers to Liatoukine; a post that secretly involved a security role, which given her criminal past she was well suited for.

"Yes," replied Liatoukine, "but not just at the moment, there are too many eyes on me at the moment due to this election. Let it be as planned."

Natasha nodded. "We have the St. Petersburg rally to plan for," she said.

The Russian vampire nodded as the car continued its journey to their electoral HQ.

*Paris, 9 March*

The Countess Irina Petrovski looked around the table. Seated around the table were some of the individuals most feared by what was left of the supernatural community. Feared due to their effectiveness in eliminating many of the most the hostile elements to humanity—especially vampires. Here there were aristocrats like herself and millionaires, policemen, spies and others including descendants of people who had fought supernatural evil. She was one such descendent as well as being a Countess and millionaire. Everyone was here. She decided to open the meeting.

"Ladies and gentlemen, how good it is to meet again."

She was immediately interrupted.

"Could we not have done this online? The secure technology exists. I had intended to attend an important debate this afternoon at the European Parliament in Brussels. And putting us in one place does make us a target."

The accent was Germanic and came from a well-dressed man right at the other end of the table. The Countess understood that he was making a genuine point—but also that this was a unspoken, although minor, challenge to her authority as chair of the meeting and de facto leader of the group.

"My dear Baron Vordenberg," she replied, "we all recognize the important work you do at the European Parliament. Your dedication in promoting links between the old Habsburg states within the European Union is most commendable—and something still greatly needed after the ravages of communism. However, meetings by electronic means are too prone to being tapped. We don't keep written minutes for similar reasons."

Another voice spoke up. The Countess saw with pleasure that this was her old friend Karl—a senior member of the BND[10].

"Technology can still be hacked. We have to use it sometimes but not for a meeting like this. It would be unfortunate if a recording of a meeting were made public—technology can still be hacked. Discussing the destruction of supernatural beings? Vampires? The press would have a field day portraying us all as deranged fantasists. The days of official groups dealing with such creatures are long gone—you of all people should know that."

The Baron knew what he meant.

"Yes, one of my ancestors did command the Austro-Hungarian Empire's department for dealing with dark forces. The dissolution of the Empire saw the end of that. My ancestor, however, would certainly have been in favor of using modern technology today, especially to defend ourselves against the Russians, let alone the supernatural"

The Countess saw her chance to end this diversion.

"Technology, Baron, that our subject today may well have the capability of intercepting. He is the ex-KGB officer now turned oligarch Boris Liatoukine, also known to quite a few people as 'Captain Vampire.' He has eluded our efforts at eliminating him over the years. Now he has a candidate in the Russian presidential elections in which Vladimir Putin can no longer stand due to constitutional term limits. This has caused great concerns among many of us. How can we deal with the situation? I have asked Karl to give us his view—his work at the BND gives him an insight."

---

[10] Germany's Federal Intelligence Service.

The Countess noted that the Baron clearly did not press his points over and above her introduction.

Karl proceeded to give his views, not giving the Baron any opportunity to interrupt him.

"Boris Liatoukine is of course known to us all as a vampire, a role he has been active in for quite possibly over 300 years. His main motivation is power—but from behind the scenes. However, he is also a proud Russian—which may seem strange given that his country has a strong religious objection to his identity. It would seem that Liatoukine simply ignores that part of it. He is also a survivor and a pragmatist. We believe he joined the KGB—then the OGPU—in the 1920s. He fought the communists as a White officer and was tracked down by the Soviet spy Von Bork, whom I believe gave him little choice but to work for him. Subsequently he managed to replace von Bork in 1979 by killing him. With the end of communism, he took full advantage of the changes and became an oligarch."

"We know all this," said the Baron, taking advantage of a pause.

"We indeed do," responded Karl. "However, I wish to make a point. Liatoukine has survived many threats. He has had setbacks, but always finds a way ahead. He certainly can be destroyed, but any attempt now would likely fail. His long experience almost gives him a special extra sense. As a presidential candidate, his security will be more heightened than usual. A failed—or even successful—attempt now at assassination by us would be exposed as a Western plot, which would be essentially true. That could have dangerous international repercussions. It is not worth it, not least as Liatoukine is not expected to win. He is slated to come third, behind the Communist candidate Kuragin. He is only there as nationalist candidate to drain votes from those unhappy with Putin's candidate—Kirill Bezukhov—rather than seeing them go to any potential real rival. Bezukhov is determined to win outright in the first round, and Liatoukine is to ensure that. We should wait until the election has passed, then consider how to proceed."

There were murmurs of agreement around the table.

"I must agree with that assessment," said the Countess. "We cannot act now, but after the election we must certainly prioritize his destruction. Before we take a vote, are there any other views?"

She was not surprised when the Baron spoke up.

"As has been pointed out," he said, "Liatoukine has survived many attempts on his existence over the decade—centuries even. Unorthodox methods should be considered. This election gives us a special opportunity to neutralize Liatoukine. If we do nothing, then he will have more influence than ever as a reward for helping Bezukhov. The election of Bezukhov will be a disaster for the West—the advancement of Liatoukine within the Kremlin court would be catastrophic also. He will use his influence to promote Russian aggression even further."

The Countess knew well that the Baron's distaste for Russia rivaled—if not exceeded—that for the supernatural.

"I am well aware of Russian behavior which I directly fought during the Cold War," she stated. "Even then, we had to make sure not to provoke them too far."

The Baron knew he needed to be careful. The Countess's record was well respected and, despite her age, she was she still sharp and looked younger than her years. He himself was not old enough to have played the kind of role she did in the past.

"Of course, we are all aware of your achievements, Countess," he said, "but please allow me to outline my plan."

She made a hand gesture indicating he should proceed. He then outlined his plan. When he had concluded, the Countess spoke:

"That plan—assuming it would even be successful—would have the very real effect of inflaming tensions between Russia and the West with unpredictable consequences. Exactly the sort of thing we are trying to avoid as we have just discussed." She was clearly irritated. "Let us proceed with a vote. All in favor in not making any attempt to neutralize Liatoukine during the Russian elections?"

All bar Vordenberg raised their hands.

"I think that settles it," the Countess said, not wanting to proceed with those against.

"I bow to the wisdom of the group," Vordenberg said, smiling.

He was aware the Countess was much too influential and respected to be easily defeated. Now, it was best to change the mood.

"With the business out of the way, it is time for refreshment. If we move to the adjacent room, a buffet has been prepared. I have also brought along some wines from my personal wine cellar."

The mood immediately changed, and even the Countess smiled.

Later, after the buffet, Baron Vordenberg got into his chauffeur-driven BMW 8.

"My apartment, Jacques," he instructed.

As the car moved off, he took out his mobile phone and switched off the intercom on the soundproof partition between him and the driver. He wished privacy. He dialed a number.

"The meeting, as predicted, did not go well," he said. "We will proceed to Zagreb. It is time to talk to Lady Ruthven. "

Meanwhile, Karl had driven the Countess back to her Paris residence. As he saw her to the door, his mobile phone rang. He looked at the caller's name and took it. The Countess waited; she sensed this was important.

Karl finished the call. He looked at the Countess and said:

"Irina, there is bad news about Father Joseph…"

## 10 March

Baron Vordenberg was on his private jet en route to Zagreb. He was reading news of the death of Father Joseph, a respected figure in Moscow, in an Austrian newspaper. There was no hint of this being a murder; the priest was reported to have died from natural causes. But the Baron knew better. He had, along with the Countess, tried to discourage him from attempting to kill 'Captain Vampire.' They knew the vampire would not be so easy to kill. The weapons they had supplied him were for defensive use only.

"Unfortunate news regarding Joseph," said his aide.

"Yes", replied Vordenberg. "We had warned him. Now we have lost the best contact in we had in Russia." He looked at the newspaper again. "Natural causes it says here. Given that he was an admirer of Putin, no one will think he was murdered. How ironic; he was killed by the very creature the West thinks of as a lesser evil than Bezukhov."

His aide looked puzzled. "If Father Joseph was a Putin admirer, how did he come to work with the network?"

"The network is dedicated to eliminating vampires and the like," the Baron replied. "Father Joseph understood that, and set aside his politics. Our network being informal helped this; we do not even have a name. With the supernatural fading away, there are less and less experts to deal with the matter, and fewer still in Russia. Why? Because we think Liatoukine had them eliminated—at least those he could not recruit. We have few people left in Russia now. It becomes ever more important to neutralize Liatoukine."

The Learjet soon landed at Zagreb's Pleso airport, where a car was already waiting for the Baron to take him onto his next destination.

At her Paris residence, the Countess took a call. Her phone indicated from whom it was: Boris Liatoukine. They had spoken in the past, making vague threats against each other. She picked it up and spoke in English:

"How can I help you, Mr. Liatoukine?"

The voice on the other end replied in English. "How kind of you to offer to help me, my dear Countess. I will come to that in a moment. I just wished to call to give my condolences over Father Joseph, who died very recently. He was well known in my country. I believe you were friends?"

"We had met a number of times," the Countess replied icily.

Liatoukine continued, "Yes, I thought as much. His death was... a waste. He had much to offer the world. It is in his spirit that I propose that relations between Russia and the European Union—and perhaps our British friends as well—should change. We could have relations based on 'you leave us alone, we will leave you alone.' We could solve many conflicts. What would you think of such a proposal? I know you have great influence in certain circles."

"You seem very certain of victory, Mr. Liatoukine," the Countess replied. "I had read that you are likely to come third, and indeed that your candidature is merely to ensure that voters none too keen on Bezukhov will vote for you, thus ensuring that votes will not go to any possible real challenger."

Liatoukine laughed. "Of course I intend to win! However, if God decrees I should lose…" the Countess winced as no doubt the vampire intended, "…then I am sure that my advice on many matters would be highly sought after."

"Thank you for calling me, Mr. Liatoukine. I will consider what you have said."

She hung up on him. She understood very well what he meant. He was after some kind of truce between himself and the network. Surely, this indicated some kind of weakness? Regardless, it could not be countenanced. And yet, it was true that, whilst they had come close to eliminating him in the past, they had not been able to do so. Liatoukine was certainly capable of eliminating some of the network—as clearly he had done with Father Joseph.

She had never been too keen on the priest's Russian nationalist views, especially his views on her beloved Poland. However, they had both put that aside in order to cooperate against the supernatural, and she had respected him for that. He had been told not to attempt an assassination—he was frankly not capable of dealing with a vampire of Liatoukine's stature. She was sure that this was what provoked Liatoukine to murder him. His death—amongst many others—should be avenged.

Liatoukine had proved to be someone very difficult to kill. A truce could well be exploited by him to continue murdering his opponents. No, there could be no truce. However, this was still a sensitive time. Effectively, there was a truce due to the decision not to go after Liatoukine during the election. What to do next? She hoped that Baron Vordenberg would do nothing foolish.

In Moscow, Liatoukine switched off the phone. With him was Natasha.

"Do you think she is interested?' she asked.

"Probably not at the moment," he replied. "However, she and the others may well reflect over the death of Father Joseph and finally realize that co-existence is the best option. After all, have they not virtually won? There are but a handful of vampires in existence now. Yes, I seek power in the form of influence, but it is very much on human terms."

"You seek power, but this is an election you wish to lose," said Natasha, teasingly.

"Indeed it is. The powers that be want someone to make sure that those electors who want a slightly 'gentler' nationalism, but not a Western stooge. This is a favor to the Kremlin. I do not appreciate the limelight, but not doing it would make me enemies, and given that I have been promised influence and a free hand for my business activities, this is good for me. The polls have Bezukhov first, Kuragin some way behind in second position, and myself a bit past that in third place. So far, the plan goes well."

"Just as well for you—if you won, the scrutiny from home and abroad from the intelligence agencies and the media would soon find out that you are not quite human," Natasha said.

"Yes," laughed Liatoukine. "Not that Bezukhov has a clue. It grates having to do this for him. He affects an aristocratic air. I knew his ancestor, a Count—Bezukhov was descended from one of his illegitimate son. Even the name was taken decades after Count Bezukhov's death. He doesn't mention that when he talks about his aristocratic heritage in his campaign rallies!"

She joined in with his laughter.

"Now," he said, "have you made security arrangements for the rally in St. Petersburg?"

She nodded and started to give him the details.

Baron Vordenberg's car arrived at its destination in Zagreb. It was an old building in central Zagreb near Ban Jelacic Square, dating well back into the Austro-Hungarian Empire when it was used for military purposes. The Baron took pleasure in the fact that this building was still in use. In his soul, he was an Austro-Hungarian; his family had served that Empire for generations. One ancestor had commanded the Empire's division that dealt with supernatural threats, using this very building. Then, the Great War had come and that had been the end of the Empire—an empire which had certainly been better than the fascism and communism which had followed it—of that Vordenberg had no doubt.

A private security firm now used the building. The Baron was pleased with this company; he owned majority shares in it and it made money—enough money to be able to provide security for the secret basement.

He and his aide went down the stairs to the basement, and through the security doors. A guard escorted them. The structure was clearly old, but supplemented by modern reinforced doors and various technological devices. It was a prison.

"You know, Boris Liatoukine himself came here in the past as a visitor?" the Baron said to his aide.

The aide looked startled.

"Oh yes," continued the Baron. "He came officially as a Russian officer. A record of his visit was made. A vampire held here died during his visit. Somehow, he avoided suspicion, no doubt using his powers. The Habsburg's supernatural department ran this place. Now, that department has gone, but the values of the Empire are still with us, and now we maintain this place privately."

His aide was used to this; Baron Vordenberg was well known for his Habsburg nostalgia.

They swiftly came to one particular door. A security guard was there waiting for them. He opened the door—which on the inside was lined with silver and had a crucifix on it, with garlic hung on it for good measure. Ahead of the door was a further door constructed entirely of a reinforced plastic. Behind it, seated in a chair, was a beautiful young brunette, seemingly no more than twenty. Behind her, there appeared to be the fashionable room of a larger apartment.

The Baron and his aide sat down in chairs opposite her.

"Good evening, Lady Ruthven," said the Baron.

"Good evening, Baron," Lady Ruthven replied in a cut-glass English accent. "I was told to expect visitors. No doubt you want more information from me? Over the years, I rather think that I have told you everything I know."

"Not information this time, but rather a favor, shall we say," the Baron replied. "It would see your freedom—for a time."

Lady Ruthven was slightly startled by this—although she did not show it. What did this Austrian aristocrat mean?

"Go on," she said.

"You have cooperated with us before. When we captured you, you gave us information regarding other vampires and others, enabling our network to locate and eliminate them."

She interrupted him.

"Oh yes, I don't have any loyalty to other vampires. My husband killed me and then abandoned me, not bothering to see if I returned from the grave. I took the name Lady Ruthven—perfectly legally, given that he was a Lord. We are fellow aristocrats, you know, *Baron*"

He ignored her comments and the emphasis on his title. In his non-public circles, he was called Baron; but in his political life he could not use it, due to Austrian law not recognzing such titles.

"In return for your cooperation, we allowed you your continued existence," he stated.

"And in luxury too," she replied, waving her arm at the rooms behind her.

The Baron resumed talking.

"The information you gave us has helped reduce the numbers of vampires to an even lower level than there were previously. However, our holding up our end of the agreement demonstrates that not only are we not genocidal in intent, but that we can be trusted."

Lady Ruthven nodded her head cautiously.

"We want you to help us neutralize Boris Liatoukine," he said.

"Thank you for visiting me, Baron Vordenberg. I really must get back to watching something on the television," she said and then got up to go.

The Baron was ready for this.

"Fail to cooperate, Lady Ruthven, and you will find many of your privileges curtailed."

Lady Ruthven got back in her chair.

"You said that you could be trusted. I see now that is not true."

"Your privileges and existence were dependent on telling us everything you knew about your fellow vampires. Upon closer inspection, it seems that those you did provide us information on those who happened to be enemies of yours. We know that, in the early 2000s, you had business dealing with Liatoukine in London. You never mentioned this to us. As such, we feel that some curtailing of your privileges may be in order, if not a stake through your heart."

The vampire did not like the sound of that. What he had said was perfectly true. She had refrained from mentioning her dealings with Liatoukine—which were both amicable and profitable—not out of any loyalty, but purely due to the fact that the notorious 'Captain Vampire' was both powerful and hard to kill. She did not want the remotest chance of making an enemy out of him. She would not give in to the Baron just yet.

"I am immortal, A few years here will hardly affect me. Just moments in time."

As soon as she said it she realized just how weak that comment was. The Baron smiled and responded:

"First of all, if we liked, we could destroy you at will." He pointed upwards to the ceiling on her side of the wall. "The fire sprinkler system is linked to a supply of holy water. We turn it on—no more Lady Ruthven. Or we could just starve you by denying you the animal blood we supply you with. Alternatively, you help us and your privileges shall remain intact. More importantly, you get to see the outside world again, and if it goes well you will get to go on other missions."

She could see she was defeated.

"Very well," she said. "Tell me how I will not simply escape you the moment I am let free for this 'mission' of yours?"

It was the Baron's aide who answered. He opened a briefcase he had with him. Inside where two small capsules nestling in foam.

"These implants will be placed in your neck and stomach," he explained. "They are lead-covered and contain holy water and shards of silver. They have small explosives contained within them which we can detonate via a satellite signal. Once you have concluded your mission, we will remove them. They will be triggered if tampered. Further, the devices will receive a regular signal. If they do not get that signal, say, because you decided to enter an area where such signals are blocked, they will detonate after a certain time."

"How long?" Lady Ruthven asked.

"That is for us to know," the aide replied, smiling. "It could be seconds, minutes, hours... Probably best for you to simply make sure that you do not 'accidentally' enter a signal-free zone, such as a metro station for example. Although, if the mission does require it, we will make sure it won't go off in any such circumstances. Provided we know beforehand, that is. We will implant a communications device also. This all being said, your body will eat at them, to purge them from your system. The capsules have a coating made to a certain formula which will hold out for about ten days. When it eats through, the anti-tamper mechanism will be triggered. However, if you complete your task, the capsules will be removed well before then."

Lady Ruthven did not like any of this. However, she gave the only answer she could.

"Very well," she said.

*St. Petersburg, 13 March*

Boris Liatoukine stood in front of the monument of Tsar Nicholas in St. Isaac's Square. This was familiar ground. He had been here when the monument was being constructed. In fact, he knew Nicholas I personally. Tonight's rally for his candidature would play on Imperial nostalgia. Although, of course, the audience would not know just how nostalgic Liatoukine was, or rather why. He thought back to those times. They had certainly been better for him. A long period of power and status, and Imperial adventure. He remembered in particular his operations in Rumania. Crushing the locals was always something he had enjoyed. He had found some kind of accommodation with the Soviet regime, but he was happy enough it was over. The Imperial age was gone—but the compensation of being an oligarch was reasonable. He even had a wife for a while. He had divorced Magda fairly recently, most amicably. She had played her part well, and there was no need to liquidate her. He would have kept her on for the election had he known he was going to be a candidate. Still, she gave excellent comments about him to the media when they contacted her.

His thoughts were interrupted by his cellphone ringing. He answered, and recognized the voice immediately—his contact in the GRU[11].

"Greetings, Boris. I take it the preparations for tonight's rally are to your satisfaction?"

"There are indeed," said the Russian vampire, looking at the workmen putting up the last of the crowd barriers.

He had ensured that the rally would take place in the evening—when he had more power. It was best to seem as invigorated as possible at such events.

"Excellent, Boris. We notice that the West is increasingly interested in your candidacy. You are being spoken highly of amongst human rights groups. Perhaps you should cultivate these contacts?"

Liatoukine knew what he meant—trying to cultivate them for GRU purposes. This would be going too far in their arrangement. The last think he wanted was to be associated such groups, a sure way of being portrayed as a stooge for the West, something that could be easily used against him in the future.

"No, my friend," Liatoukine replied, "I have no desire to encourage such elements. Furthermore, if I were to be seen as working for the West, I am sure I would lose the votes of those patriots who are not happy with the leading candidate for any reason."

"Of course, of course, Boris. We would not wish to do that. We are keen to have your candidacy to be a success. We will be in touch again soon."

The caller rang off

Natasha approached the Russian vampire. She had been looking over the preparation for tonight.

---

[11] Russia's external military intelligence agency.

"Our GRU friends again?" she inquired.

"Yes," he replied. "It is fortunate that we have others on our side from within the Kremlin. The GRU never really forgave the KGB—or rather myself and Von Bork—for monopolizing supernatural affairs. However, with the general skepticism towards such matters that has grown over the years, that antagonism should have gone, and yet the GRU are still a little unfriendly."

"There are still people around who are aware of the reality of the supernatural—or rather what's left of it," Natasha replied. "Perhaps there are such people left in the GRU?"

"Perhaps. In the time before leaving the KGB, I had eliminated a few such people. It could just be coincidental—general antipathy towards an ex-KGB man. Whatever, I think our GRU friend will have to shock his colleagues and die young, just as soon as this election business is over."

He changed the subject.

"Is my speech ready?"

She nodded. They moved away from the monument and towards the nearby parked campaign bus. On its side it had a picture of Liatoukine, looking stern, with the slogan "To a better Russia" on the side. Liatoukine liked the slogan—it could mean anything to anyone.

Once on board the bus, they looked over the speech.

"We will need to make some amendments here. A little more criticism of the West. Given the GRU's behavior, it is best to make any attempt to portray me as in the pay of the West look absurd. Here, it should say…"

He stopped suddenly, looking around. Natasha was suddenly on alert too. They had both sensed something...

Lady Ruthven put her binoculars down. If she had had her sniper's rifle, she could have taken a shot there and then. However, that was not the plan. Clearly, Liatoukine and his lackey had sensed her presence—and the element of threat, simply by her looking at them. It is possible they would take further security precautions.

She decided not to tell Baron Vordenberg that piece of information. Best not to upset anyone who could destroy her at the touch of a button. She had broken into this room; it had a perfect view of the monument. Unfortunately it also had a perfect view of the St. Isaac's Cathedral which overlooked the moment. It was far enough to do her no harm, but it made her feel uneasy. Her target was a lot closer to the Cathedral, although clearly it did not entirely inhibit his powers. She would return later—fully armed. She would fire the shot—a silver bullet—and then she would leave rapidly. Her vampiric speed should get her out of danger quickly. Furthermore, she had changed form—she was now a bit taller and blonde. Lady Ruthven thought this prudent; it would be unfortunate indeed if Liatoukine somehow saw her and recognized her before she completed the operation.

The doors to the apartment opened—two Moscow police officers walked in. They saw the petite woman in front of them and kept their guns holstered.

"What are you doing here?" one of them asked.

Lady Ruthven bluffed. "I am looking after the property for the owners," she said.

The officer replied, "No, you are not. They have said nothing about you. Are you foreign?"

He put his hand on his pistol. His companion started to talk on his radio. They were clearly checking the area ahead of the rally. And as good as her Russian was, she could not hide her English accent. She had to act fast.

She ran towards the officer with the radio. At high speed she covered his mouth and switched off his radio. She stared into his eyes.

"Silence!" she hissed.

She had the power of mesmerism, and she only needed it to work for a moment whilst she dealt with the other officer.

The other one was astounded. What was he seeing? She moved so fast—like a blur. Whilst she was in front of him, dealing with his colleague, he grabbed at her, but she knocked him flying.

He smashed to the ground, but still had his wits about him. He pulled his gun out of the holster and aimed it at the woman in front of him. She was smiling, and looking at him. Her eyes seemed to bore into him.

"Fire, then," she said.

He looked fearful—and then pulled the trigger. And then realized his gun was missing. The woman had it. She was tossing it up and down in her hand.

"Get up," she said.

She then spoke to the other officer, still standing there.

"Get onto the radio. Tell them all is well, the person was just an employee on the stairs."

After he had done so, she spoke to both of them.

"Why are you here?" she asked.

They both answered at the same time.

"Quiet. Just you," she said, pointing at the officer who had tried to shoot her.

He responded, "The occupants downstairs had seen you on the stairs and did not recognize you. They called the police. We were checking on the area and were able to respond swiftly."

"Very well," Lady Ruthven said. "As far as anyone was concerned you only came across another employee. The people who made the call—where are they?"

"Downstairs" came the answer.

"Please invite them in," she said.

They did as instructed, and a man and a woman came in. The vampire swiftly mesmerized them. It transpired they were the only ones who had noticed her.

*Excellent*, she thought. *And most convenient*. The man had made the call. She said to him:

"It turns out the person you saw earlier was in fact your colleague here, who had business on this floor—that would be plausible, wouldn't it?"

They both nodded. She continued:

"Good. Make up something more detailed if anyone asks, but say nothing if no one does. Forget me, and any other sightings of me. Off you go now."

They went off.

"And you two," she said to the policemen, "will ensure that this area is regarded as fully checked—and you will respond to any calls or commands from me, whilst telling no one of me. Resume your duties."

They did so.

*Splendid*, thought Lady Ruthven. Her mesmerism powers were strong as ever, despite her ten-year incarceration in that Zagreb dungeon. She liked little tricks such as taking a gun off someone whilst they were under her influence. Their bemused looks when she took them out of their trance were also amusing. Now she had two policemen to help her with tonight's events... that would make things a lot easier.

No wonder Baron Vordenberg wanted her for this job—such powers were most useful for an assassination. The Baron would not doubt affect to disapprove, if she told him, but he should be grateful that she had killed no police or members of the public—as he had demanded.

As she left, she noticed a window was tinted slightly green. It was an occasional giveaway for some vampires. It could be controlled, she had done so for many years, but it seemed that being let out meant some lapses. She would need to concentrate more on that—which was difficult given the intensity of her task.

St. Isaac's square was crowded that evening. Boris Liatoukine was pleased. He was less pleased about St. Isaac's Cathedral being lit up as well—but there was nothing he could do about that. He decided not to keep them waiting. He stood on the platform, and began his speech.

A distance away, Lady Ruthven was looking down her telescopic sight. She could see him making the speech. She could hear him through an earpiece connected to radio coverage. It was up to her when she should take the shot. She settled on firing when he said something particularly irritating.

Liatoukine was thinking that the speech was going down well. He had spoken of the need of to maintain defenses, to preserve Putin's achievements, and to stand up to the West. It was now time to differentiate himself from the leading candidate, and make a gentle gesture towards the West—but not too much.

"We must take a new approach to the West. Yes, they do accuse us of interfering in their elections. They even blame us for Jeremy Corbyn becoming the British Prime Minister!" The crowd laughed. "I will look into the matter, but I also expect them to look into their interference in our own elections—the funding of 'activists' and radio stations..."

The crowd roared wildly. Now, however, for the fig leaf to the West.

"However, whilst the West are most certainly guilty of human rights violations, can we honestly say we could not do better? Even in the KGB, I was always concerned about the well-being of our citizens. Now, I see our society must develop further. Russians must not fear voicing their opinions. Please believe me, the cause of human rights is very dear to my heart."

He clasped his hands over his chest. The crowd applauded. Lady Ruthven rolled her eyes and then pulled the trigger.

Liatoukine heard the crack of the rifle in the distance and, due to his heightened vampire senses, saw the bullet coming straight at him. He moved slightly, and the bullet missed his head and smashed into the set behind him.

For a moment there was silence and bewilderment in the crowd. Natasha leapt onto the stage, along with FSB[12] bodyguards. They grabbed Liatoukine to move get him off the stage. But he used his strength to move them back. He spoke into the microphone:

"My friends, please leave immediately and in an orderly fashion. Your safety is paramount."

He then let himself be rushed off the stage.

In the back of a police car, still listening to radio coverage, Lady Ruthven laughed at Liatoukine's attempt to play the concerned candidate. The car was driven by the policemen whom she had mesmerized earlier. They thought they were driving a lost British journalist to safety, rather than helping an assassin escape.

---

[12] Federal Security Service of the Russian Federation, the internal successor of the KGB.

Later, in a secure location in St. Petersburg, Liatoukine awaited a report from Rostova. She came in.

"The would be assassin has of course got away. The Police and FSB seem to have no idea as to who it was. However, the bullet has been retrieved."

She showed Liatoukine a picture on her phone.

"A silver bullet?" he asked.

"Yes," she replied. "It seems this is an attack against you as a vampire. Unfortunately, someone has seen fit to decide it would be good to quickly reveal this to the press."

Liatoukine grunted. "It looks like my nickname of 'Captain Vampire' is going to be wheeled out to a greater audience than ever. This is the Countess's work."

"Are you sure? Could it not be the GRU?"

"No, they would not dare, given Bezukhov is my ally. Now, I must be seen by the public, no matter that I do not intend to win—I must not be seen as being weak. However, first I must make a call."


The Countess was watching television coverage of the incident, with news coming in constantly. Already, the Russian vampire was being portrayed as a hero for his telling the crowd to leave. Despite the late hour in St. Petersburg, it appeared that Liatoukine was going to make a press appearance. She wondered if he had set all this up for himself. Did he really want to win? Her phone rang. It was Liatoukine.

"My dear Countess! Another failure of your group, it seems."

"I have no idea what you are talking about," she replied.

"Yes, you would say that," he responded. "However, I think the silver bullet used was a clear enough response to my offer of good will. I will send my own message back in good time."

He hung up.

A silver bullet? The Countess realized what must have happened.

"Vordenberg!" she spat.

In St. Petersburg, Liatoukine switched off his phone. He and his entourage were on board his campaign bus. They got off outside the Mariinsky Theatre, its neo-renaissance façade making an excellent background for media pictures as intended. The press had already been alerted. They jostled around him Liatoukine. The vampire was pleased—he had made clear his instructions that the journalists were not to be pushed away. He must be seen to be fearless, not so much for the election, but more for not showing any public weakness to his enemies. Many questions were being thrown at him. He was able to create a small space in the crowd by raising his hands. His power as a vampire was largely responsible, although the assembled throng believed they were showing respect.

"My friends! I am pleased to be with you. I am delighted that my supporters only suffered minor injuries rather than anything more serious in their rush to avoid this would-be assassin. I expect the authorities to do their job properly and apprehend the criminal. For too long this kind of thing has gone on in our country, with the perpetrators getting away. Well, no more! When I become President, yes, I will stand up to the West, and yes, I will promote Imperial Russia's values. But I will also insist on human rights in our country, for the ordinary Russian to not live his life in fear. I will set up a commission to defend human rights and investigate corruption. I will not take a penny from the West for this. Now, I must return to my headquarters—my staff are frightened and distressed, and I must see to their well-being."

As he moved back to the bus, journalists shouted questions. He ignored them, but then one pushed forward, sticking her microphone under his nose.

"The police say that the bullet used was made of silver. What do you say about that?"

Another journalist shouted from behind, "Is it because you were known as 'Captain Vampire' when you were in the KGB?"

Liatoukine smiled. "If a silver bullet was indeed used, this can only point to the mental health of the perpetrator. We all know from the cinema that silver bullets work only on werewolves, not vampires!"

The crowd burst into laughter, allowing Liatoukine to get back on board the bus.

"How little do they know," said Natasha as he sat down.

"Quite," he replied, laughing.


In Paris, the Countess was controlling her fury. Had Vordenberg gone mad? She knew he advocated extreme methods against the network's foes, in particular vampires. Furthermore, he had a particular animus against Russians. She sympathized to a degree; but communism had been defeated, and they still had to cooperate with a few Russians in dealing with supernatural forces.

She took a call. It was Karl.

"I've made checks on the Zagreb detainment center. The prisoner we are interested in is officially still there. However, one of my sources in the prison has informed me that Vordenberg met with her and subsequently, she left. Orders were given that no one was to report her departure for security reasons. It is clear that he is proceeding with his plan."

The Countess knew that Karl maintained certain informal sources in the network. A good intelligence officer, he did not simply take the word of people.

"Karl," she said, "We have to stop Vordenberg. Where is he?"

"He is in St. Petersburg as a member of a European Parliament election monitoring group. He was a last minute addition to the team. I am having the whole team monitored, but beyond that I cannot do more. To target him with resources would invite many questions—he is very well respected. Trying to suggest he is involved in an assassination would not go down well—let alone discussing the... particulars of things."

Despite the secure line, Karl was still circumspect with his language.

"Berlin would have me removed," he concluded.

"Do you have any suggestions?" she asked.

"You could try and talk to him. Bluff that you will expose him. Or reason with him. It might work."

"I have tried to call him, Karl. He did not answer. I am disinclined to continue."

She had certainly been displeased by having been ignored. She was not accustomed to that.

"I will continue to monitor the situation," Karl continued. "I will see if there any other avenues to pursue. However, I fear we may be able to do nothing. It could be that we have to hope that Vordenberg succeeds completely in his plan, with no trace back to us... Irina, there is one thing that plays in our favor. It seems that western diplomats and some of the non-governmental organizations they back are now seeing Liatoukine as the candidate to back, despite his known KGB past, his dubious dealings as an oligarch, and his nationalism. His talk of human rights and rapprochement with the West has convinced them that he is probably the best option. Even though it is known he is simply trying to drain support from the communist candidate in order to for Bezukhov to get more votes—they are even trying to doubt this."

"Please tell me you're joking? No, I can well believe it—their hypocrisy and naiveté is nauseating. How on Earth does this help us?" she asked, exasperated.

"It means that it less likely that the attempt to kill him will look like a Western plot," Karl answered, "but more possibly a business rival—or some lunatic, given that a silver bullet was used. Even the Russian state could now be blamed. However, I can certainly push the idea of a business rival. I will brief some of our friends in the media. I am, of course, looking into helping us increase our own security, given Liatoukine's threats to us."

"Thank you Karl. That is most considerate. Goodnight."

She put the telephone down. The Countess was unused to feeling powerless. What could be done?

### 15 March

In Moscow, Baron Vordenberg was meeting with Lady Ruthven in Alexander Gardens, near the Kremlin. She had some concerns about the location.

"Baron, as a member of the EUP monitoring team, are you not aware that the FSB are monitoring you?"

"Of course, they are! That is why we are meeting here. I also have an electronic device on my person which will interfere with any devices pointed at us. Furthermore, there is nothing suspicious. You are a journalist from the *New York Times*. Why should I not be meeting you?"

Lady Ruthven was grateful that, at least, he was being discreet in conversation, not mentioning the fake ID she had been given. She had also used her powers to change her appearance. A little taller, with blonde hair and changed features. She had not changed accent however; it would sound fake whatever she tried.

The Baron looked over to a couple also walking in the park. He gave them a cheery wave. They ignored him.

"They are FSB. Are you deliberately trying to antagonize them?" asked Lady Ruthven.

"What does it matter? They would not dare to arrest us!" he exclaimed.

Lady Ruthven was none too sure about that.

"Will you be at the TV debate on Friday night?" he asked, knowing the answer.

"Yes," she said. "I will be reporting on it for my paper."

"Security will be tight of course," he said. "After the attempt on Liatoukine's life, and the failure to capture his assassin, there is some nervousness. You know, Putin did not bother with debates back in 2018—his stature and poll popularity meant he did not need it. Bezukhov does not quite have that lead, despite being ahead in the polls. He is attending this final one in order to show he doesn't fear the other candidates. Not in the least due to Liatoukine looking like a hero after the attempt on his life."

Lady Ruthven nodded. "Liatoukine has taken a few votes off Bezukhov. But he has taken rather more off the communist. He may even come second in the polls, but Bezukhov will come well ahead. With Putin's endorsement and his anti-Western rhetoric, I can't see him losing. If Liatoukine really is Bezukhov's man, he is doing the job we expected."

The Baron smiled. "And I certainly expect you to do yours. Perhaps you could deal with these two? I will see you after the debate."

He strode off.

Lady Ruthven strolled over to the FSB couple. She spoke to them. And then she left, knowing that the FSB records would show that Baron Vordenberg had met with a journalist from London's *Daily Telegraph*. He would not be linked to a fake *New York Times* reporter. However, she was unhappy with having had to meet him at all. He was too confident and reckless. He just wanted to remind her he was in control, regardless of the risk o the FSB observing. This whole plan was dangerous. However, she had no choice but to go through with it. She had everything planned —her powers should see that she came out of this well. The world would be hunting a fake *New York Times* journalist with blonde hair. She would not be resuming this form again. Still, she knew much could go wrong—but she had no choice. Vordenberg's devices implanted in her body had seen to that.

Liatoukine sat in his campaign HQ. He and Natasha were in an office. Through the glass doors they could see the campaign workers outside in the open plan area busily concerning themselves with election matters. They were preparing for the big event tonight.

"Bezukhov will be there tonight. His first and only of these debates," said Liatoukine. "It seems the polls show that the public want him to do so. He's not quite as popular as Putin was, which must annoy him. I am not to outshine him tonight. Irritating, but I should be able to manage it."

"You will need to be careful, Boris," said Natasha. "You've appeared in all the debates, cultivating your 'democratic' credentials. You did well, and the polls place you a close third. You need to tone down the performance—we cannot have you suddenly chasing down Bezukhov."

"I will deliver my part of the bargain," he replied. "In any event, I can't see any great polling change. Bezukhov will win, Kuragin will come second, and I come third—with the Kremlin owing me a lot. Perhaps the first favor I shall ask is the liquidation of a member or two of the Countess's network? A couple of unfortunate accidents perhaps, if not any poisonings. Perhaps I could request the GRU does it? That will teach them to treat me with more respect."

"We've been assigned further FSB agents for security reasons. No doubt this is genuine after the attempted assassination and so on, but they must have orders to keep an eye on us in a more political fashion."

Liatoukine nodded. "Yes, Bezukhov is no fool. Still, I have my friends in the FSB which has allowed us to oversee security. However, there have been renewed attempts to look more deeply into my—and your—backgrounds. This also includes efforts by foreign services such as MI6, the CIA, the BND and all the rest. It has been ensured that they only received the material we wish them to have. Decades upon decades of practice will mean our covers will withstand a degree of scrutiny, but not much more. The sooner this election is over, the sooner I can fade back into background—or at least what is possible. Wealth and a degree of influence is all a vampire can achieve; too much power and profile means more scrutiny from the world, and in this new era of social media, that could be dangerous to one's health."

Natasha smiled, "If you do win, we could always say that claims of vampirism are 'fake news,'"

Liatoukine laughed. "Yes—but that won't work with the intelligence services who may get so suspicious that they may take any information from people such as the Countess's network seriously. Another good reason to kill a few of them."

There was a knock on the door.

"Time to head for the studio," Natasha said.

Lady Ruthven arrived at the Russia TV studios in central Moscow. She was part of a small group of western journalists permitted to cover this last of the debates. She was accredited with the *New York Times International Edition*. It was known that this was Liatoukine's favorite international newspaper. No doubt Vordenberg thought it amusing to associate her with the newspaper. It could draw Liatoukine's attention. It had not done so, but this again showed how reckless the Baron was.

Now, it was time for her to get through security. A matter made easier by her vampiric powers. In that, at least, choosing herself as the assassin made sense. She had a firearm in her bag, next to her laptop. It was made out of a plastic that would resist electronic detection, but would certainly not elude the eyes of the police searching through her bags.

She approached the security gates. She could see that there was a queue for the bag search. She waited for her turn. The police officer at the search desk started to open her bag. She immediately used her mesmerism.

"All perfectly safe," she said, looking directly into his eyes.

Without a beat, he looked into her bag, took out all the items, bar the gun, and then nodded her to the next stage.

She quickly put her items back in the bag. *That was easy*, she thought. Clearly Liatoukine had not used his influence to place people more resistant to mesmerism here, assuming he had any that is. He probably thought that it was a human assassin who was after him—as the Baron had reasoned.

She then set to placing all her items in a tray for the electronic scan. She left the gun in the bag, with her laptop. The tray went through. She walked through the metal detector and scan on her body. No problem there. She was waved through to where the other journalists were collecting their things from the trays that had passed the scan. She felt nervous. Had her tray not gone through yet?

It did not come out from the machine. A policeman from behind the machine stood up. He held up her bag.

"Whose bag is this?" he asked the journalists.

"Mine," Lady Ruthven said.

She moved towards the police officer. She was prepared to get out fast. If the policeman had spotted the gun, he had probably already alerted his colleagues. She would have to use whatever supernatural violence to escape, and just hope Vordenberg won't detonate the devices in her.

The police officer handed her the bag.

"It contains your laptop. The instructions on the notice in front of the machine are clear. You must go back, and place the laptop into a separate tray."

"Yes, of course. My apologies, officer."

She went back to the end of the queue for the machine. Vordenberg's gun would not doubt pass security again, she thought. Where did he access such weaponry, she wondered, as well as her impeccable credentials? He may be reckless, but he certainly had resources.

Finally clearing security, she proceeded into the studio. Here, she would carry out the assassination. Her escape plan was crude and simple: After firing the weapon, she would use her strength and speed to exit the studio. The first moment she was unobserved, she would change form into someone else. Someone older, with short black hair. Her jacket was reversible; she would look wholly different. Shorter even. To all intents and purposes, the assassin would have disappeared into thin air. Any bullets fired into her by the police would be disintegrated by her metabolism.

She took her seat. Despite being coerced into it, she was excited by what she was going to do. As far as she was concerned, Liatoukine's fate was sealed.

The press and studio audience were mostly seated now in the TV studio. Final checks were being made on the set. Natasha Rostova walked around the set, consisting of seven podiums for the seven candidates. She looked at each of the bottles of water as she walked around. She sensed nothing from them. No holy water in them.

The communist candidate, Kuragin, had sent a young representative today, rather than himself—one Boris Drubetsky, claiming a lack of respect from others. He had a glass of water thrown into him by a woman candidate in a previous debate and used this to back out. Natasha thought that his ego was indeed damaged by this, but also that his debating skills were not up to the level of the others. He would lose votes for that. Probably to Liatoukine or Bezukhov. Either way, it would help Bezukhov to get over the 50% and win the first round.

Her thoughts returned to security. She could not notice anything wrong, and the water bottles were safe. Hopefully, the police and FSB had done their jobs—they seemed competent.

She went backstage. Liatoukine was waiting his dressing room.

"Is all well?" he asked.

"As far as I can see," she replied. "Still, be ready for anything."

"I always am," he replied.

He pointed to the grey streaks in his black hair and beard. "Does this look alright? I am probably the only candidate who dyes his hair to look older. Unavoidable given that I am known to be old enough to have been in the KGB. However, do I look distinguished or just older?"

Natasha knew he had a vain streak.

"You look fine," she said. "Very distinguished indeed. Just don't try to over-shadow Bezukhov."

Liatoukine nodded—perhaps a little reluctantly thought Natasha.

"*The New York Times* wants an interview with you," she said. "They are very keen on your liberal values. Perhaps straight after the debate?"

Liatoukine smiled. He had been reading the international edition of that newspaper since it was founded in 1887 as the *Paris Herald.*

"Is the journalist here tonight?" he asked.

"Yes, he is," she replied. "The press list also shows a freelancer for the same newspaper; she is doing more general coverage of the election, apparently."

"Of course. The newspaper understands Russia is a great power and needs extensive coverage," he said.

Natasha noted the vampire's strange patriotism. If the Russian people found out what he was, he would not last very long.

An electronic buzz came on.

"Time to put on the show," Liatoukine said.

Lady Ruthven watched the candidates take up their positions on the podiums, formed into a semi-circle. She was glad that they had come on at last; she was getting tired of the journalist next to her, from a British broadsheet.

"You are from the *NYT*? You must know Jim then? He's got an interview for Liatoukine for your paper, he says."

"We don't really know each other; we are working independently on our own stories," she said.

Her neighbor seemed to accept that, then started to gush about Liatoukine.

"Isn't it wonderful what he is saying about human rights? Imagine if he could win!"

"He was in the KGB," she replied in a bored tone of voice.

"Oh, yes, but that was long ago! Look what he says now!" he replied, not put off by her attitude.

She could not believe the stupidity of this man. She was relieved when, at that moment, the candidates came on. To applause, they all went to their individual podiums, laid out in a semi-circle. The moderator, a well-known Russian TV political correspondent, started to introduce the proceedings.

Lady Ruthven felt into her handbag for the gun. It was a handgun; there was no way a rifle could be used. However, as a vampire, she knew her senses would enable her to hit her target accurately. She could take the shot now; but no, she wanted to watch them speak for a bit.

Also watching—albeit on TV—was the Countess. Her phone rang. It was Karl.

"I am in Zagreb, Irina. I have used my contact in Vordenberg's security firm to find out more. Explosives are implanted into Lady Ruthven which will release silver and holy water, and even bits of garlic, if detonated. This can be done by a signal from here. I think I can get into where their control room is."

"Do so immediately," she replied. "Detonate the device. Even if she is in the audience for this debate, better she blows up there than carry out the assassination."

"Agreed. I will proceed."

He hung up and walked into the building. Time was against him; perhaps he should not have wasted time calling the Countess, he thought.

In Paris, the Countess continued to watch the debate. They had no choice but to kill Lady Ruthven. She had no real sympathy for the vampire, but the network had given their word that they would permit her continued existence. It was Vordenberg who was forcing her to do this. However, an assassination tonight at the debate would have destabilizing effects for Russia. They had no choice. Vordenberg would also somehow have to be dealt with. She watched the screen intently.

In the studio, Lady Ruthven continued to watch the candidates giving their opening speeches. All dull. However, they were now arguing with each other. This was amusing—the assassination could wait for a short while.

In Zagreb, Karl entered the prison. The guards knew him; after a cursory security check, they let him through. They had no problem with his pistol.

Karl was pleased; he had ensured in the past that his clearance with this company permitted him to carry a firearm in the building, as a defense against the creatures kept prisoner. Waiting for him, was his contact, one of the Baron's security analysts.

"Which way, Vojna?" he asked.

Wordlessly, she pointed up a flight of stairs. They rushed up onto the first floor. There was a guard by a door.

"I'm sorry sir, no one can enter this room. Direct orders from the Baron."

"I have clearance to go anywhere in this building," Karl said, in perfect Croatian. "Given to me by the Baron himself."

"Except in here, sir," the guard replied.

Karl had no time for this. He pulled out his pistol from his shoulder holster.

"Open the door," he said, pointing the weapon at the unfortunate guard's head.

Karl's man took the guard's weapon from his belt and gave it to Vojna. The guard wisely let them in.

The room was small, but there was a communications set-up complete with live TV coverage of the debate on a large screen. There were two technicians seated by it. There were startled to see Karl waving a gun at them and one of their analysts holding a gun at their guard.

In Moscow, Liatoukine was making a point.

"People say that I have sold out to the West in the last few days. This is not true. Yes, I accept some criticisms from the West…"

He was cut off by hisses from the members of the public in the audience.

"…but I do so only on our terms. I will also bring back Imperial codes of honor! I will mix the best of the past with the future!"

"A future determined by the West," shouted Drubetsky.

He was a man in his 20s with no experience of the ideology he believed. Clearly, thought Liatoukine, he was going to try and make a mark for himself whilst his boss was too proud—or rather too cowardly—to turn up tonight. However, his implication of treachery could not go unanswered.

"Boy," said Liatoukine clearly trying to patronize, "I proudly served Russia in the KGB for years, risking my life for the motherland. I saw your ideology from the inside. It failed Russia in the end and was worthless. Like you."

Liatoukine had surprised himself; there was real anger in his words.

Drubetsky spluttered. "How dare you! Stalin saved us from the Hitlerites! The world feared us! You insult the dead who fought the fascists! I will treat you how we have been treated!"

He flung his glass of water at him. The audience laughed. Liatoukine took out a handkerchief and slowly dried his face. He was truly angered now. He simply glared at Drubetsky. The audience fell silent—they could sense something.

The young man could see nothing but Liatoukine's eyes, which suddenly looked like those of a cat. He was consumed with fear, yet did not know why—except that he knew he had provoked something terrible.

He started shaking, and then walked off the stage at speed without saying anything.

Liatoukine turned to the camera that was on him and smiled.

"I suppose that's why some people call me *Captain Vampire*!"

The atmosphere broke and the audience laughed again. Liatoukine had turned a potential humiliation into a triumph.

Bezukhov decided he had better weigh in—he was displeased that the limelight was off him. He was also annoyed that Liatoukine had just made a big impression, and that he was being overshadowed.

"Only one person can maintain and increase the strength of Russia," he said. "He is before you. Unlike the two bickering candidates we have seen, I respect everything that makes us strong. I am no communist, but I recognize their achievements in defeating Hitler, putting the first man into space—and most of all, keeping the West at bay!"

There was applause. None of the other candidates interrupted. Not even Liatoukine. He knew his role—and it was not to try and win this debate. However, it rankled that he had to give way to this man—someone who was nothing more than the illegitimate descendent of a Count the vampire had little time for.

"However," continued Bezukhov, "there was much to be said for the Imperial age, especially in regards to the monarchy. I will set up a commission—perhaps we can restore something of the aristocracy—in a purely ceremonial role of course."

The moderator, who himself had felt a little side-lined, intervened:

"Are you suggesting the establishment of a new Tsar?" he asked.

"There are no living relatives," Bezukhov replied, "but we could perhaps establish something from the surviving relatives of aristocratic families, who knows?"

Liatoukine could contain himself no more.

"You mean yourself, don't you? What, the country will crown you Tsar?"

As he said it, he knew the deal for influence was over.

Bezukhov took this challenge on.

"My dear Liatoukine, I have my duties as a politician to consider—such a thing would not be on my mind. Perhaps you are thinking of such a role?" he gestured to Liatoukine's hair. "With your talk of Imperial honor, perhaps you can remember those years?"

The audience laughed. As did Bezukhov, who shot a glance at Liatoukine at the same time. The vampire was unnerved—did Bezukhov know what he was? A joke at his expense—or something more?

He then noticed something on one of the studio monitors near him. It was an audience reaction shot—of laughter—but there was a strange tint of green. It seemed to be more intense at the edge of the screen, especially on one woman, whose features he could just make out. A technical hitch or the presence of a vampire?

He scanned the audience and spotted the woman. Lady Ruthven sensed his eyes. She looked at him. They made eye contact. All this happened in a moment, during the laughter.

*Time to do the job*, she thought.

She stood up and pulled out her firearm from the bag and pointed it right at him.

In Zagreb, Karl knew he had to act fast.

"Detonate the device," he said to the men at the table.

They did not move—they were calling his bluff.

"The red switch," said Vojna.

Karl moved forward.

In Moscow, Liatoukine leapt from the stage into the audience—he would not run from her, but would take her on directly, even if that meant his own death. He would use his powers to elude the silver bullets.

Then she moved her arm away. And fired at Bezukhov.

The FSB were already hurtling towards the candidate to protect him. They were too late. Bullet after bullet—not silver, this time, Liatoukine noted—smashed into his body. Bezukhov was propelled backwards, and then the last bullet hit his head, blowing the back of it off onto the set and the unfortunate moderator's face.

There was pandemonium, screaming and shouting. Liatoukine pushed passed the audience, even stepping on some of them to get to the assassin.

Lady Ruthven herself had already been on the move, heading along her row to a side exit. She looked back, and saw Liatoukine racing towards her. She was surprised. She and Vordenberg had expected that he would have allowed himself to be taken to safety by the

FSB. However, she was prepared for any encounter with him. She did a high kick at him.

The end of the heel caught his face—burning him. He staggered back slightly and then realized the stiletto heel had silver at the end of it.

Lady Ruthven did not press home the attack, but decided to take advantage of his momentary hesitation to head for the door. Liatoukine was even faster. He managed to grab her arm and pull her around. She seemed familiar.

"Who are you?" he demanded.

She looked him right in the eyes and opened her mouth.

Then she exploded.

Liatoukine was flung back. He could feel bits of sliver and even holy water burning on his face. It burned badly, but not enough to kill him. His vision became blurred, but in front of him, he could still see the assassin, now a skeleton, writhing in white flame, somehow still screaming.

She collapsed over two rows of seats. The flames died out and there were just bones, then ash.

Liatoukine stared. He knew what had just happened. The bullets were aimed at Bezukhov, but they may have well just been stakes to his heart.

The FSB got to Liatoukine and pulled him away.

In Zagreb, Karl's finger was still on the depressed switch. He was staring at the screen, which had gone to a news studio with a newscaster relaying what had just happened, already showing slow motion of the assassination.

One of the technicians had grabbed his arm as he tried to press the switch. Karl had shot him in the leg. In the ensuing melee, the assassination had taken place. Karl had hit the button too late. The fight had distracted him from the screen in those precious seconds; he had heard the shots, but was firing his own gun at time. It was only the replay that confirmed that he had been too late. Baron Vordenberg's insane plan had succeeded. Now, he could only pray.

At the EU's observer headquarters in Moscow, Baron Vordenberg was watching what had happened. All the staff were in shock at what they had just seen. The Baron, however, was well pleased. He would find out later what had happened to Lady Ruthven—his intention had been to honor his part of the bargain with her. Despite her death, he was delighted. The plan had worked, as he knew it would.

### Paris, 17 March. Election Day

The Countess and the Baron met in the Luxmebourg Gardens. Anywhere indoors would have been too risky, due to possible surveillance. They started walking together. The Countess said nothing; she was going to let the Baron start to explain himself.

"After the assassination," he started, "all the EU observers were kicked out promptly. Some Russians think the West was behind it."

The Countess looked at him coldly.

"They are not wrong," she said.

Vordenberg laughed. "Not officially! The EU—and Washington—did not do this, and indeed have no idea of who was responsible." He laughed again. "One popular theory is that rogue British elements are responsible." He grinned at the Countess. "Perhaps we can push that theory through your friend Karl? It would teach the British a lesson. That would be a splendid bonus!"

The Countess could barely contain her fury.

"What you have done is create international tension, and it looks like Liatoukine will become President, thanks to your turning him into a hero!"

The Baron was not concerned with her anger.

"The tension will blow over. You fail to see that many objectives have been achieved. We have neutralized a dangerous Russian nationalist. Did we need another Putin? And yes, Liatoukine will become President. The scrutiny he will be under will soon see him found out for what he is—and neutralized. There will be a renewed belief the supernatural—at the very least amongst the intelligence services. That will be invaluable in dealing with the remaining such creatures that exist."

"And what might be the consequences of all this? The ones we cannot foresee? We could have dealt with Liatoukine in time," the Countess said.

"In time?" the Baron looked incredulous. "We—and others—have spent years trying to eliminate Liatoukine, and have consistently failed. You saw what happened when Lady Ruthven took a shot at him. I knew it would fail, the point being to ensure everyone—especially Liatoukine—would think there was a threat against him, rather than Bezukhov. If Bezukhov had won, the vampire would have had even greater power. No, action had to be taken! He will be disposed of, very likely by his own countrymen. The GRU are not fond of him. He is beyond our reach, but not theirs. He can't mesmerize or kill them all. And when he is gone, Russia will be weakened. Let them try and interfere with our elections then!"

"You are wrong. You should be held to account," she replied, not accepting anything he said.

"For what? For defending Europe against Russia? I would be applauded as a hero. Further, although you voted against my plan, you and the others all knew about it. And without the resources of the group, I could not have achieved what I have. If there is any accounting in the way you think, you and all the others will go down with me." He paused. "Perhaps it is time for new thinking at the top of our network."

The Countess looked at him. He was reckless. However, his plan had worked—on its own terms—so far.

"I think not. Good night, Baron."

With that, she strode off.

The Baron was pleased. He had no doubt his plan would continue to succeed. His fellow Habsburgians in the EU parliament would be horrified by his actions if they knew—but he did not need them. The others in the Network would come round to him. With their support, he knew he could achieve much more.

*Moscow, Election night, 17 March*

Boris Liatoukine looked out onto the stage from the window of the room next to it. He would have to go out there very soon to address his supporters.

Natasha Rostova was in the room. For the last few minutes, they had been watching TV coverage of the final vote counting.

"They all think you are a hero," she said. "It's not every presidential candidate that tackles an assassin and suicide bomber."

"That is the only story that makes any sense," said Liatoukine. "However, whilst that is the current speculation, many aren't quite believing it. I spoke to my FSB contacts today. Whilst they are briefing the public that it was some kind of incendiary device that she had on, they themselves do not accept that as fact. They are pouring over this. The TV footage is repeated endlessly around the world, blurred and green tinted as it is. The world does not know what happened, and unfortunately, they are not going to brush it under the carpet either. They are determined to know. One theory is that I was responsible!"

"Not surprising," said Natasha. "The security devices in this room will block any listening devices—our team did find a couple earlier. Whether that is the usual sort of listening or something of greater interest, I cannot say."

"Oh, I am sure it was," he replied. "It has been made known to me that there will be a delay in providing me with the nuclear codes and so on. They claim to be updating systems. Perhaps they are. Such matters are in the hands of the GRU. Bezukhov leant towards them, and after that debate, I wonder if he knew something."

"I thought all the files of your old department were destroyed? You had seen to that?" Natasha asked.

"Those in the FSB and SVR[13], yes. Or rather I appropriated them. However, I had rather less influence in the GRU. Stalin had our Vampire City destroyed with an atomic device in 1953. It is not likely that the GRU had no information about that. I was kept out of that operation, but such information would be evidence of the su-

---

[13] The Foreign Intelligence Service of the Russian Federation, the external successor to the KGB

pernatural. GRU, FSB, SVR, the western intelligence agencies. Eventually, they will put it all together. The discrepancies in my past will no longer be overlooked. The medical checks and so on. And what kind of Russian President tries to avoid the church as much as possible? My time is limited.

"The FSB and SVR insisted that the election should go ahead as planned, believing they can control me. However, they are looking very hard at the circumstances of the assassination. And if some supernatural files do still exist, they may no longer dismiss as them as lunacy."

"You could run," said Natasha.

"Like you plan to? I am aware of flights to London in your original name of 'Polly Bird' in a few days' time. Don't look so surprised; my FSB friends are always on the lookout for certain names I have given them. A bit sloppy, using that name?"

"I can be a bit nostalgic. Or rather, I had no time to create a new identity for myself," she replied.

"Do not concern yourself over it. You may leave; but I expect you to resign, saying that your job is over and you have had other offers. Not overly convincing, but rather better than you simply disappearing. As for me, running? No. I will not run away. I doubt it would be possible now, anyway. After me, they would come after you."

"They will never catch me," Polly Bird replied.

Liatoukine's cellphone rang. He looked to see who was calling.

"Our friend, the Bolshevik Kuragin. I assume he is calling to concede defeat." He switched him off. "To Hell with him."

He looked up at the TV coverage. The figures on the screen were clear; he had won outright with 54% of the vote. There would not be a second round.

The crowd outside had seen the news. "Boris! Boris!" they were chanting. He walked out of the room. He strode by himself onto the wings of the stage and walked straight on. The crowd roared in a frenzy.

No, he would not run away. The impersonal forces of history had crushed the supernatural. And now, those same forces had come for him. He would face fate right in the eye. Whatever else, he had made his mark. For however short a time, he would be ruler of Russia. Now, he would tempt the fate that delivered him here, and to the Devil with the consequences.

"My friends!" he said to the crowd, "I am so pleased to have been elected your President. You know, they once called me 'Captain Vampire.' Well, now they can call me 'President Vampire'!"

# Afterword

## Brian Stableford's introduction to
## Captain Vampire

Marie Nizet's *Le Capitaine Vampire*, originally published in Paris in 1879 by Auguste Ghio, was lost to sight for more than a century. The Bibliothèque Nationale has no copy, nor has the British Library or the Library of Congress. The book was rediscovered by Radu Florescu, a Rumanian scholar who had made something of a specialty out of researching the historical background of Bram Stoker's *Dracula* (1897) and the Voivode on which the eponymous character was modeled, Vlad Dragul, *alias* the Impaler. One of Florescu's successors, Matei Cazacu, appended a reprint of Nizet's novella to his own compound biography (in French) of the historical and literary figures, *Dracula* (2004), and included a chapter in his commentary speculating about its possible influence on Stoker.

Cazacu's research into Marie Nizet's background revealed that she was born in Brussels on January 18, 1859–which means that she had not long turned 20 when *Le Capitaine Vampire* was published, presumably having written it at 19. Her father, François-Joseph Nizet (1829-1899), was a lawyer whose numerous political pamphlets, of a fervently patriotic stripe, had won him an appointment as the joint curator of the Bibliothèque Royale; while occupying that position, he published various scholarly works in the fields of bibliography and history. Marie's younger brother, Henri (1863-1925),

269

also embarked on a literary career as a journalist and novelist.

Although Henri remained in Brussels to pursue his studies, Marie went to Paris to complete her education, where she cultivated a strong interest in Rumanian culture and folklore. In 1878, she published a volume of poetry entitled *România*; Cazacu observes that many of its inclusions are based on native ballads celebrating the continual wars of independence fought against the Turks of the Ottoman Empire, but that her political commentary takes even greater offence at the treatment of Rumania by the "great powers" whose international conferences strove to settle "the Turkish question" in the 1870s–with the eventual result that Rumania became a pawn of Russian imperial ambitions in the Russo-Turkish war of 1877-78, which forms the historical background of the story told in *Le Capitaine Vampire*.

Marie Nizet never visited Rumania; her knowledge of the country and its predicament was very largely based on information provided by two close friends: Euphrosyna and Virgilia Radulescu, the daughters of the late writer and fervently anti-Russian political agitator Ion Heliade Radulescu (1802-1872). Radulescu was considered to be the foremost 19th-century representative of Rumanian culture; he founded and edited the first Rumanian newspaper and played a leading role in the 1848 "Muntenian revolution," becoming a member of the provisional government set up thereafter. He was well-known in France, and contributed articles to many of the leading French newspapers.

For Marie, under the spell of Euphrosyna and Virgilia, Rumania became part of that Parisian land of dreams called "the Orient," to which many Parisian writers made imaginary pilgrimages, if not actual ones. She seems to have found it very easy to empathize with her friends' patriotism, and their indignation at the Tsar's abuse of his Rumanian allies. The centerpiece of her story–the fulcrum around which everything else is organized–is an account of the storming of the Gravitza redoubt on September 11, 1877, when several regiments of the Rumanian army were ordered by their Russian commander-in-chief to lead a dangerous assault that had a tremendous cost in human lives.

Cazacu, whose only focus of interest is the character of "Captain Vampire" himself, suggests that the inspiration for the novella might have come from one of Ion Heliade Radulescu's poems, *Zburàtoral*, which describes a young girl's sexual awakening in response to the visitation of an incubus. Nizet's novella has a very different theme, though, and the most obvious literary influences manifest in the novella are two of Charles Perrault's didactic fairy tales, known in English as "Cinderella" and "Little Red Riding-Hood."

In studiously echoing these moral tales, Nizet is not attempting to produce an "art fairy tale" of the kind beloved by some Romantic writers, but quite the reverse; she refers to the stories primarily to mock and deny them, calling attention by contrast to the fact that real life is not at all like a fairy tale. Although its plot has supernatural elements, and its antagonist is manifestly demonic, the eponymous monster is part of a more elaborate pattern of symbolism whose purpose is to bring out the horror of actual events. First and foremost, and in its very essence, *Le Capitaine Vampire* is a war story, and a very striking one. In its method and tone alike, it was way ahead of its time, and the principal reason for the book's rapid descent into obscurity might well have been its discomfitingly cynical treatment of the ugliness of

271

warfare–a treatment that must have seemed more than slightly shocking as the composition of a young woman of 19.

The possibility of Nizet's novella's possible influence on Bram Stoker cannot be sensibly discussed without extensive reference to its plot, so that sort of speculation is best left to an afterword, where it cannot spoil the reader's enjoyment in advance. It is, however, appropriate to offer a brief consideration here of the earlier history of French vampire fiction, in order to identify the groundwork on which Nizet might have been able to draw in selecting and shaping her key motif.

Cazacu observes that Marie Nizet's text does not employ any of the Rumanian words associated with vampire folklore–he lists *strigoï, vârcolac, moroi* and *nosferatu*–but only the word "vampire" itself. He notes that the word is of Slavic origin, but that is unlikely to be of any significance; by 1879 it had become commonplace in French parlance and it is with its French meaning that Nizet concerns herself. Indeed, she makes no reference at all to vampire folklore, although almost everyone else who wrote 19th-century French fiction featuring vampires seems to have had some knowledge of the contents of Dom Augustin Calmet's classic treatise on the subject, first published in 1746, even if that information had been filtered through the popular collection *Infernaliana* (1822; belatedly attributed, perhaps dubiously, to Charles Nodier).

*Infernaliana*'s selective recycling of Calmet's "case studies" includes a substantial chapter on "Vampires de Hongrie," which is presumably responsible for the fact that most 19th-century French vampire novels feature Hungarian vampires rather than Rumanian ones. Nizet shows not the slightest evidence of familiarity with

*Infernaliana* or its source, or of having taken any notice of such elements in later texts shaped under its influence.

There were, however, other significant inputs to the development of the French literary mythology of the vampire, of which the most important was John Polidori's novelette *The Vampyre* (1819), which was rapidly translated into French. *The Vampyre* gave rise to several imitative works, including two successful dramatic adaptations, both entitled *Le Vampire* and both produced at the Porte-Saint-Martin theatre, in 1820 (a version adapted by Achille Jouffroy d'Abbans, Jean-Toussaint Merle and Charles Nodier) and 1851 (a version further adapted by Alexandre Dumas and Auguste Maquet).

Although it is highly unlikely that Nizet had seen the play performed, she might well have read the script of Dumas' version in the 1876 edition of his collected plays, just as she might easily have read a translation of Polidori's original. Both texts feature male vampires, as Nizet's does, but this was relatively rare in early 19th-century French literature; the texts she could have found even more easily–including Théophile Gautier's *nouvelle* "*La morte amoureuse*" (1836; tr. as "*Clarimonde*" or "*The Dead Leman*") and two poems from Charles Baudelaire's *Les fleurs du mal* (1857), "*Le vampire*" and "*Les métamorphoses du vampire*," employ the word in a psychosexual context with respect to female temptresses (although Baudelaire's use of the masculine pronoun suggests that it is male lust rather than the female object of desire that he is characterizing as vampiric).

The only other text Nizet is likely to have run across which features a male vampire is Paul Féval's *La ville vampire* (1867 as a serial), whose first book version was issued in 1875 and must still have been available for purchase when she arrived in Paris. Although Féval's novella is a historical comedy parodying the excesses of English Gothic fiction, it does have two features that are found nowhere else prior to 1879 and which are reproduced in *Le Capitaine Vampire*: the vampire's ability to be in two places at once, and an extensive exercise in symbolism that makes vampirism a lurid exaggeration of various sorts of human depredation, including those associated with warfare. The former is trivial, but the latter may be more significant.

The word "vampire" was extensively used in a metaphorical sense before 1879. Baudelaire's use of it as a symbol of the male response to female sexuality reflected a trend that eventually gave rise to the American use of the term "vamp" as a description of predatory women—especially those featured in the cinema—but the more frequent and lurid application was in socialist rhetoric that represented capitalists as "bloodsucking" predators. Karl Marx's *Das Kapital* (1869; French tr. 1873; English tr. as *Capital*) makes continual reference to proprietors as "vampires."

Nizet gives no clear evidence of being a revolutionary socialist, in spite of being fervently anti-aristocratic and pro-proletarian, but Ion Heliade Radulescu had played a leading role in the local version of the wave of revolutions that swept Europe in 1848, and his daughters would certainly have been familiar with contemporary revolutionary rhetoric. This influence could have combined with that of *La ville vampire* to make it seem very appropriate to Nizet to symbolize the ultimate Russian bogey-man as an aristocratic vampire.

Brian Stableford